Dream Jumper

By Jacqueline Richardson

This book is dedicated to Brittany and Blake – the two brightest little stars in my universe. You need not seek greatness, for within you greatness already resides.

Also by Jacqueline Richardson:

The Burning Side
Beyond Reason
The Time Thief
The Time Thief: A Change of Face

Preface

From the start, I feel it is important to inform you that I am not a physicist. This book deals with a few complex theories of physics, and though I have tried to stay true to the basic principles of these theories, and have tried to avoid turning this into science-blasphemy rather than science-fiction, I cannot assure you that you will not find fault in some of my explanations. I have researched and studied extensively to maintain the integrity of each theory to the best of my abilities for the purposes of this book, but if you are unhappy with whatever liberties I may have taken, don't knock down my door. This is a work of science-fiction, not a physics textbook. This book is meant to stimulate your mind – to make you ponder your place in the universe, to make you question the beliefs you hold so strongly yet have never truly contemplated. It is meant to introduce you to a new way of thinking, on a grander scale than usual. Above all else, this book is meant to entertain, and perhaps spark your interest in the sciences.

Chapter 1

Jenson was staring down the barrel of a sawed-off shotgun, and the woman wielding it appeared to be deranged. She had wild, curly blond hair, cold blue eyes, and slightly masculine features. He raised his hands defensively, unable to recall how he had arrived in this situation. He seemed to be in an abandoned warehouse.

"What are you?!" she demanded, shoving the barrel of the gun closer to his face.

"Jenson Thorne," he said hesitantly. He began to slowly step backward.

"Don't move!" she shouted, and Jenson froze. "I didn't ask who you were. I said *what* are you?!"

He didn't know how to respond. "Um, a 32-year-old artist?"

The strange woman scowled at him and reached for a flask at her hip, keeping the gun on him. She popped the top off with her thumb and suddenly splashed the contents onto Jenson's face.

"What the-?!" Jenson hurriedly wiped the liquid from his face. It was only water. He looked at the woman incredulously.

"Well, you pass the holy water test. Hold this for me, will you?" She lowered the gun and handed him a shiny, silver colored knife. As he slowly reached for it, she quickly sliced the blade across his palm, drawing an instant stream of blood.

"Ouch! Dammit, what the hell?!" he growled angrily as he pulled his wounded hand close to his chest.

"You're just a human?" she said, sounding surprised.

"What the hell else would I be?!" He was certain now that she was deranged.

"Well, you aren't the demon I'm after. Come with me." She turned and walked away from him, into a long, dark corridor.

"Wait a minute! What is going on here? Where am I? Who are you?" He hurried after her.

"I'm Kristine. You were possessed by a demon, but it's apparently moved on to somebody else. Just stay with me and you'll be fine." Kristine walked on with purpose, constantly monitoring her surroundings.

Jenson was about to speak when she suddenly stopped and halted him with a raised hand. Without warning, she dove into a room on her left. Jenson heard gunfire and shouts, both male and female. He quickly contemplated whether to run away or help, but, being the good Samaritan he was, he ran into the room. He found Kristine standing over a large man on the floor, who had several bloody bullet wounds in his chest.

"Who is he?" Jenson demanded.

"Not who. What." Kristine turned toward him and smirked. She wiped her brow with the back of her forearm, still clutching the shotgun, and walked past him, out of the room. He took one more look at the body on the floor, then went after Kristine.

"That was a demon?" he asked when he caught up to her.

"Well, unfortunately it *was* a person, but there was a demon inside of him. I had to kill him to stop the demon. That could've been you, you know."

As Jenson tried wrapping his brain around what had just happened, he heard a strange but familiar beeping sound. "Do you hear that?"

"Hear what?" Kristine asked, giving him a strange look.

Yeah, I'm the crazy one, he thought to himself in the seconds before he woke up.

Jenson reached over and shut off his bedside alarm clock. As he lay in bed, trying to regain his senses, he thought about how oddly realistic his dreams always seemed to be. Other than having an outlandish theme, it had seemed like he was having a real experience. He looked over at his girlfriend, Maggie, who was still asleep. She always looked so lovely when she was sleeping, with her long dark eyelashes resting peacefully upon her lower lids, hiding her big, deep blue eyes. Her short, blondish-brown hair was in a disheveled mess around her small, lightly freckled face, and her full pink lips were parted slightly. He wasn't sure why he loved the way she looked in the morning, but he had a feeling it was because he was the only one who ever got to see her in such a state of disarray. The moment she woke up, she always ran straight to the bathroom to shower and straighten her hair and cover her face with makeup. She never lounged in her pajamas, not even on weekends, and she refused to go camping or stay anywhere that she couldn't perform her morning ritual. She was high-class, and while he loved that about her when he had her on his arm at his art shows, he couldn't stand it at home. He loved her, but it didn't mean he had to love everything about her.

He sluggishly climbed out of bed without waking Maggie, for he knew that he'd never get in the bathroom if he roused her now. They had a party to attend that afternoon for his grandfather's 90th birthday in Jenson's hometown, and with a 180-mile drive in Michigan's unpredictable autumn weather, he knew he'd have to make his shower quick if they wanted to arrive on time.

He lumbered to the bathroom in their small, one-bedroom apartment and switched on the blinding light. He blinked at himself in the mirror, wondering if the dark circles under his bright hazel eyes would fade by the afternoon. He'd started a new painting the previous night, a wilderness scene (which was his subject of choice), and once he'd started, he had a hard time putting down the brush. Despite the sleep deprivation, Jenson thought he still looked pretty good. He had a perfectly symmetrical oval-shaped face, a straight, narrow nose, and a strong, slightly cleft chin. His skin naturally retained a light, sun-kissed glow all year long, which made his fair-skinned Maggie envious. He was well built and just tall enough to be taller than his long-legged girlfriend when she wore high-heels. Whenever he asked Maggie, who was a successful marketing agent, why she was with him, an up-and-coming artist, she would just laugh and tell him that he was the best eye candy she could ask for.

As Jenson brushed away his morning breath, he began to feel a dull ache behind his right eye. He cursed himself for staying up so late the previous night, because he knew that ache would only intensify. By the time he emerged from the shower, the ache had turned into a sharp pain that had spread to the entire right side of his head, and his vision had become compromised in his left eye. As always, his lack of sleep had brought on a vicious migraine. He swallowed more than the recommended dose of pain medication, as was always required to tame his migraine pain, and commenced his typical morning routine.

Once he was clean-shaven and had gelled and spiked his short brown hair, he woke up Maggie. When she rolled over and looked at the clock, she reprimanded Jenson for allowing her to sleep so long.

"Damn it! I have less than an hour to get ready! I knew I should've set my own alarm," Maggie complained as she hurriedly grabbed an outfit she had set out for herself last night and stomped to the bathroom.

As Maggie showered, Jenson sat in the bathroom and talked to her. "I had a really crazy dream last night."

"And how is that different from any other night?" she replied from behind the floral shower curtain.

"It's not, I guess. But in this one there was a weird lady who was killing demons."

"You've been watching too much TV. How much of your painting did you finish last night?" Maggie changed the subject, straight to business as usual.

"I got the background completed, but I didn't get to bed until after 3 AM. And now I've got a pounding migraine to reward me for my hard work."

"That's unfortunate, especially since you're going to have to drive. I'm going to have to do my makeup in the car because somebody didn't wake me up when they were supposed to."

Jenson sighed and went back into the bedroom to pack his duffle bag. He noticed that Maggie already had two suitcases packed and sitting by the bedroom door, and wondered why she would need that much luggage for a one-night trip. He shook his head and commenced his own packing.

When Maggie had finished blow-drying and straightening her hair, she came out of the bathroom. With one look, she displayed her disapproval of his attire.

"Please tell me that isn't what you're wearing."

He looked down at his plain gray t-shirt and his favorite blue jeans. "I guess not," he replied in annoyance. After three years together, he should've known that she would object to him wearing casual clothes to an "event." He quickly threw on the dress slacks and blue, button-front shirt she tossed onto the bed for him. He hoped his brothers wouldn't give him too much grief for his outfit when they got to White Dove.

Waiting for Maggie to pack up her last few items, Jenson thought about how nice it would be to see his brothers. He and his brothers had scattered throughout Michigan over the years, and now it was rare that they were all together. They all enjoyed each other's company, despite their differing political views and paths in life. His oldest brother, Billy, was divorced and in the process of beginning his own farm. Pete was his next oldest brother, married, with two young boys and a successful career as an automotive technician. His youngest brother, James, was an electrical engineer straight out of college with a lively personality and currently single. The one thing they all had in common, however, was that they loved to sit up all night and drink a 30-pack of beer together, talking about anything and everything that came up – whether it be cars, politics, guns, or even science. Jenson was looking forward to spending time with them tonight.

Jenson carried all the luggage out to the parking lot, and after Maggie insisted upon them taking her car (since it was the nicer of the two, and she was all about keeping up appearances), he packed the vehicle while she sat in the passenger seat and began applying the layers of makeup she thought was required to make her look beautiful. As he climbed into the driver's seat, he had to pause for a moment because the minor change in altitude from a standing to sitting position caused his head to throb painfully.

"Come on, we're going to be late," Maggie said impatiently as she brushed mascara onto her eyelashes.

Biting his tongue, Jenson rubbed his forehead, started the car, and headed to the expressway.

Once Maggie had finished her makeup, she reached over and put a disc into the CD player. It was an artist of the pop genre, which Jenson couldn't stand. If he dared to suggest that they listen to his rock music, though, he knew he would be starting World War III. Instead, he turned the volume down slightly and tried to start up a conversation so he didn't have to listen to her bubblegum pop.

"I'm pretty excited to see James's new house, aren't you?" Jenson asked.

"Yeah, but I'm not so excited about his big dog and his roommate. I mean, who buys a house and then moves their roommate into their house with them? I still think it would've been better if we had just booked a hotel for the night," Maggie replied.

"It'll be fine. His dog is nice, and I like his roommate. Craig's a bit wild, but he's a lot of fun. Craig is just living with him until he can afford a place of his own. Besides, if we stayed in a hotel, I wouldn't get to hang out with my brothers, and you know that's important to me," Jenson reminded her.

"I know, and that's the only reason I agreed to stay there. But his dog does *not* like me. She stands up and stares at me every time I move, like she's about to bite my face off. It's unnerving. And I don't think Craig likes me either," she said.

Jenson knew Craig didn't like her, and suspected that James's dog, Scooter, didn't like her either, but he would never tell her as much. In fact, he knew that no one in his family, including his parents, was very fond of Maggie. They thought she was too high-maintenance, stuck up, and, to quote Pete, "bitchy." But Jenson loved her, despite her difficult personality, and his family supported his choices, regardless of whether or not they thought they were right.

"I'm sure that's not true," Jenson lied. "Everybody likes you. You worry too much. You just need to relax." When Maggie remained silent, Jenson tried another avenue. "So how's work been going?" That subject always sparked Maggie's interest.

He wasn't disappointed. Maggie talked for thirty minutes straight, pausing only to make sure Jenson was still listening. As much as he didn't like listening to her talk about work, he liked listening to her music even less. Neither, however, helped his pounding headache.

By the time they had put 150 miles between themselves and their apartment, the gas light came on in Maggie's car. As Jenson watched for the nearest exit, Maggie reprimanded him for failing to fill up the tank before they left. He ignored her and rubbed his forehead, thinking that a break from the car was exactly what he needed right now. When he finally saw an exit ramp, he pulled off the expressway and found the closest gas station. It was small and slightly run-down, but he didn't care. He just needed to get out of the car.

When the gas tank was filled, Jenson leaned down and tapped on Maggie's window. "Are you coming in?"

Maggie just looked at the building and wrinkled her nose in disgust, shaking her head. Jenson didn't press her any further and went inside. He headed straight for the coffee station and filled up the largest Styrofoam cup they offered with the pungent, black sludge that passed for coffee at gas stations. It might taste terrible, but he hoped the caffeine would help dull his migraine. He brought his coffee to the cash register and placed it on the counter without looking up. He dug into his pocket for his wallet.

As he rubbed his forehead and thought about how much he dreaded getting back behind the wheel, he didn't notice when the woman behind the counter asked him a question.

"Hello?" she said, waving a hand in front of his face.

"What? I'm sorry-" he began, then froze when he looked up at her face. With the spotty vision in his left eye, it took him a second to realize that the woman before him was the same blond-haired demon hunter from his dream.

"I asked if we've ever met before. You look familiar..." She stared at him for a moment, then realization spread across her face. "Holy crap, I had a dream about you last night!"

Jenson just stared at her, not knowing what to say.

"Yeah," she continued, "we were hunting demons! It was awesome. I almost killed you. Weird, huh?"

"Yeah, weird," he said slowly. Should he tell her he had that dream as well, or would it just make him sound creepy? He was in shock. This couldn't be possible.

"Maybe remote viewing isn't such a fallacy after all. Anyway, that'll be $44.62." She popped her gum and stood there, just looking at him like nothing strange had happened at all.

He paid for his purchase, trying not to stare at the woman, and walked out the door, looking back once just to make sure his eyes weren't playing tricks on him. It was definitely the same woman from his dream.

When he returned to the car, his hands were shaking. What had just happened? How could this woman, whom he was certain he had never met or even seen before, have had the same exact dream that he had in the same night? And what was remote viewing?

"Maggie, you won't believe what just happened."

Chapter 2

Maggie looked at him, eyeing the cup in his hand. "Did you find a cockroach in the coffee? Because I would definitely believe that."

Jenson shook his head impatiently. "No. Remember that dream I was telling you about this morning?"

"Vaguely. Something about killing demons?"

"I dreamt about a woman who was some kind of demon hunter. And just now, when I went up to pay for the gas and coffee, I saw that the woman behind the counter was the *same* woman from my dream! She looked exactly the same, just dressed differently. And then you know what she said to me? She said that she'd had a dream about me last night and that she and I were hunting demons, and that she almost killed me in the dream. That was exactly what happened in my dream! It's like we had the exact same dream in the same night! I've never even seen this woman before in my life!" Jenson was almost to the point of hysteria.

"What? That is unbelievable," Maggie agreed. "I don't even know what to say. She just came out and told you that as you were checking out?"

"Yeah!"

"Did you tell her that you had the same dream?"

"No. I thought she might think I was making fun of her or messing with her if I did. But she mentioned something about remote viewing. Have you ever heard of that?" Jenson wondered.

"Is that where you see other places, like a psychic or something?"

"I don't know. I've never heard of it before," Jenson said. "I've got to say, though, that my interest is piqued. I want to find out more about this. What could this mean? Could I be psychic?"

Maggie raised one eyebrow. "It's pretty crazy, I'll admit, but I don't know about you being psychic. Besides, how would you even find out more about it? It was one strange occurrence."

"When we get back home, I want to research it online. I want to see if anyone else has had anything like this happen to them. I want to know if it's something psychic, or paranormal, or if there are any theories out there about something like this."

"Great, but let's worry about it later. We're half an hour behind schedule right now. We should get going," she urged.

Jenson spent the rest of the trip lost in his own thoughts, wondering how two strangers could end up in the same dream at the same time. He was bothered by Maggie's borderline indifference toward the situation. How could she not be rattled by this? It was the strangest thing that had ever happened to him. His head was spinning with the possibilities, but he shared none of his ideas with her. Was it possible that he was psychic, and that the dream wasn't actually his own? But he had been a part of it. It wasn't like he was just dropping in and watching someone else's dream. Or maybe he did drop in on her dream, and when he did so, he altered it somehow by putting himself into it. By the time Jenson arrived to the restaurant where his grandfather's birthday party was being held, his head was reeling from more than just the migraine.

He and Maggie hurried into the restaurant, as they were more than thirty minutes late for the party. When they walked into the back room where his family had congregated, Jenson was relieved to see that there were two open chairs for them at the long banquet table. He quickly wished his grandfather a happy birthday, then took his seat next to Maggie, as she had already settled in next to his tall, red-headed mother, Carla.

"Sorry we're late," he apologized to his mother as he sat. "We had a late start this morning."

"That's fine. The servers haven't even been back here to take our orders yet," Carla said. "So how was the trip? You look ill, Jenson. Are you alright?"

"I'm fine. I have a bad migraine, though, and something really weird happened on our trip that rattled me a little. But other than that I'm ok."

"What happened?" Carla inquired.

Jenson told her about the dream and the woman at the gas station. "Have you ever heard of such a thing?" he asked.

"That's wild!" Carla exclaimed. "Remote viewing, huh? Do you think it's possible?"

"I'm not even sure what it is."

"Don't quote me on this," she said, "but I think it's when you mentally travel to another location and can see what's going on somewhere far away from your physical body. I actually had a friend when I was younger who claimed that her father could do that. She even told me once that her father had accurately described what she'd done in school one day, like he had been there with her. I always thought she was pulling my chain."

Jenson was floored. "So this could be a real thing? I've got about a million questions floating around in my head right now, and if I could find at least one direction to start looking for answers I would be happy."

"I don't know if remote viewing would exactly explain what happened to you, since it was all in a dream, but I think that's where I would start looking to get some ideas," Carla opined.

From across the table, Pete took interest in the conversation. "Did I hear you guys talking about remote viewing?" After Jenson filled him in on what had brought them to that topic, he replied, "Man, that's crazy! You know, I had something weird happen recently with my dreams, too. I kept having dreams with one song in them that kept repeating, the same song every time, and then a few days later I heard that the bassist for that band had died. It was weird because I'm not even a fan of that band, so it's not like I would've been listening to their music or anything."

As Jenson was about to reply, his Uncle Rick stood up and gathered everyone's attention for a short speech he had prepared for Jenson's grandfather. When the speech was over, the servers began making rounds and taking orders, and the remote viewing conversation was put on the back-burner for the rest of the afternoon.

After the party, Jenson and Maggie headed to James's house, which was in Brighton. It was about an hour's drive from White Dove, where the party had been, but was a fairly central location for the brothers to gather for a night before going their separate ways again. That evening, once Pete and his wife, Rhonda, had put their children to bed in one of James's guest bedrooms, Craig, Rhonda, Maggie, and the four brothers all retired to the garage to socialize. They sat in canvas camping chairs as James handed out cans of beer from one of the cases they had purchased from a gas station up the street. The ladies sipped rum-and-coke from tall glasses and talked mostly only to each other as the brothers and Craig talked about Pete's latest car project – his Subaru STI.

As the evening wore on, the garage began to resemble a bar scene, with loud rock music blaring from James's CD player on a shelf and noisy laughing and conversation. The air was filled with a thick haze from the cigarettes Pete, Craig, Billy, and Rhonda were smoking. Jenson wished he could partake in a smoke, but he knew that the second he lit one up, Maggie would shoot him an angry glare and give him grief the rest of the weekend. He liked to smoke when he drank, but Maggie found the habit disgusting and banned him from smoking in her presence. He hoped she would go to bed soon so he could open up the pack of cigarettes he had secretly purchased at the gas station when they'd gone to get beer. He knew she wouldn't stay up past midnight, since she stuck to a strict sleeping schedule. He kept his eye on the clock on the wall, waiting for the hands to point to twelve.

Finally, as expected, Maggie excused herself shortly after midnight. He waited until he was sure she had gone to bed before excitedly ripping open his pack of cigarettes and lighting one up. He sighed contentedly, watching the smoke roll away from him with his exhale.

"She still won't let you smoke?" Billy ragged. "Man, she's got you on a short leash, buddy. You know, it's only going to get worse if you marry her. Trust me, I speak from experience!"

"Hey, I'm not ring shopping yet," Jenson replied.

"Do you think you two will ever get married?" Rhonda asked. "You've been together for like three years, haven't you? Hasn't she even suggested it?"

"Not once. I don't think she's in any hurry either, which is fine with me."

"I don't think you guys should ever get married," Billy declared. "I mean, Maggie's hot and all, but I think you'd regret it after a year or two."

Jenson was beginning to feel agitated. He understood why Billy felt the way he did, as his experience with marriage had left a sour taste in his mouth, but Jenson wasn't seeking marriage advice. His relationship with Maggie was his own business, and he didn't want to discuss her less-than-appealing qualities with everyone right now.

Pete seemed to pick up on Jenson's aggravation, and he quickly changed the subject to maintain the peace. "Hey, Jenson, did you tell everybody else about that crazy dream thing today?"

Jenson was glad for the shift in conversation. He hadn't told them about the dream, so he shared it then. When he had told his story, everyone was shocked.

Craig asked, "Was the cashier's name Kristine too?"

"I don't know," Jenson replied. "I never asked her what her name was. I didn't even think to ask! That would've been even better if I had found out that her name was Kristine!"

James chimed in, "You should stop back at that gas station on your way home tomorrow. It would be interesting to know if she had the same name."

Jenson agreed. He wondered if Maggie would object to returning to the run down station. She probably would.

"So why do you think that happened?" Rhonda asked.

"I'm not sure, but Mom and I were talking about remote viewing and wondering if that was a possibility." He explained to Rhonda what remote viewing was as his mother had explained it to him. "I just don't know if that particular phenomenon explains exactly what happened to me, though. It wasn't like I was *seeing* her doing things in real life. I was actually there, interacting with her, in a whacked out dream with demons in it. I think there has to be something else, some other way of explaining it."

"Maybe it's some kind of psychic connection, where both of your brains somehow joined the same wavelength and allowed you to both interact in one dream," James suggested.

"Like some kind of extreme telepathy," Jenson added.

"Yeah, exactly like that!" James replied.

"I can think of a few women I'd like to connect wavelengths with," Billy commented.

"I bet you can," Rhonda teased, rolling her eyes.

"What about the dreams you had, Pete? What do you think that was?" Jenson asked, trying to get the conversation back on track.

Pete told everyone about his dreams and about the bassist of the band dying. "I think it might've been a premonition, but I don't know how or why I would've been keyed-in to that information."

"That's really weird," Craig said. "I've had a dream like that, where you dream about something happening, and then you get Déjà vu when it happens in real life. I wonder if every case of Déjà vu is because you dreamed of it before it happened."

"What I want to know is *how* things like that happen," Jenson said. "After what happened to me, I'm kind of obsessing over it. There has to be more to dreams than just your mind cycling through the information you picked up throughout the day. I mean, when I was little, I had a dream that my godfather was on a train with a bunch of people I had never seen before, and it was like I was just floating there, watching him. Then suddenly the train exploded, and I woke up. A few days later, he died of an aneurism in his heart. The strange thing was that I hadn't even seen him in a long time prior to having that dream. Why would I dream that? What would've made my brain just suddenly bring him up, especially when he wasn't a big part of my life anyway?"

"You dreamed of Uncle Ed dying before it happened?" Billy asked. "You were so little when it happened, I'm surprised you remember him, let alone a dream you had about him."

"Yeah. I always remembered it because I always thought it was weird. His funeral was the first one I had ever been to."

"Maybe it's God's way of preparing you for something before it happens," Rhonda conjectured. "He shows it to you in a dream so it's less devastating when it happens in real life."

"But why would He try to prepare me for a bassist dying? I didn't even like that band," Pete countered. "I don't think my dream was any kind of divine message. Maybe some are, but I doubt that mine was."

"Ok," James jumped in, "this might be the beer talking, but I have a wild idea. What if there is an inherent knowledge, on some other plane of existence, that we can all tap into without even knowing it. Knowledge of what has happened, what is happening now, and what will happen in the future –"

"Like a physical manifestation of destiny?" Pete proposed.

"Sure, why not. And what if we sometimes accidentally tap into that information when we're dreaming, and that's how we get our premonitions? It could happen all the time, but we only take notice when it affects us directly in our own lives." James took the last swig of his beer, then pointed to no one in particular. "Wrap your mind around that one!"

"Let me get this straight," Billy said as he lit up a cigarette and handed James another beer. "We psychically connect with other people while we're dreaming *and* we look up the skirt of destiny? Maybe that's why I'm always still so tired in the morning when I wake up," he joked.

"That's kind of a funny way to put it, but seriously, have you ever noticed that sometimes when you've had a lot of dreams in one night, you do wake up tired?" Craig said.

"Yeah, that happens to me!" Jenson exclaimed.

"Me too!" James said.

As the conversation slowly shifted to less theoretical topics, Jenson thought about all the things he wanted to research online when he got home the next day. He wondered if he would be able to find anything that would satisfy his questions, or if he would just end up with an even greater obsession for answers. He had a feeling that he had discovered something of great importance, and he knew he wouldn't be able to stop obsessing over it until he figured out exactly what his brain was doing while he was sleeping. There had to be more to it than what he had learned about sleep in Psychology 101.

The next morning, everyone went out to a local restaurant for a greasy breakfast to remedy their hangovers. Maggie, of course, had no such ailment, and she had a fine time teasing Jenson about his puffy eyes and sallow complexion.

"You look like a zombie," she jested after they gave the server their orders.

Jenson looked around the table at his brothers, and, for once, he had to agree with her. "We might look like shit today, but we were geniuses solving the mysteries of the universe last night."

"Converting alcohol to urine isn't exactly a mystery of the universe," she teased.

James overheard their conversation and chimed in, "We might've been drunk, but it doesn't mean we didn't have an intelligent discussion. Well, at least until Pete decided it would be cool to turn my deodorant can into a flame thrower. It was all kind of downhill after that."

After a fairly quiet breakfast, the brothers said their farewells and Jenson and Maggie hit the road. Jenson's head was pounding, again, but he insisted upon driving. He wanted to stop at that same gas station and find out his cashier's name, and he knew that if Maggie was driving, she would probably turn down his request to stop. He was afraid she didn't understand how important this mystery was to him.

Jenson waited until they were only a few miles from the exit where the gas station was before he revealed his plan to Maggie. She didn't seem as irritated about it as he had expected, but she wasn't overly supportive either.

"Is finding out her name going to change anything?" she asked.

"Yeah, it is. If her name is Kristine, then that's even more evidence that my dream was something out of the ordinary. I just need to know. It's important to me."

As he pulled off onto the correct exit, his heart began to race. When the small, dilapidated gas station came into view, he felt adrenaline begin coursing through his veins. With shaky hands, he steered the car into the drive and parked at the pump. He gassed up the car, frequently looking at the building, trying in vain to see the cashier through the window. Finally, the tank was full, and he headed inside.

His heart dropped when he saw a young, short, pudgy man standing behind the counter. He looked around the small store, but there was no one else in the building. Disappointed, he grabbed a candy bar and went to the counter.

As the attendant initiated the transaction, Jenson asked him, "Wasn't there a woman working here yesterday? She had short, curly blond hair."

"You mean Kristine?"

Jenson felt his stomach turn.

Chapter 3

The attendant continued, "She works here a couple days a week. Did she do something to piss you off? She does that a lot."

"No, nothing like that. I was just curious. She looked a little familiar, that's all," Jenson replied, trying to keep his wits about him. He grabbed his receipt from the attendant's fat sausage fingers and started to walk out the door.

"Dude, you forgot your candy bar," the man called after him, but Jenson ignored him. He had no appetite at the moment and knew he needed to hurry to the car to sit down. His legs were suddenly shaky and threatened to buckle beneath him.

When he made it to the car and plopped into the driver's seat, Maggie gasped.

"Your face! God, you look so pale! Are you ok?"

"Her name is Kristine."

"Shut up," Maggie replied, surprised.

"Seriously. The guy behind the counter told me. I honestly didn't expect it to be true."

"Wow. You must be psychic!"

Jenson didn't reply. He started the car and drove back to the expressway. Maggie tried to start up a conversation with him a few times on the way home, but he was too befuddled to maintain one. He had just received further proof that he had experienced something beyond explanation, and it consumed his thoughts. When they arrived home, Maggie had to call after him to remind him to grab the bags from the car, as he was already running toward the apartment to get on his laptop and begin his research. He hurriedly returned to the vehicle and took two of the bags, leaving the last bag for Maggie, and ran toward the apartment again. He heard an exasperated grunt from Maggie, but he was too excited to care.

Once inside the apartment, he dropped the bags on the floor in the kitchen and sat down at his desk in the living room. He stared at his laptop screen, trying to sort through the jumble of ideas in his head, and ignored Maggie's complaining regarding his placement of their bags. He decided to perform a search on remote viewing and dreams, just to see what came up. He was surprised by the overwhelming number of theories he found. As he sifted through all the information, trying to weed out the plausible from the insane, he came across a theory that intrigued him: alternate realities and alternate dimensions. He ran a search using the topics of mind travel, dreams, and alternate dimensions, and what he found greatly interested him. He read about how many of the great thinkers and geniuses in history allegedly had their moments of enlightenment and strokes of genius while in a deep meditative state. Einstein would sit in a chair silently and run "thought experiments" for hours. Leonardo da Vinci would lie in his bed with a lit candle at his feet and stare at the light that flickered off the ceiling until he fell into a meditative state. Socrates would reportedly stop in the middle of what he was doing and stand still and silent for long periods of time, oblivious to his surroundings, as a deep thought overtook him.

Jenson was fascinated by all of this, but one story in particular caught his attention. Srinivasa Ramanujan, the Indian mathematician, claimed that all of his brilliant, groundbreaking formulas and equations came to him in his dreams when the goddess Namagiri revealed them to him. Some of his formulas were subsequently proven to be correct, and some of them are still in the process of being proven. In the articles he read about Ramanujan, the theory of the Akashic record was also mentioned. He learned that a Hindu legend describes the Akashic record as a plane of existence that holds all of the information of the universe. The articles he read postulated that Ramanujan and other geniuses may have been able to connect with this realm of knowledge while in deep meditative states. As he read this, he was reminded of James's theory of the "plane of destiny."

Only a few days ago he would have thought all of this information ludicrous. After his experience, however, he found himself nodding enthusiastically in agreement as he read each article. He felt like he had just arrived at the greatest "Aha!" moment in his life. What he was reading was making sense to him.

After several hours of staring at the computer screen, Jenson's eyes were beginning to ache, and his stomach was growling incessantly at him. When he looked at the clock in the corner of the screen, he was surprised to see that it was already past 9PM. He decided it was time to take a break. He stood up from his computer chair and headed to the kitchen. As he sat on a stool at the bar in the tiny kitchen, a bologna sandwich in his hands, he pondered the validity of what he had read. The theory of alternate realities and mind travel were interesting, but did it exactly explain what had happened to him? If his dream with Kristine had taken place in a shopping mall or a meadow, he might've believed it did. But demon hunting? Was there really an alternate reality where people hunted demons?

Maggie strolled into the kitchen and stood with the refrigerator door open, contemplating what to make herself for dinner. She looked at Jenson and furrowed her brows.

"A bologna sandwich for dinner?"

"Why not? It was quick and easy. I would've made you one too, but I know how you detest heavily processed meats," he replied.

"Damn right I do. I shouldn't even allow them in the apartment. Do you have any idea how bad that stuff is for you?"

"Yep. You've told me many times."

She sighed disapprovingly and removed a bag of salad from the fridge. As she poured the contents into a bowl and began sprinkling sunflower seeds and frozen peas over it, she asked him how his research was going.

"I found a lot of interesting information." He shared with her what he had learned about alternate dimensions and the habits of certain historical figures. He was pleased to see that she was showing some interest in what he was telling her.

"So you think you travelled to an alternate reality?" she questioned as she stood across the bar from him and munched on her salad.

"I'm not sure. If that was the case, then that would mean that Kristine would've had to have travelled too, at the same time, to the same place."

"Do you suppose that's why you had such a bad migraine yesterday morning? Maybe your brain did do something extraordinary, and your migraine was due to whatever it was that you did," Maggie theorized.

Jenson hadn't even considered that possibility. Whenever he had a migraine, it would start in the morning shortly after waking up. But it usually happened after a lack of sleep, which was exactly what had happened yesterday.

"I think my migraines are from a lack of sleep, but I guess I can't rule anything out right now."

"Maybe your brain is more likely to do its weird psychic thing when you are overtired, when you go to bed too late," she reasoned.

Jenson was surprised at her ideas. He hadn't expected her to actually get involved in helping him figure out theories. She was an intelligent woman, but physics, psychology, and astronomy weren't subjects in which she had ever shown an interest. She was usually more into economics and political science than physical and applied sciences. He was glad for her interest and input, and it was times like this that made him remember why he loved her.

"I do have my craziest dreams when I'm overtired," Jenson acknowledged.

"Are you going to do any more research tonight?"

"I don't think so. I'll go to the university tomorrow and search their databases for any scientific papers relating to the theories I read online. For now, though, I think I'm going to go to bed. I think a good night's sleep will do me good."

"Agreed. Just try not to do anything too crazy in your dreams tonight," Maggie teased.

As Jenson lay in bed that night, he wondered what his dreams would bring. He felt slightly apprehensive about falling asleep now that he knew his brain might do something psychic or supernatural while he slumbered, but he also knew he had nothing serious to worry about. He would still wake up in the morning, regardless of what transpired in his dreams. He thought about all the outlandish dreams he'd had throughout his life and wondered if any of them had anything in common with the dream from two nights ago. He often dreamed of strangers, so was it possible that those strangers were real people, like Kristine? He also had dreams that were so jumbled and nonsensical that he could barely piece them together when he woke up and tried to remember them. Were those dreams anything special? He continued to think about his past dreams as he drifted into a deep sleep.

Jenson walked out of his bedroom into a living room that he knew to be his, unaware that it was completely different than the living room he was used to. It was filled with people that he knew to be his roommates, though for some reason he couldn't remember any of their names. Two young men were planted on a green plaid couch, watching a football game on the wide-screen television. One man was tall and thin, with a long face, bright blue eyes, and short blond hair. The other was shorter, with dark hair, a five o'clock shadow, a stocky build, and dark brown eyes. They both sported football jerseys and had beers in their hands. A third man, about the same age as the other two, was walking out of the kitchen with a long-neck bottle of beer and a bag of beef jerky. He was rather tall, with a muscular build, and had a round, bearded face with a pug nose.

"Hey, Jenson, come watch the game with us," the muscular one said, gesturing for Jenson to join them as he plopped down on an old leather recliner next to the couch. "Dave and Tom here are rooting against our team. I need some backup."

A female voice then came from the kitchen, "No amount of backup is going to save your team from losing!" Jenson watched as a woman stepped around the corner from the kitchen and came into the room. He was instantly attracted to her. She was tall, thin, and beautiful, with long, voluminous, dark brown hair that hung down to her large, perky breasts. She had a rich, honey colored complexion and large, deep brown eyes that hinted at a Latino heritage. Jenson was mesmerized, and though he knew she was his roommate and that he must've seen her every day, he felt like he was seeing her for the first time. She was wearing a low-cut, v-neck t-shirt that exposed a small amount of cleavage that Jenson had a hard time keeping his eyes away from. As she turned to set her beer on the coffee table, he noticed how tight her jeans were and how perfectly shaped her bottom was. He looked away to avoid staring, and walked to the couch where the first two roommates were seated. They moved over to allow him seating space. As Jenson sat and watched the football game with them, it didn't occur to him that he didn't particularly enjoy football. He spent much of his time stealing glances at the lovely brunette to his right, whom he soon found out was Andrea.

Before he knew it, the game was over. To celebrate their team's victory, Dave and Tom invited the others to join them at the bar for drinks. The five of them walked to a bar only a few blocks down the street from the apartment. It appeared that they lived in a busy downtown area of a large city, which Jenson didn't find strange in the least. As they sat at the bar, talking about the next big game and their Super Bowl picks, he noticed that Andrea, who was seated at the barstool next to him, wasn't joining in the conversation.

He turned to her and asked, "Why so quiet?"

She looked him in the eyes, distress written on her face. She then took a sideways glance behind her. "My ex is sitting back there with his new girlfriend. You know, the one he cheated on me with."

Jenson took a quick look behind him, but he didn't see anyone familiar. Though he couldn't remember any details, he seemed to know what she was talking about. "Maybe they'll leave soon," he said.

"I doubt it. If he sees me, he's going to stay as long as he can just to make me uncomfortable. You know how he is."

"You want to go? I can take you back to the apartment if you want," he offered.

"Yeah, I think that's a good idea."

Jenson told his buddies about the situation, and they promised they'd meet them back at the apartment before too long.

At the apartment, Andrea flopped down on the couch and started to cry with her face in her hands. "God, why does it bother me so much? I should be glad that she stole him away from me. He was such an asshole! He was always cutting me down and picking fights with you guys. It was exhausting to be with him. Why the hell do I still have feelings for him?" she wondered aloud.

"It's hard to get over somebody that you loved, even if he was a terrible person. I know exactly how you feel. But I promise you, someone wonderful will come into your life and completely wipe those remnant feelings off the map," Jenson consoled.

"I don't know if 'love' is what you would call it. He was too horrible to love. It was more of an attachment, I guess you could say. It's just hard to sever that attachment and be alone, you know?"

"You're not alone. You have all of us," he reminded her.

"I know. I'm lucky you guys didn't allow him to push you away from me, or I'd have absolutely no one right now. Thank you for that," Andrea said as she smiled at him through her tears. Jenson noticed that she was one of those rare women that could still look beautiful when she was crying.

Jenson reached over and pulled her to him. He wrapped his strong arms around her dainty figure and held her against his chest in a comforting embrace. He lightly kissed the top of her head, discretely inhaling the lovely floral scent of her hair. He then rested his cheek against the spot he had kissed, and held her while she cried. He realized that he badly wanted to be the man that made her forget all about her feelings for her ex.

When Jenson awoke the next morning, he clearly remembered the dream. He could even remember the way Andrea's hair had smelled. He looked at the empty spot in the bed where Maggie had been, and thought about how different Andrea had been from his Maggie. She didn't resemble Maggie at all, and in his dream it appeared that Andrea hadn't been wearing a spot of makeup. Andrea also seemed much more free-spirited and more open to discuss difficult emotions than Maggie. With Maggie, the only time Jenson knew something was bothering her was when she was being exceedingly difficult, and when he would try to pry from her what was truly bothering her, she'd close up and refuse to talk about it. Even when they had first started dating, Maggie never would have been able to have a conversation with Jenson like the one he'd had with Andrea. He couldn't help but notice the strange longing he felt for Andrea, even though he was now awake.

He wondered if this dream had been anything like the demon-hunting dream. Was Andrea a real person? If she was, and he ever met her, he worried what it would do to him. He loved Maggie, he was sure of it, and he was a faithful man. But he had to admit that he was mesmerized by the woman from his dream, and it would be difficult for him to forget her.

When Jenson went into the bathroom to use the toilet, Maggie was still in the shower. She heard him come in.

"Any crazy dreams last night?" she asked.

Jenson knew better than to share his dream with Maggie, so he told her, "Not that I can remember."

"Yeah, me neither. Though I never remember my dreams the way you do, anyway. I don't think I even dream half the time," she said as she shut off the shower. She pulled back the curtain and stepped out of the shower, quickly wrapping her towel around herself. "So what are you going to be doing while I'm at work today?" Maggie inquired.

"I'll work for a while, but I'm anxious to do some more research. I think I'll go to the university library today to see what kind of articles I can find in their online databases of peer-reviewed journals. I'm not expecting much, but we'll see."

"Why do you need to go to the university for that? You have a computer here."

"I don't have remote access to the database since I'm not a student anymore. You need a student ID and password to get onto the library's database if you aren't on one of the campus computers."

"Oh, I see. Well, good luck with that. I hope you can find something. But do make sure to get some work done too, because I don't want you to get so sidetracked by this dream business that you put your art on hold. You have a gallery show in three months, remember?" she said.

"I know," he replied reproachfully. "I'll get my work done." He felt like she was treating him like a child, telling him he had to eat all his peas before he could have ice cream.

To prove his ability to prioritize, he left the bathroom and went straight to his work corner in the living room. He wished he could call it a studio, but it was more of a nook. He had his table, which served as his easel because he preferred to paint with his canvas lying flat rather than upright, and a wide array of brushes and paints scattered about upon the table. He sat down in his creaky wooden chair and looked at the wilderness scene upon which he had been working. He wondered if there was anywhere on earth that looked exactly like that scene. Had his mind completely fabricated the landscape, or had he seen it somewhere? Perhaps he had seen it in a dream, or *visited* it in a dream. He squeezed some paint onto his palette, selected a brush, and began blocking in the moose that would be the focal point of the piece. He heard Maggie dashing about the apartment as she hurriedly grabbed her briefcase from the counter in the kitchen and her lunch from the fridge. She was cutting it close on time, as usual, so she gave Jenson a quick kiss on the cheek and ran out the door, barely getting "I love you" out of her mouth before the door slammed shut behind her.

Jenson felt a familiar calm wash over him that always presented itself when Maggie left the apartment. He subconsciously kept himself tensed whenever she was around, and it wasn't something he could control. He wondered if he would feel the same way if he lived with someone more like Andrea.

As Jenson painted, his mind became focused on his work, and for several hours he wasn't plagued by thoughts of his problems. He was calm, centered, and happy. When his subject was completed, he looked up at the clock on the wall. It was already lunch time, which meant he needed to put down the brush and head to the university. From his experience as a student, he knew that if he didn't get to the library before 2 PM, there would be no open computers. He quickly changed into some presentable attire, foregoing his shower for the sake of time.

Once he found an open parking space in the metered lots at the school, he deposited two hours' worth of change into the meter and walked toward the library. He felt a strange nostalgia as he walked the familiar sidewalks and navigated his way through the bustling crowd of college students. It had been ten years since he last stepped foot on campus, but his college days flooded back to him like a tidal wave. He hadn't realized until that moment just how much he missed those days. It was a time of fun, friends, women, and few real-world responsibilities. Now here he was, ten years older, not much richer, and a hell of a lot less happy. What had happened? He ignored the little voice in his head that shouted *Maggie!*

When he entered the expansive library, he was immediately disoriented. The layout of the first floor had been changed, and he had to refer to a map on the wall to locate the computers. He trudged up two flights of stairs and, after several minutes of searching, found one open computer. He sat down and began his search for answers.

An hour and a half later, Jenson was feeling discouraged. He'd read through several dry articles that had sounded promising in the abstract, but had revealed nothing of interest within their pages. Finally, however, as he was scrolling through the journals one last time, just about to turn over his computer to an awaiting student, an article caught his eye: *Dreamscapes as Parallel Universes* by Dr. Donald Wesson. He let out an audible gasp of excitement, ignoring the strange looks it had earned him. He quickly opened the link and began scanning the pages. He was not disappointed. Dr. Wesson's paper was hypothesizing that the mind, when in a certain state of sleep or meditation, may be able to transport an individual's consciousness into another reality. Through his research, he had discovered that certain individuals exhibited strange brain function patterns occasionally during their dream state. When they were in such a state, they were exceedingly difficult to awaken, and when they were asked to recount their dreams, there were similarities in the descriptions. The dreams always contained people the dreamer didn't actually recognize from real life and seemed more real to the dreamer than most dreams.

Dr. Wesson's article went on to describe several cases in which he had trained individuals to practice lucid dreaming so as to consciously gather information from their dreams. In many instances, the dreamer was able to learn something in their dream about which they had no knowledge before falling asleep, then accurately describe it once they were awake. In one case, the individual was asked to look up and memorize pi to the fifteenth decimal place, and after a dream that produced strange brain functions, he woke up and correctly wrote out pi to the twenty-third decimal place. The individual claimed that in the dream he actively found a computer and looked up the number online and memorized it to as many decimal places as he could.

Before he was able to finish the article, Jenson noticed that he was almost out of time. His meter would be running out soon, and he knew that an expired meter always resulted in a parking ticket due to the heavily patrolled parking lots at the university. He quickly printed out the article and ran to his car. He drove home with an excitement akin to a child on Christmas Eve.

Jenson sat at his computer desk at home and continued reading Dr. Wesson's paper. He was intrigued by the accounts of Dr. Wesson's study subjects and the information they were able to gather in their dreams. According to Dr. Wesson, he always asked his subjects to gather information on mathematical formulas and equations as it was generally accepted that math was the language of the universe and should remain constant regardless of what universe his study subjects visited in their dreams. At the end of the article, the subject of the Akashic record was introduced. Dr. Wesson indicated that he believed that such a plane of existence was entirely possible, if not probable, and planned to focus future research efforts to discover it.

When he had finished reading the paper, Jenson wanted more. He needed more. He felt like he had just discovered a rich vein of coal, but knew that if he dug deep enough, he'd find diamonds. Dr. Wesson's paper proved to him that he wasn't crazy – or, if he was, then there was someone else out there who was just as crazy. He had to tell Maggie what he had discovered.

"I'm busy, dear," Maggie greeted him when he called her cell phone.

"I know, but I found something amazing," he replied. "There is a scientist who actually studies the very same thing I experienced! I just finished reading his paper, and it validates everything I suspected."

"Huh, I didn't expect that," she replied simply.

"I didn't either, but it's true. I need to know more, though. I can guarantee this guy knows more than what he put in his paper. Who knows what he could have discovered in the five years since this paper was published?"

"Well, maybe you should try to contact him. He might be interested in what you have to share," Maggie suggested.

"I know, I was thinking the same thing. I have to get involved in some way. I just hope I can find a way to get a hold of him."

"Sounds like you've got work to do, then. I'll talk to you when I get home tonight. Good luck," she said before ending the call.

Jenson turned on his laptop to begin tracking down Dr. Donald Wesson online. When he ran a search of his name, he was surprised to find more than one Dr. Donald Wesson. After reading about each of them, he almost fell out of his chair when he found the Dr. Wesson he sought. He is a physicist who specializes in quantum theory, and he is located at the University of Michigan – two hours away from Jenson's apartment.

Chapter 4

Jenson couldn't believe his luck. If Dr. Wesson was still performing his dream studies, Jenson might actually be able to participate, given his locale. He desperately needed to convince Dr. Wesson to meet with him. He was too obsessed with this subject now to just let it fall by the wayside, and he had to find a way to contact him.

Finding contact information for Dr. Wesson was easier said than done. Jenson was unfamiliar with which avenues to follow for finding contact information for someone. It took him almost an hour to finally dig up an email address, but when he did, it took him even longer to compose an intelligent letter that would be taken seriously. He didn't want to sound like a raving lunatic, even if that was how he felt.

Dear Dr. Wesson,

My name is Jenson Thorne. I recently had the pleasure of reading your article entitled "Dreamscapes as Parallel Universes" in the November 2010 edition of the *Journal of Quantum Physics*. I came across the article as I was doing research to better understand a peculiar event that occurred in my life this past week. I had a strange dream one night before a long road trip, in which I met a woman I had never seen before in real life. The next day, when I stopped at a gas station I had never been to, I met the woman from my dream. Strangely, she revealed to me that I looked familiar and then went on to tell me about a dream she'd had of me the night before. It was the same dream I'd had. The strangest thing about the instance was that her name was the same name with which she provided me in the dream. I can only conclude that somehow we met in the same dream at the same time. Your article and studies greatly intrigue me, and I wonder about the possibility of speaking with you about my incident and perhaps becoming a part of your study on dreams and alternate dimensions. I look forward to hearing from you and I appreciate your time. Thank you.

Jenson signed off and provided his email address, phone number, and mailing address. After clicking the "send" button, he felt his stomach tie into knots. How long would it be before he heard back from Dr. Wesson? Would Dr. Wesson take him seriously, or just delete his email and move on? He was determined to find out what Dr. Wesson knew, so he wasn't going to allow himself to be ignored. If need be, he'd become a pest until Dr. Wesson had to acknowledge him. For now, though, he played the waiting game.

When Maggie came home that evening, she didn't ask Jenson about his day or try to follow up with him regarding his research and Dr. Wesson. She simply announced that he was to get showered and dressed immediately as she had made plans with one of her friends to meet her and her husband for dinner, then she disappeared into the bedroom to change her clothes. He followed her into the bedroom.

"Seriously?" Jenson asked in disdain. "I can't stand Heather, and her husband is even worse. I don't even remember his name."

"Dick."

"What?" Jenson replied abashedly.

"His name is Dick."

Jenson laughed at his misunderstanding, then said, "Fitting. But why do I have to go? I'm pretty sure they can't stand me either."

"You're going," she said firmly as she rummaged through his clothes in the closet. "It's weird to go out with a couple and not have your own date. Then you just feel like a third wheel."

Jenson sighed heavily and grabbed the clothes Maggie had picked out for him. As he turned to leave the room, he mumbled, "You didn't even ask about my day." She said nothing.

In the car, Jenson told Maggie about the letter he sent to Dr. Wesson. If she wasn't going to ask about it, he was going to make her listen anyway.

"I tried to make it short so he might actually read the whole thing, but I hope I put in enough details to get him interested," Jenson said. "I just hope he responds, one way or another."

"What if he doesn't?"

"Then I'll keep trying. Dreams as an alternate reality is a hugely amazing idea, and if I can help in any way to prove it is real, I need to."

"So his paper was pretty interesting?" Maggie inquired.

"Incredibly so!" He enthusiastically described the contents of the article to her.

"That's pretty weird. But how did he know that his test subjects weren't just going home, looking up the numbers or equations, memorizing them, and then going back in and reciting them at the next experiment? Mathematical equations are easily accessible online."

"He covers that issue in the paper. All participants were given a different value or equation to look up each time they were monitored – one they claimed to have no knowledge of beforehand – but what's more interesting is that they were only able to accurately describe what they were asked to learn when they'd had a dream that produced the unusual brain patterns. And they weren't notified of when they'd had such a dream until the entire experiment was over. Also, the people who never showed signs of unusual brain patterns weren't able to provide the correct answers. Statistically, it was more significant than just mere chance or coincidence."

"Still, though. It just seems a little too easy to falsify," Maggie said. "I just don't want you to get too caught up in something just because you want to believe it to be true."

Jenson tried to control his irritation. "Well, I need some direction to go on this, and right now, Dr. Wesson is the only legitimate lead I've got."

"Legitimate might be a strong word for now," Maggie replied as she checked her hair in the visor mirror. "The restaurant is right up here. Please try to be nice tonight."

"I'm always nice," Jenson stated begrudgingly. He was too annoyed to notice the irony.

Jenson tried to keep a pleasant smile on his face as he and Maggie were seated in the restaurant. Heather and Dick were already there, waiting for them. Jenson instantly remembered why he disliked the couple when Dick's first comment to him involved a jibe about being fashionably late. Jenson looked at his phone and saw that he and Maggie were actually five minutes early.

"Well, better to be fashionably late than pathetically early." He followed up with a falsely good-natured chuckle. Maggie shot him a look. It was going to be a long night.

As he sat and listened to the usual dry, boring conversation, he tried to mask his displeasure with a fake smile. Dick turned to him as Maggie and Heather gossiped about one of their other "friends," and said, "So what have you been up to? You've had a smile on your face all night, so it must be something good."

"Oh, I've been working on my paintings for my upcoming art show, as usual."

"I've never understood that artsy thing. I mean, it must be difficult to sell a painting in this day and age with high resolution photography. Do you find that to be the case?" Dick said condescendingly.

"Not at all. You'd be surprised at what someone will pay to own a piece of what another person created by hand. I find it's more of a higher class market that my work appeals to." Smile.

"I suppose. After all, look at the crap Picasso put out and his work is worth millions of dollars." Smirk.

"Indeed."

After a long silence, Dick asked, "So do you have any other hobbies, aside from painting?"

Jenson fought the urge to argue that his painting wasn't a hobby, it was his livelihood, and instead said, "Well, I've been doing some research into parallel universes lately. Are you familiar with the theories of parallel universes?"

"Oh, I don't believe in all of that nonsense. God created the Earth and the universe, and I don't believe that we as mere humans are capable of understanding His divine processes, or should even try. We have the Bible to tell us all we need to know."

"If we never tried to understand the world and universe around us, we wouldn't have the medicines that save our lives, the electricity that powers your big-screen television and lights your home, or the carbon fiber on your expensive Porsche. We would still think the world is flat and burn women for witchcraft. Don't you find it a bit ironic that the people who fight so strongly against science are doing so while living comfortably with the products of its progress? It's like raging against the machine while using the machine. Or like drinking a cup of coffee every morning and saying, 'Wow, I sure hate coffee.' Science is a necessary and inevitable aspect of human existence. Why would God give us such wonderfully efficient brains and limitless curiosity if we weren't supposed to use it? It is what makes us human and not just animals," Jenson argued.

"And often it is that same dangerous thirst for truth that makes us act more like animals than humans," Dick replied matter-of-factly.

"I find it to be quite the opposite, actually. It seems to me that many of the atrocities against our fellow man throughout history have been done in the name of religion and the rejection of truth."

Maggie interrupted, "Wow, it sounds like you guys are having quite an involved conversation there, but I must interject for a minute. Dick, Heather just told me that you are taking her to Italy for your anniversary this year. Tell me about your itinerary! I would love to see Italy."

Jenson tried to cool his boiling blood as the other three at the table talked about Venice and Rome. He was by no means an academic scholar, but it burned him to his bones when others were so hypocritical as to scoff at science yet reap the benefits that science offers. If you don't believe in the science it took to create the smart phone, then maybe you shouldn't be allowed to use smart phones, he thought. He wasn't an atheist, but he felt that a belief in God and science were not exclusive of each other. How could someone be so close-minded?

He avoided conversation with Dick the rest of the evening, and for Maggie's sake, he kept all responses civil and simple. By the time they got into the car, however, Maggie was fuming anyway.

"You embarrassed me horribly tonight! I told you to be nice!" she scolded.

"So I'm just supposed to let Dick just treat me like a chump and say nothing? I wasn't being any more rude to him than he was to me. It's not like I punched him in the face, and believe me, it crossed my mind," Jenson defended.

"I'm sure I'll be getting a call from Heather tomorrow about what happened tonight. I'll be surprised if they ever want to have dinner with us again."

"Mission accomplished," Jenson chuckled.

"This isn't funny. God, I can't take you anywhere."

"And I didn't ask you to. Actually, I specifically remember asking you to *not* take me," he reminded her.

"So you did this on purpose, to get back at me for making you accompany me?" she asked accusingly.

"No, I honestly didn't. I'm sorry you are mad, but I'm not sorry for defending myself and my views. I wish you would do more of that so I didn't feel like it was always you and your friends against me."

"This is the problem, Jenson. I shouldn't *have* to defend you. You should just be nice and try to get along with my friends."

"It's hard to get along with someone who belittles me and thinks that I'm beneath them. And that describes every one of your friends."

"That's not true. They just don't understand you yet because you never give them a chance to. If you let them get to know you like I do, they would really like you," Maggie said.

"I doubt it. The moment they find out I'm not a successful lawyer or businessman, they completely disregard me and treat me like a lowlife. I've just stopped trying. After three years, dear, you should understand that I'm never going to fit in with your crowd. I've just accepted it as an inevitability."

"I just wish you would try harder."

Jenson gave up. He knew there was no point in continuing the argument, as it was going nowhere. At this point, Maggie was just trying to make sure she had the last word, so he let her. He spent the rest of the ride home in silence, stewing.

When he and Maggie returned home, he went straight to his laptop and checked his email. There was no response from Dr. Wesson yet. He'd expected as much, but still felt disappointed. While he was online, he decided to see what he could find out about lucid dreaming, as Dr. Wesson had mentioned in his paper that it was a technique his study subjects used in their dreams to remember to gather the information that Dr. Wesson had requested.

Jenson found several informative websites and bookmarked them all in his browser. He then began reading through them. He found that learning to become lucid in dreams was a far more involved process than he had imagined. It required a dedicated schedule of checking to make sure you were actually awake by looking for cues throughout the day, such as checking your watch two or three times in a row to see if the time changed too quickly, or reading something several times to see if the text changed. The process for purposely trying to have a lucid dream, from what he read, was to do it when you've just awakened from a dream and remembered it clearly. You were then supposed to recall the dream as vividly as you could, then try to fall asleep again with the intention of looking for signs that you are dreaming and trying to imagine what you want to happen in the dream once you enter into it again.

As Jenson read this, he wondered how well these techniques could really work for a dream that caused an actual out-of-body experience to another dimension. From the information he was reading, the lucid dreaming was supposed to keep you conscious of the fact that you were dreaming and allow you to do anything you wished. But if you were actually in another dimension, would the dream cues actually work? The dreams that supposedly transported an individual to another realm were described by Dr. Wesson as being very realistic. The dream Jenson had had seemed incredibly real when he was in it, but when he awoke, he knew it had been very different from the world in which he lived. He doubted, however, that the watch technique or the re-reading text technique would have worked in his dream, or any other mind-transporting dream. That would likely only work in an actual dream. So how did Dr. Wesson train his study participants to become lucid dreamers in another world? He desperately wanted to know.

After gathering all the information he could stand to read, Jenson leaned back in his computer chair and clasped his hands over his forehead. He tried to relive his dream, attempting to remember anything about the dream that would indicate that it was different from any other dream. One thing came to mind: in his dream, he'd had a choice as to whether or not he went into the room after Kristine killed the demon. He remembered clearly that he actually weighed the options in his head, and had made a conscious decision to go in because he wanted to make sure that nothing terrible had happened. He could have run. He had been in control of himself. In most of his dreams, everything flowed as if he were watching it in a movie, with no conscious decision-making. The script had already been written and he was just acting out what was supposed to happen next.

As he thought more about his dreams, it occurred to him that his dream of the beautiful Andrea had been of a similar caliber. He'd consciously tried to find a face he recognized when

Andrea had pointed out that her ex boyfriend was in the bar. He'd consciously decided to take her back to the apartment instead of making her stay at the bar. He'd had choices, and hadn't blindly done whatever was scripted for him. Did that mean that Andrea was real? Was she a real person that just happened to be in the same dream as he, like Kristine? The thought had crossed his mind after he had the dream, but now he truly believed it. And it excited him almost as much as it scared him.

He jumped when Maggie walked into the living room.

"Whoa, jumpy aren't we? Did I catch you doing something bad?" she teased.

"No, no. I was just lost in my thoughts and I didn't hear you coming."

"What were you thinking about so hard?"

"The only thing I've been able to think about lately: my dreams, and what they've really meant all my life."

"You need to find something else to focus your attention on for a while. This whole thing is consuming you."

"I'm still getting my work done, though. Did you see how much I got done on my painting today?" he asked.

"I did, but ordinarily you would be painting again tonight, not sitting in front of the computer, staring off into space. I'm just concerned."

"If I hadn't had to go out and get insulted by Dick all evening then I might've had time to do both," he said, smiling smugly.

"Do we really need to go there again, Jenson?" Maggie asked curtly.

"Nope, we sure don't. Why would you bring it up?" he teased.

"You're not as cute as you think you are."

"I'm only as cute as *you* think I am." He wondered if she would understand that he was actually referring to her controlling personality.

"Damn straight."

That night, Jenson contemplated whether or not to attempt lucid dreaming. If he was serious about getting involved with Dr. Wesson's research, then it was something he should probably begin learning. As he closed his eyes, he focused on the fact that he was going to sleep, that he would be dreaming soon, and tried to remain conscious of it. An indeterminate amount of time later, he realized he was half asleep and thinking about dinosaurs. He tried to regain control of his thoughts and began the process again as he tried to fall asleep.

When he woke up in the morning, alarm beeping, he knew he had failed. He remembered the dream he'd been having, though, so he did what he had read he was supposed to do. He got out of bed, leaving the alarm for Maggie to deal with, and went to the kitchen, still in his skivvies. He grabbed a pen and notepad and began writing down the dream as best as he could remember.

I was not an actual participant in this dream, and it played out as though I was watching it as a movie, yet it was as though I was still there. A silent, floating observer with no body. It started out in a room that resembled a classroom, and a woman was giving birth, surrounded by people assisting her. Suddenly there was a huge burst of light, and everyone in the room died except for one man, who happened to be a cop. Then there was an entire family that appeared, seeming to have come from the light, and they looked to have poor hygiene, were overweight, and dressed in ragged clothing. There was a woman, her husband, and several children. I got the feeling that they were evil, and they had actually been what the woman on the floor had given birth to. They saw that one man had survived the explosion of light, and they set out to kill him, as for some reason they wanted no survivors. They wanted no one to know of their existence. The cop escaped and suddenly his partner was with him. They then began chasing after the family and the entire family disappeared into a blast of light again. The cops ran around through a school that I recognized as my old elementary school, then they went through some unfamiliar, run-down buildings. Somehow they came to the realization that this family was able to travel through space in a manner like teleporting. The cops then investigated several strange incidents in which houses had been raided with no apparent point of entry, and all that was taken was food. The cops discovered that the evil family members were using their space jumping skills to steal mass quantities of food, which they ate like gluttons. The rest of the dream was all about the cops and the family trying to kill each other.

When Jenson was finished, he read through what he had written. It sounded incredibly crazy, and he was quite certain that his dream hadn't been of the mind-travelling kind. At least, he hoped it wasn't. If he had been able to become lucid during this dream, what could he have done? He wasn't even really there, and had no body to control. Would he have been able to influence any of the events that occurred in the dream in any way? It was just a strange dream, even for him.

He went back to the bedroom while Maggie was in the shower and tried to go back to sleep. He ran through the dream over and over again in his head, trying to bring about the same dream as suggested by the websites on lucid dreaming. Unfortunately, he just wasn't tired enough to fall asleep again.

When Maggie came back to the bedroom to get dressed, she said, "You're going back to bed? Don't you think you should get some work done since I apparently kept you from it yesterday?"

Jenson sighed and climbed out of bed. He didn't tell Maggie that he was trying to have a lucid dream, as that would only exacerbate her obvious foul mood. Instead, he said, "Yes, dear. I'll get right on that."

"Don't 'yes, dear' me. I know you're being sarcastic."

"I'd never dream of it."

After Maggie was gone, Jenson showered and dressed. He checked his email only to be disappointed again. He didn't feel like painting at the moment, so he sat in front of the television and searched the channels for something interesting. He ended up watching a program that discussed the theory of ancient astronauts, which theorized that aliens had visited earth several times throughout ancient history and had influenced the evolution of mankind and culture. He wondered what Dick would have to say about it, and made a mental note to bring it up next time he had the pleasure of spending time with him. Jenson imagined it would make for an eventful evening. How could Maggie even suggest that he didn't try to get along with her friends?

He finally pulled himself from the couch and checked his email again. When he still found no reply from Dr. Wesson, he felt frustrated. He knew it had been less than twenty-four hours since he emailed the man, but he was anxious to hear something. Annoyed, he went to his painting table to work and clear his mind.

***

Over the next week, Jenson was disappointed each time he checked his email, which was often. He continued to record his dreams, but he still had no luck in bringing about a lucid dream. None of the dreams he had seemed to be like the demon-hunting dream or the Andrea dream, either. He began to lose a little of his passion for his dream research, and he considered giving up on the entire endeavor as he felt that he was going nowhere with it.

One night, however, about three weeks after his initial obsession began, his passion was reignited. He was walking down the sidewalk of what he knew to be Main Street in the dark, alone. None of the street lights were lit. The cars parked along the curb were covered in dust and debris, as though they hadn't been moved for some time, but he found it to be nothing out of the ordinary. He felt a tangible sense of anxiety and fear, because he knew there was danger about. People were infected in this area, and he shouldn't be here, but he pushed on because he was looking for someone important to him. He couldn't remember who it was he sought, but he felt that he would know when he saw her. It was definitely a woman.

Suddenly, from his left, he heard quick footsteps of someone running. He ducked into a nearby shop in which the door had been left ajar. It was incredibly dark inside. He waited next to the door until he heard the footsteps run by and fade into the distance, then peeked out. He saw no one on the street, so he continued on his way. When he came to a tall brick building on the corner of Main Street and Ash Street, he saw her. It was a beautiful brunette, but she wore dirty, ragged clothing. She was standing next to the building and gesturing wildly to him to hurry to her, but she said nothing. He ran to her, and she grabbed his hand and pulled him through the doorway into the building. She quietly shut the door behind her. Jenson followed her down a short flight of stairs, stepping over garbage and paper waste, until she brought him into a small room, dimly lit with candles.

"Did you get the antibiotics?" she asked him in a hoarse whisper.

He searched the pockets of his worn corduroy jacket and found a small bottle of gray and white capsules.

"Oh thank God." She took them and rushed to the corner of the room where a young girl of about fourteen was lying on an old, dirty mattress covered in blankets. As she gave the feeble-looking girl one of the capsules, she said to him, "We need to get out of here soon, Jamie. This place is riddled with the infection."

"Natalie," the girl said weakly after swallowing the pill, "I can't ask you to stay here with me. You and Jamie should just go. I'll catch up when I can."

"We're not leaving you," said Natalie, the beautiful brunette. She looked at Jenson with concern in her big brown eyes.

"She needs water," Natalie said to him. He saw a bucket on the floor that appeared to be filled with water and grabbed it, bringing it to her. She grabbed an old coffee mug from the floor next to the mattress and dipped it into the water for the girl. The girl sat up and drank the water down in a few big gulps, as though she hadn't had anything to drink in days. Then the girl lay down and closed her eyes.

Natalie stood up and walked to Jenson. She wrapped her arms around him and hugged him tightly. He felt her body begin to shake with silent sobs as she buried her face in his old jacket.

He embraced her and kissed the top of her head, inhaling the scent of her hair. Suddenly, he felt a strange sensation, like that of Déjà vu. And he remembered.

"Andrea?" he said as he looked down at her.

"What? Andrea?" she said as she looked up at him, her face full of tears and confusion.

It was her. He remembered. He remembered everything.

Chapter 5

The woman he had known to be Andrea stared at him, a look of horror beginning to contort her features. "No, not you. This can't be," she said in dismay as she backed away from him.

He was perplexed by her behavior. "Yes, Andrea, it's me! I met you in another dream, a few weeks ago. We were living in an apartment together with a few other guys. You remember?" He was certain she was remembering.

"Confusion, hallucinations, strange behavior...oh, God, you're infected! No, this can't be," she began to sob.

The girl in the corner bolted up. "Natalie, you have to do it! Do it now! Kill him before he infects us!"

Jenson was horrified. "No, I'm not infected! I'm fine! Let me explain!"

He took a step back when he saw Andrea, or Natalie, unsheathe a large knife that was strapped to her leg. He hadn't even noticed she had it before now. She advanced toward him.

"I love you, Jamie. I'm sorry," she said as she came at him suddenly.

He turned to run out the door, just as he felt a searing pain in his back.

Jenson's eyes shot open as he gasped in a lungful of air. He was in his bed in the apartment. He looked over and saw Maggie was just beginning to sit up.

"What the hell was that, Jenson?" she asked, annoyed.

"It happened again. I had another dream," he said as he tried to catch his breath. His heart was pounding in his chest.

"Another dream? You mean like the Kristine dream?" she said groggily as she settled back into bed.

"Yes. I know it for sure, because..." he hesitated. He didn't want to tell her about Andrea. Or was it Natalie? What was he supposed to call her now?

"Because what?"

"I just know. It was different. I remembered everything about this life, and the dreams, and I was able to control myself completely and had total awareness of everything." He climbed out of bed.

"Where are you going?" Maggie asked.

"I have to write it down. I need to record this."

"Can't you do it in the morning?" she called after him as he left the room. He didn't bother to answer.

In the kitchen, he retrieved the same notepad in which he'd been recording his other dreams. He sat at the counter and wrote out every last detail he could remember. When he was done, he set the pen on the notepad and stared at the pages before him, wondering what he could learn from his latest dream. He had met Andrea again, but she had a different name, a different life. She had called him by a different name - Jamie. But he had been Jenson in the first dream in which he'd seen her, hadn't he? He then had a startling thought. If he were truly visiting other dimensions, were those dimensions still existent when he woke up? If so, what happened to the Jenson or Jamie in the dream dimensions when he awoke? Did they just disappear? Or were those dimensions created by his mind entirely? Was that even possible? He couldn't wrap his head around it. Who and what were the Jensons and Andreas and Kristines of the dream dimensions?

Jenson went to his laptop and composed another email to Dr. Wesson. He was now more determined than ever to find answers.

Dear Dr. Wesson,

My name is Jenson Thorne, and I emailed you several weeks ago about a strange dream I'd had involving a woman whom I later found out to be a real person I had never met before. I have read your article entitled "Dreamscapes as Parallel Universes" in the November 2010 edition of the *Journal of Quantum Physics*, and found it to be most intriguing, as I stated before. I am emailing you again as I have not received a reply, and I am growing desperate for answers. I would also like to tell you that I've had another dream that I believe to be out of the ordinary. I met a woman in this dream that I'd met in a previous dream, and in the midst of the dream, I remembered everything about my current life, my previous dreams, and the woman. She had a different name, though, as did I, and it raised a lot of questions that I was hoping you might be able to answer. What and who are the people I see in these dreams? Am I still me? And if I am, what happens to the "me" in the dream "world" when I wake up? Do these dimensions still exist after I awaken? I would greatly appreciate a response, as I feel I would have a lot to offer to your field of study. I look forward to hearing from you soon. Thank you for your time.

He signed off, again leaving all of his contact information. As he returned to bed, he wondered if Dr. Wesson would ever respond. He needed to talk to him, but how did he get him to return his emails? Perhaps emails wouldn't be enough, but what would it take? Would he have to drive to the University of Michigan and find his office? If that was what needed to be done, he would do it.

In the morning, Jenson slept in while Maggie showered and got ready for the day. It was Saturday, but she preferred to wake up to the alarm every day of the week, even when she didn't have to work. When she came into the bedroom, she sat down on the bed and woke Jenson.

"Honey, I need to talk to you."

Jenson sat up and rubbed his tired eyes. "What's up?"

"I'm a little worried about your renewed obsession with this dream world thing. You were just starting to forget about it and get some work done, but after last night, I'm afraid you're going to fall back into a rut. Dr. Wesson never emailed you back, so can't you just let it go? This is a dead end for you, I can guarantee it. I let you indulge in your curiosity for a while, but it's time to move on," Maggie said.

"You don't understand, Maggie," Jenson replied. "I can't just stop and forget about this. These dreams are going to keep happening to me, and now that I can recognize them while they're happening, I can't stop trying to figure out what they are and what they mean. It's like an itch I have to scratch."

"Some itches shouldn't be scratched, Jenson. What do you hope to learn, to accomplish with pursuing this? You can't make money with it. It isn't going to help pay our bills, so you need to stop putting your work aside to focus on it. Your art show is less than two months away, and you still need to complete almost twenty paintings."

"I know that, and I will get my work done. But haven't you ever had something you felt passionate about, something that was bigger than yourself, bigger than your job? How amazing would it be if I helped to discover a truly ground-breaking theory in the world of physics? Aren't you curious to know if there really are multiple dimensions out there, with endless possibilities?"

"It would be interesting to know, but I fail to see how it would be beneficial to you and me."

"Not everything has a dollar value, Maggie. Not everything has to result in a paycheck. You've never done something just for the sake of knowledge, of understanding?" Jenson was surprised at how incredibly superficial Maggie was being. How could she not see the importance of it all?

"When you get obsessed with something, it consumes you. This is a bad time for you to get immersed in something so absurd."

"A bad time, hey? So when would it be a *good* time for me to get immersed in something *absurd*?" Jenson retorted.

"Never, ideally, but two months before an art show is especially bad timing. Now, I hate to do this, but I'm revoking your laptop privileges for today. I want you to paint today. Promise me."

Jenson scoffed. "What am I, twelve?"

"I think we both know the answer to that," Maggie rejoined.

Once Jenson sat down at his painting table, the day flew by. He only put down his brush to eat and to use the bathroom, but even in those short breaks, he found his mind returning to last night's dream. He had decided to keep calling the woman from his dreams Andrea, as it was the name that first came to mind when he pictured her face. Was the world he visited last night a real place? It was a terrible, depressing place. He remembered the cars, the shops along Main Street, the street lamps, and concluded that if it were a real place, then it must have been similar to many other American small towns before the infection. What was the "infection," exactly? Andrea had tried to kill him when she thought he was infected, so it must be something exceedingly horrible.

He thought about the beginning of his dream. He had somehow known that he needed to be wary when he was on the street, and had some knowledge that an "infection" existed. How had he known that? And how had he known he was looking for someone, and that he would recognize her when he saw her, but not know what her name was, where he was, or anything else about his situation? He was puzzled. If that dream dimension had been created solely by his mind, wouldn't he have known more about what was going on? But if it wasn't created by him, then how did he come to be part of it? The Jamie he had been in the dream seemed to already have an established identity and life before Jenson entered the picture. So who was Jamie? Did Jamie look like Jenson? He hadn't actually seen his reflection or really tried to look at himself, so he didn't know. He could've been in an entirely different body than the one he knew. And what about the searing pain he'd felt before he awakened? Did Natalie actually stab Jamie? If there was a real Jamie, was he dead now? There was so much he still couldn't figure out.

In the evening, he quickly checked his email while Maggie was in the bathroom. He wasn't surprised to see no new messages in his inbox. He closed the laptop and returned to painting, hoping to distract himself from his disappointment.

To keep Maggie happy, Jenson painted every day, morning to night, for the next week. He was able to complete ten paintings in that time. Unfortunately, that was the only thing he was able to accomplish that week. He'd had no interesting dreams, and Dr. Wesson still ignored him. His frustration with the matter had hit a peak, and he was ready to sit down and have a serious conversation with Maggie. He had done what she'd asked, and now he needed something from her.

"How was your day?" he asked her at dinner as they sat across from each other at the small café-style table in the kitchen.

"Not so great. My boss had a major stick up her ass today, and everybody paid for it. She actually made a comment to me that my perfume was too fruity and I was never to wear it again." When Jenson gave her an odd look, she said, "Seriously. Too fruity. She's nuts."

"That's an unusual complaint. But on a brighter note, I've finished ten paintings this week," he said proudly.

"Great! Halfway there! See what you can do when you focus on your work?"

"Yeah. I figure I can have everything ready by the end of next week, which would leave me a month and a half of downtime before my show."

Maggie stopped eating and looked at him. "I can guess where you are going with this."

"Well, I'm doing what you wanted me to do. I was hoping I could get you to do something for me now, as a reward," he said hopefully.

She seemed hesitant. "Before I agree to it, what do you want me to do?"

"In your line of work, you've gotten really good at finding a way to get a hold of people when you need to. I was wondering if I could get you to track down Dr. Wesson's phone number for me." He smiled at her as sweetly as he could.

Maggie took a bite of her pasta and stared at Jenson while she chewed. He waited patiently, knowing she was drawing out her answer purposely. Finally, she swallowed and said, "Fine. But I want you to promise me that you will finish all of your work before you call him. I want every painting completed." Her demands were set.

"I can do that. Thank you, honey."

"Just don't make me regret doing this for you."

Jenson worked tirelessly through the next week to complete his paintings. Each day, when Maggie returned home from work, he asked her if she had Dr. Wesson's number. Her reply was always the same: "Are you done with your paintings?" When he said no, she said no. When Thursday evening came around, however, he had a different answer.

Jenson was waiting in the kitchen for her when she came through the door.

"Did you get his number yet?"

Maggie frowned and asked, "Did you finish your work yet?"

"Yes. I've finished every last painting. Now please tell me you have good news for me."

"Really? All of them?" she asked doubtfully.

"Yes! If I were going to lie to you, don't you think I'd have done it already?"

"Alright. I've got his number for you." She opened her briefcase and pulled out a yellow sticky note with a phone number and "Dr. Donald Wesson, University of Michigan" scrawled upon it.

"Thank you, honey!" he exclaimed as he snatched the paper from her and grabbed his cell phone from the counter.

"Are you seriously going to call him right now? Aren't we going to eat dinner?" Maggie asked.

"I've been waiting for this moment for over a month now. Dinner can wait."

Jenson carefully dialed the number, checking twice to make sure he had every number entered correctly before pressing "send."

He put the phone to his ear and smiled at Maggie as he listened to the ringing on the other end. Maggie rolled her eyes at him and started getting things prepared in the kitchen for dinner. He didn't let her annoyance frustrate him this time. He was too excited. However, with every unanswered ring, he felt his heart drop a little. After eight rings, his call was sent to voicemail.

"Doctor Donald Wesson, leave a message." The voice was deep and curt.

When Jenson heard the "beep" that indicated he should begin speaking, he suddenly didn't know what to say. He sputtered for a moment before he found his words. "Hi, this is Jenson Thorne. I've emailed you several times, Dr. Wesson, about some dreams I've had, and I was hoping to have a chance to speak to you about your studies. I'm interested in being in your experiments. Please call me back," he pleaded. He left his phone number and ended the call.

He sat for a minute, feeling let down. Maggie, however, had no intention of letting him wallow in his disappointment and ordered him to get up and help her with dinner.

"I probably sounded really stupid in that message. I wonder if I should call back and leave another message," Jenson fretted.

"So you can sound stupid twice? No, leave it alone. If he's interested, he'll call you back. He's probably home eating dinner at this time of night anyway."

Jenson said no more on the subject, knowing Maggie was tired of hearing about it. He listened to her complain about work and her boss all evening, though he had a hard time concentrating on the content of her monologue. He could hear her voice, heard her speaking words to him, but if she were to ask him to repeat what she'd just said, he could not. Luckily, she didn't seem to care if he was part of the conversation. She just wanted someone to talk at, and she talked at him until she went to bed. He wondered if she even noticed that he had said barely a word the entire time, and concluded that she likely did not.

As he sat on the couch by himself, staring at the television, he wondered what his future would bring. What would become of his relationship with Maggie? At this point, he felt like he was more of a pet to her than a boyfriend. Her needs always came first, in every aspect of their relationship. Her career, her friends, her wants and desires, all took precedence over him. He had become an afterthought in her life. He had become so used to it that he had forgotten what it felt like to be important to someone, to be the main focus, and not just a side note. He had gotten a taste of what that felt like in his first dream with Andrea. He had felt needed. For the first time in a long time, he had felt like someone actually wanted him around instead of just tolerating his presence. And it felt wonderful. Would he ever feel like that again with Maggie? Had he ever felt that way with Maggie? The longer he thought about it, the more he wished he wasn't thinking about it.

He was surprised out of his depression when his phone suddenly rang. He furrowed his brow as he looked at the screen. The clock said 11:18 PM, and the number was unfamiliar. He considered letting it go to voicemail, as he usually didn't answer such calls. At the last minute, however, he decided to take it on the off chance it was Dr. Wesson.

"You called me earlier?" the man on the other end responded brusquely when Jenson answered.

Taken off guard, Jenson asked, "Is this Dr. Wesson?"

"Last time I checked."

He didn't know what to say next. The conversation was already incredibly uncomfortable and awkward, and the ensuing silence on the other line only made it worse.

"Um, yes, I called you earlier this evening. I just wasn't expecting you to call me back tonight."

"Call me tomorrow then. I'll be around."

"Oh, no it's fine –" Jenson said, but it was too late. Dr. Wesson had already hung up. He looked at his phone to make sure the call had ended, and when he saw that it had, he looked around in bewilderment. What the hell had just happened?

He looked at the number Dr. Wesson had called from, wondering why it didn't identify it as a known contact on his phone. When he had called Dr. Wesson earlier, he had saved the number to his phone. He discovered the number Dr. Wesson had called from was a different number than the one he had called. A cell phone perhaps? He tried to select the number to save it as a contact, and when he did so, he accidentally called it. When he realized what was happening, he hurriedly stopped the call. He hoped to high heaven that the call hadn't actually rung on Dr. Wesson's end. He was off to a blazing start with this whole endeavor, and he knew Dr. Wesson must be exceedingly impressed with him already.

Jenson put his phone on the coffee table in front of him to prevent anymore mishaps. He sat back and rested his head on the back of the couch, staring at the ceiling. Despite his embarrassment, he felt excited and was pleased that Dr. Wesson had called him back. He was going to be a difficult man to work with, Jenson deduced, but he had a feeling that the things he would learn would be well worth it. He wanted to rouse Maggie from her sleep to tell her he'd finally spoken to Dr. Wesson, and that he was finally moving forward with this adventure, but he thought better of it. She wouldn't care. She'd be annoyed that he was bothering her with his nonsense. He desperately wished he had someone to share in his excitement.

Lying in bed later that night, Jenson found he was unable to sleep. In his mind, he played out several scenarios depicting the possibilities of his impending conversation with Dr. Wesson. He tried to figure out the best way to start the conversation, and wondered how much information Dr. Wesson would disclose to him over the phone regarding his research. From Jenson's brief experience with the man, he concluded that he wasn't exactly a chatterbox, and would probably leave most of the talking to Jenson. He knew he should have some notes prepared before he called Dr. Wesson, just to help keep him focused and prevent himself from jabbering like a moron. He needed to persuade Dr. Wesson to meet with him and include him in his studies, and that wasn't going to happen if he thought that Jenson was a nitwit. His mind worked at prioritizing the main focal points he wanted to address with Dr. Wesson, but he fell asleep long before it was finished.

In the morning, Jenson awoke half an hour before Maggie's alarm was set to go off. He slipped out of bed without waking her and went to the kitchen. He sat down with his breakfast and a notepad and wrote down his latest dream. He was sure it was not a mind travelling dream, but there was one part in it that he found very strange.

I was an active participant in this dream. It was a zombie apocalypse, and I was on the run with a small group of people, none of whom I knew except my mother. We were all on a city bus, which apparently was still running its route, and we were getting ready to head out of town to seek a more rural safe haven. Before the bus left, however, a small mechanical toy horse approached the bus, and it was repeating my name. I knew in the dream that this was a "message horse," and I went out and grabbed it. I brought it back onto the bus and pressed a button to listen to the message. It warned me that if I did a certain thing, which I can't remember what, then someone would die. We set out then, and we found ourselves on a tree-lined country road. We came to a haunted house (the Halloween attraction, not a real one) and checked it out. It appeared to be safe, so we made it our shelter. Soon, however, a group of 40 or more people showed up and wanted in. My group argued about whether to let them in, but then a "message horse" appeared on the doorstep and told us we needed to let the group in. As they all piled into the house, which was a normal house inside, by the way, I was worried about how loud they were. I was afraid they were going to attract zombies with all the noise. I was sitting with my group, discussing the newcomers, and I made a minor contribution to the conversation. The strange thing was, when I spoke, it was like it was the first time I was actually AWARE of myself in the dream. I felt strange, like I had just realized my own existence when I heard my own voice speak. And I realized it was the first time I had actually spoken in the dream. I had just been watching or surmising everything else. It was then that I started to notice how loud the newcomers were getting, and I ran around the house yelling for everyone to shut up. When they did, I could still hear a man talking and singing from somewhere in the house. I followed the noise, and eventually found an old man sitting on a toilet in a closet. He wouldn't stop talking, so I started slapping him, over and over, until he finally shut up.

Then we were all drinking and having a party, like a celebration of the end of the world, and I farted and everyone started cheering for me.

Jenson laughed to himself as he wrote the last sentence. He would never understand where his brain came up with such ridiculousness. He had yet to meet someone who was willing to admit that they regularly had dreams as vividly detailed and ludicrous as his, but he was hoping that would soon change. Perhaps it was the fact that his mind was able to create such bizarre fantasy worlds and scenarios that made him capable of performing the mind travel that Dr. Wesson studied.

While he had the notepad handy, Jenson decided to jot down some bullet points he wanted to make sure he discussed with Dr. Wesson. He wanted to know what kind of studies Dr. Wesson was currently performing, whether he had learned anything new since his 2010 paper, and if he were willing to take Jenson on as a study subject. He also wanted to make sure he told Dr. Wesson about his three strange dreams in which he suspected he may have mind traveled, and about his lucidity at the end of the third dream.

He heard Maggie's alarm going off in the bedroom, and he suddenly felt nervous. He had been excited to tell someone about Dr. Wesson calling him last night, but now that Maggie was available to speak to, he was worried she was going to find a way to make him feel ashamed for his excitement. It was a skill she had mastered easily. He waited until he heard the shower running before he went into the bathroom to talk to her.

"You were up early today," Maggie said when she heard him enter.

"I woke up at 5:30 and couldn't go back to sleep. Dr. Wesson called me back last night."

"Really? Wow, I wouldn't have thought he'd call back...so late."

Jenson knew she meant that she didn't think he'd call back at all. "Yeah, he seems like a strange guy. It was the most awkward and short conversation I've had in a while. I'm supposed to call him back today, and I'm kind of nervous about it. What if he doesn't want to involve me in his study?"

"Well, then I guess it wasn't meant to be. What exactly would being 'involved' in the study entail? Would that mean you'd be driving back and forth to U of M constantly?"

"I don't know yet, but I'd like to at least go there to meet him. Even if he doesn't want me to be part of his study, I'd like to sit down and talk with him about his research."

Maggie didn't respond immediately. "Well, whatever makes you happy. Just as long as it doesn't get in the way of your work or cost us too much in gas money. I've been hearing rumors that corporate is talking about cutting back hours at work, remember? We need to be smart with our money until I know for sure that my job is still secure."

"Driving to U of M isn't going to break the bank. Don't worry, it's not like I'm going to be sinking thousands of dollars into this. I just need some answers. And I need you to be supportive of me." Jenson said.

"I am supportive, but I want to make sure you're going to be smart about this. I don't want you getting sucked into something that isn't going to…"

"Make us money?" Jenson finished her sentence for her.

"That's not what I was going to say. I was going to say I didn't want you getting sucked into something that isn't going to help your career. If people find out that you're a part of some crazy psychic mind traveling study, that's not going to help your image."

Jenson had to take a deep breath to keep from losing his temper. "It's not crazy. It's a legitimate scientific study. And who cares what people think? Why does anyone have to know what I do in my private time anyway?"

"Ok, then. As long as it is restricted to your private time. Just don't let it distract you from your career goals, that's all I'm saying."

"Not everything in life has to revolve around a career for financial gain, Maggie. Sometimes you have to do things for yourself, for the sake of curiosity and personal growth.

Sometimes you need an adventure to add a little excitement to life. I'm sorry if I'm not as career-driven as you are."

"Don't get mad at me for being career-driven. For a woman like me, a career is the most important thing I can do for myself. I grew up this way, and my experience in life has taught me that a career will never wake up in the morning and decide it doesn't love me anymore, so it should always be top priority."

Jenson was taken aback. "So your career is more important to you than I am?"

"Not more important, just important in a different way."

"Well, I still love you, and always will. And while a career might not decide it doesn't love you anymore, your boss can certainly decide she doesn't want you anymore. Nothing in life is certain." With that, Jenson left the room.

He went back to the bedroom to lie on the bed. He was fuming. He had always feared that Maggie's career was more important to her than he was, but he'd never expected her to say it. She'd tried to candy-coat it when he called her on it, but he knew what she really meant. If her company wanted to send her to Japan or Europe or Peru, she would go in a heartbeat without giving one thought to whether he would go with her or not. And if he didn't go, she still would. She'd leave him behind with nary a second thought, like a pet that was no longer convenient to care for. She didn't love him.

Maggie came into the room a while later, all primped and prettied. "Jenson, you misunderstood me. I love you, and you are very important to me. I think all that I've done for us should be proof enough of that."

"You mean pay our bills? Yes, I'm aware that I don't make enough money to support us and that leaves the burden to you."

"Quit being so cross. I know you are trying to make a name for yourself as an artist, and I am completely supportive of that. Honestly, if I didn't love you, would I be so supportive? Wouldn't I just tell you to go find another job and paint in your spare time? I want the same thing you do: for you to be successful as an artist. If that means that I make the money for us until that happens, so be it. I am ok with that. What is it exactly that you want from me? What is it that you want me to say right now? All I'm trying to do is keep you focused on your goals – on our goals." Maggie glanced at the clock as she waited for Jenson to reply.

"I just want you to let me do something that *I* think is important without making me feel like I am wasting everyone's time. I need you to trust that I'm doing what is best for me, and that it won't adversely affect us or our wallet. I need you to let me make a decision for myself instead of trying to control me."

"Ok. I trust you. I'm not trying to control you, and I'm sorry that's how you feel. Let's take the day to cool off, and we can talk about it more when I get home. " Maggie kissed Jenson and left the room. He heard the front door shut shortly thereafter.

He didn't feel better. He'd had similar arguments with Maggie many times before, but things never changed. They never talked about it more when she got home, and it was swept under the rug until the next argument. He just wanted to feel like he was in control of his own life, able to do the things he wanted to do, without her perpetual scrutiny. Whenever he tried to tell her that, though, he always ended up feeling like he was being whiny and needy, the exact opposite of what he was trying to accomplish.

Jenson decided it was time to end his pity party, and he showered and got ready for the day. He tried to put the unhappy morning behind him and focus on his next step: calling Dr. Wesson. He sat down at the kitchen table, notepad next to him, and looked at his phone. After contemplating which number he should try first, the office number or the cell phone number, he decided to dial the office number. No answer. He hung up without leaving a message and called the cell phone number Dr. Wesson had called from the previous night.

The phone rang once before Jenson heard, "Yeah?"

"Hi, this is Jenson Thorne. I spoke with you briefly last night, and I wanted to talk to you about your research."

"Oh yeah. So what did you want to know?"

"Well, I sent you a few emails about some dreams I'd had, and I'd read your paper from the *Journal of Quantum*

Physics, and I was hoping you could shed some light on why I had such strange experiences."

"I don't open emails from people I don't know. After that paper was published, I got flooded with emails from all sorts of lunatics and people calling me a lunatic, so I just stopped reading them."

Jenson waited, but there was only silence. "Oh, ok, um, can I tell you about the dreams, then?"

"I don't know, *can* you? Are you physically able?" Dr. Wesson asked sarcastically. "I believe the word you were looking for was 'may,' not 'can.'"

"Yeah…so…*may* I tell you about the dreams?" Jenson asked, trying not to let his irritation show in his voice.

"Sure, why not?"

Jenson told Dr. Wesson about the dreams, about meeting Kristine at the gas station, about Andrea, and about becoming lucid at the end of the second Andrea dream.

"Yeah, that sounds about right." Dr. Wesson said. "It fits with what I've seen. So what do you want to know?"

Jenson didn't know where to begin. After a brief pause, he said, "Everything."

"Don't we all?"

"I want to know what you know. I want to be in your studies. I want to find out everything I can about what happens to me when I think I'm sleeping. And I want to know who Andrea is."

Dr. Wesson said nothing for a long time. Jenson began to think he'd hung up on him again.

"Come see me. Today. We have a lot to talk about."

Chapter 6

A smile spread across Jenson's face. "Yes, ok, that sounds great! Where should I meet you? What time? I live a couple hours away, so I need enough time to get there."

"I'll see you at four at the Rookie Pub," Dr. Wesson said.

"Ok! But how will I know who you are?"

"Just ask someone when you come in. They know me there." And with that, the call ended.

Jenson looked at the clock, and realized he had only about an hour to spare before he would need to leave. He hurried to his laptop and found the address and directions to the Rookie Pub. He then sat at the kitchen table and wrote out every question he wanted to ask Dr. Wesson. If this ended up being the only chance he got to speak with Dr. Wesson, he wanted to make sure to get as much information from him as possible.

Once Jenson's list was complete, he sent a text to Maggie to let her know his plans for the day. He was surprised when she called him right afterward.

"You're just going to drop everything and go today? On such short notice?" Maggie asked.

"Why not? I have nothing else going on today. I'm anxious to meet with Dr. Wesson, and I think the sooner, the better."

"Heather and Dick are coming over for dinner tonight! I told you that last night, remember? I wanted you to redeem yourself for being so rude last time we had dinner with them, and now you aren't even going to be there? It's going to look bad."

"I honestly don't care how I look to Heather and Dick. They've already made up their minds about me," Jenson replied.

"I care what they think about you, and you could easily change their opinion if you would just try! What am I supposed to tell them?"

"Just tell them I had a meeting in Ann Arbor. Tell them it's business related if you want. It doesn't matter what you tell them, really. They don't come for my company anyway."

"Fine. But you owe me big time. Like, tennis with Dick or something."

"Yeah, that's not going to happen, but I'll rub your feet when I get home."

Jenson had a difficult time finding The Rookie Pub. Even with written directions and the assistance of his GPS, he still ended up circling around several times before he noticed the pub tucked in between a fitness club and a salon. He thought it to be an odd location for a pub.

When a server approached him at the entrance, he asked if she knew whether Dr. Donald Wesson had arrived yet.

"Oh yeah, Don's here," she said, her pleasant face suddenly taking on a look of annoyance. She pointed to an older man seated alone in the corner. "At his usual table. You want me to bring you about fifteen shots to start you out?" She smiled, but he could tell she was somewhat serious.

"No thanks, I'll be driving later. Water would be just fine."

He approached the booth, and Dr. Wesson looked up at him. "Jenson, I presume."

"You presume correctly. It's nice to finally meet you, Dr. Wesson." He held out his hand and Dr. Wesson stood and shook it firmly. Dr. Wesson was about 5'9" and a little on the lean side. He looked to be in his sixties or seventies, and a complexion that was slightly swarthy for a Caucasian man. His short hair, what little was left of it, was a salt and pepper color.

He had light hazel eyes that tended more toward green than brown, and a narrow nose. He was one of those men who had a permanent expression of aggravation on his face.

"Call me Don. Sit down."

Jenson did as he was instructed and sat across from Don in the booth. The server brought Jenson his water and a beer to replace Don's empty one, then high-tailed it out of there.

"So, Jennie, I understand you want to know everything I know," Don said before taking a long swig from his beer mug.

Jenson was not a fan of Don's nickname for him. He couldn't tell if Don was purposely antagonizing him or if he was just being weird in general. "People usually call me Jenson," he said, trying to be polite.

"Well, I'm an unusual person, Jennie."

"I've gathered that."

"Very astute. What is your level of knowledge regarding the subject of physics, quantum mechanics, and human consciousness?" Don wanted to know.

"I've never had a physics class in my life. Not even in high school. All I know is what I've read in your paper and seen on science shows."

"Level zero, then. Congratulations, you know about as much as the rest of us." Don said. "I've been studying physics for over forty years, and what I've found is that the more you learn, research, and discover, the more you understand how much you don't understand."

"You obviously know more than I do, and that's why I'm here."

"I've seen a lot of strange things in my studies, and I've made a lot of hypotheses. It doesn't mean I truly understand."

"Tell me about your studies, about your hypotheses. I want to know about the theories of parallel universes."

"Ah, where to begin? From the beginning, I suppose. First, let me say that parallel universes are not a distinct *theory* in physics. We may say 'multiverse theory,' but really it is just a part of what is predicted based on other theories in physics.

"Anyway, I was like you once. I was always a very vivid dreamer, with wild adventures and nonsensical fantasies running through my head as I slept. But one night, something happened that changed my view of dreams forever. I dreamed of being in a car accident, and it was incredibly real and terrifying. I woke up like they do in the movies: bolt upright, screaming. I was able to remember every detail. The very next day, I was in a car accident, and it happened exactly as I saw it in my dream. I spent a few weeks in the hospital, and as I lay there, waiting for my body to heal, I couldn't help thinking: how had that happened? How did I see the accident before it happened? I was already studying physics at that time, quantum mechanics specifically. When I returned to work, I started looking into the possibility of time travel, the legitimacy of psychics, and the phenomenon of remote viewing. I had developed a hypothesis that our consciousness might not be as earthbound as we typically think. There are several theories out there regarding multiple dimensions and universes and alternate realities, and I thought that perhaps my consciousness had found a way to travel from this universe into a parallel universe, or perhaps even traveled through time.

"Time, you see, is still a debatable topic. No one can say for sure *what* time really is, Jennie. Einstein thought time was woven into the fabric of space, and that time moves slower for an object accelerating than for an object at rest. Some think time is endless, some think it is finite. Some think it is simply a construct of the human mind. But no one really knows for sure, myself included. Given my experience, I understand time as something our mind can move through. We can see the past, we can see the future. The *events* that occurred in time were what interested me the most at first. I started studying psychics, and my findings were most fascinating. I did a study with subjects trying to predict the order of cards in a randomly shuffled deck. Interestingly, I found that the only time there was a statistically significant number of correct guesses was when the person in the other room, who was drawing the cards that the subject was making guesses about, actually looked at the cards before the subject made the guess. It appeared that the subjects were able to 'see' the order of the cards only if someone else saw them first. I concluded that these psychic subjects weren't able to see into the future, but were instead somehow drawing the knowledge from the cardholder's mind."

"Wow," Jenson said. "That's pretty wild."

"Exactly. That study got me thinking about the possibility of one mind connecting with another mind. I'm sure you've had this experience: you feel that something is wrong one day, for no apparent reason, then later find out that something bad has happened to someone close to you. Have you had that happen?"

"Yeah, actually, it happens in my family all the time. It happens to my mother often when something is going on with one of us kids." Jenson replied.

"It's happened to almost everyone that I've ever asked about it. That, to me, is evidence that we are somehow able to connect our minds, to collect information from someone else's consciousness into our own." Don took another long drink of his beer.

"This is all incredibly interesting, but how does it relate to mind travel to parallel universes?"

"Relax, Antsy Nancy. You want to know what I know, right? This is part of it."

"My apologies, please continue."

"I planned to. Right after I get Smiley to get me another drink." Don held up his hand, gesturing to the server. Jenson looked over his shoulder and saw the server nod toward them in acknowledgment. He also noticed that the people at a table near him and Don were staring at them.

"We have an audience," Jenson said in a low voice to Don.

Don replied loudly, "The best stories do tend to draw an audience," and he looked at the table of gawkers and raised his mug to them before swallowing the remaining contents. The onlookers quickly glanced away. Jenson chuckled. He was starting to like Don's quirks.

The server brought Don his drink.

"Thanks, Smiley," he said.

"Whatever, Don," she replied curtly.

"More flics with honey, Judy Attitudy!" Don called after her as she walked away.

"And the most flies with bullshit!" she declared without looking back.

Don smiled at Jenson. "I like her," he said. He took a drink of his new beer before continuing his story. "Anyway, where were we? Connected consciousness, yes. Well, when I considered the possibility that we are able to gather information from other people's minds, it made me wonder if we were able to actually connect with them in a way that would allow one mind to completely invade another mind. I began to think that perhaps my dream of the car accident wasn't simply my mind seeing into the future, per se , but was instead gathering the information from a version of myself in the future, or a version of myself in a parallel universe that was on a different timing of events than our own. Interesting idea, yes, but how the hell was I going to test that? How was I going to study it? I spent a lot of time pondering that.

"I started to look to my dreams for ideas. If it happened in a dream state before, it could happen again, right? Maybe that was the key. Maybe when I was sleeping, my mind was in the right state to perform this amazing feat. I started practicing lucid dreaming, and I got very good at it. Most dreams, I found, were fun and amazing when I could control what I did. But I knew when I could make myself fly, or make things turn into other things, that they weren't real. Then, one night, I had a dream in which I could not do those things. Try as I might, I couldn't make anything happen that wouldn't happen in the waking world. That was when I knew I was somewhere else, not just dreaming. I still remember it clearly, even though it was many years ago. I was in my own home, of that I was certain, but it didn't look like the house I lived in at the time. I looked in a mirror. It was me, but I was wearing an outfit I didn't actually own. Then my wife walked into the room. My wife had died of breast cancer five years prior. But there she was, alive and well. I asked her what year it was, and she gave me a funny look and asked me if I was feeling alright. I told her I was just feeling confused, and she looked worried. She told me it was November

Eighth, 2001. That was the correct date. I asked her about 9/11, and she grew even more worried. She had no idea what I was talking about. There had been no 9/11 in the world I was in. I asked her what pi was, and she replied, 'like apple pie, or 3.14 pi?' I was floored. I needed concrete proof, however. How could I find out if this was truly another world?

"Then it hit me. Math. Math is the universal language, is it not? Formulas should hold true in any universe regardless of the different day-to-day events, except perhaps in Level Four parallel universes."

"What is a Level Four parallel universe?" Jenson asked.

"It's hypothesized that there are four basic levels of parallel universes. Some physicists break these levels down even further, but they still fall under the four levels in most respects. A Level One multiverse comes from the idea that inflation of the cosmos is infinite, and thus all possibilities for the arrangement of matter are realized, producing an infinite number of universes the same as ours. In other words, at the end of our visible universe is the beginning of another, and at the end of that one, yet another. This is the most commonly accepted model. A Level Two multiverse is explained by inflation causing multiple Level One universes which have different laws of physics than ours and different rates of expansion. We can think of these as 'bubble universes.' A Level Three multiverse is in essence very similar to a Level One, but comes not from an idea of great distance, but rather of a different dimension. This approach of quantum physics is also called the Many Worlds Interpretation. For every possible outcome of a situation, decision, measurement, et cetera, a parallel universe is created. For instance, you decided to come here today, but there would be a universe in which you decided not to come. These universes can be right on top of us, but we are not able to see or interact with them. In a Level Four multiverse, mathematical principles are different and thus give rise to differences in the equations of physics. These would be the most unlike our own universe."

"I'm lost already," Jenson admitted sheepishly.

"It's quite alright. We can come back to it later. Now, back to my story…where was I?"

"You were in a parallel world where your wife was still alive and you wanted to prove it wasn't just a dream."

"Oh, yes. I wandered through the house until I found a computer. I sat down and opened the internet browser. This world wasn't so different from our own, other than some of the details. I searched out math formulas, looking for something I wasn't familiar with, something I would remember when I awoke, but something I hadn't known before going to bed. I wanted something that I knew my mind couldn't have constructed. And I found one. It was one of Ramanujan's mathematical formulas that had not yet been proven. I sat there and memorized the formula. Only when I was certain that I had it memorized perfectly and could easily and quickly recite it and write it down did I leave the computer desk. I then went back and spent as much time with my wife as I could until I awoke."

Jenson waited anxiously as Don took a break to drink his beer.

"On the edge of your seat now, aren't you, Jennie?" Don teased. "Well, I woke up and remembered the formula. I wrote it down as I had remembered it, then looked it up. It was the very same. And it had still not been proven. Interesting note, by the way, it was proven to be correct in 2012, and is used in physics in computing the entropy of black holes. I wonder if it has been proven yet in the world I visited that day."

"So that was how you were able to determine you were in another world? What if it was a formula you might have seen once, since it is from the field of physics, and you just forgot you'd seen it? Couldn't your brain have retained it and just brought it up then, even if you weren't aware that you had ever seen it or didn't remember seeing it?" Jenson suggested.

"I suppose it is entirely possible, I'll give you that, but I find it unlikely. Of course, your concern regarding the matter is the very same concern my colleagues have. They tore apart my paper, the one you read, because there existed the possibility that my test subjects did know what I had asked them to find in their dreams beforehand, but claimed that they did not. This is the reason that I haven't published any further papers on the subject, and why I no longer check emails from people I don't know."

"Can you tell me more about your studies? I had a hard time understanding some of the technical jargon in your paper. What exactly was your method?"

"I worked with a couple of neurobiologists for this study, as my area of expertise is in physics, not the brain. They helped me to develop the methods we used. First, my team and I used an MRI machine to scan the brains of our subjects while they looked at pictures, and we collected an encyclopedia of brain patterns which could later be used to translate a particular brain pattern to a particular image. Then, we were able to scan subjects' brains while they slept, and from the encyclopedia we'd gathered previously, we could roughly reconstruct vague images of their dreams. I tried to use this method to 'see' what a person was seeing when they experienced the type of dream that takes them to another universe. It didn't work, though, which, to me, proved that something interesting was going on. Instead, we could see that the dorsolateral prefrontal cortex was activated, which happens when someone is in a lucid dream, but we weren't able to read any images from the brain. It was as though the brain wasn't actually seeing what the subject was 'dreaming' about. We also noticed activity in the area between the parietal and temporal lobes, which the neurobiologists were able to tell me is a region associated with the sensation of leaving the body. I found this very interesting indeed. However, the study of the brain is still in its infancy, and our results were deemed by many to be unverifiable."

"That is interesting, and much easier to understand than what you wrote in your paper. I want to talk about how this happens, though. The woman I met in my first dream, Kristine, turned out to be a real person in this world. I'm sure I've never met her before. And she somehow was able to remember having the exact same dream as I did, except from her point of view. What do you feel happened there?" Jenson asked.

"Scientists don't *feel*. We *think*. And from what I've been able to observe through my own experience, and from the experiences of those I've studied, I've come up with a hypothesis that I haven't been able to disprove. Granted, it's damn near impossible to prove, but I'll settle for not being able to disprove it for the time being." He stopped to take another drink. Jenson couldn't help but wonder how many drinks Don had already had tonight.

Don continued, "I think what's happening in our sleep is that our consciousness, our mind, opens itself up in some way to other minds and consciousnesses that we are somehow inherently connected with. Are you familiar with quantum entanglement?"

"What do you think?" Jenson replied sarcastically.

"Thought I'd ask anyway. Quantum entanglement is, in a nutshell, when two or more objects behave in a way relative to each other, regardless of the spatial difference between them. When you influence one, the other one is influenced even though it is nowhere near the object being influenced. Now, I'm not saying that my hypothesis draws directly from quantum entanglement, but it is the basic idea of this connectedness regardless of space that I find intriguing. Additionally, we have found that the particles, or so we'll call them for Jennie's sake, in quantum field theory are not strictly in one well-defined location. A particle in your body, for instance, has a small but nonzero chance of being found in the farthest reaches of the universe right now."

"That doesn't make any sense." Jenson said with his brows furrowed.

"I know. That is the unofficial slogan for quantum physics. 'This shit doesn't make sense.' Trademark."

"Ok, so things aren't where they always seem to be, and they can be connected in a way that causes one to behave a certain way based on how the other is influenced regardless of how far away the objects are from each other...is that what you are saying?"

"For our purposes, basically yes. Now think back to what I told you about multiverses. If it is true that the universe is infinite, and therefore the matter within it infinite, then there must be an infinite number of parallel universes that mimic our own, as in Level One multiverses. There is a finite number of ways for matter to arrange itself, like a deck of cards. If you shuffle that deck of cards, or matter, an infinite number of times, there will be an infinite number of times that the deck of cards arranges itself in the same order it has been in before. There will be repetition. Therefore, if the universe is infinitely large, then there must be parallel universes just like our own. But imagine in these universes, that the parallel version of you encountered a decision just as you have encountered in this universe, but he chose a different path than you did. Now it is different, but only in the minor details. Are you with me?"

"Infinite Jensons, on infinite earths, with varying events that have brought about a different outcome than in this world. And are you saying that we are somehow connected with these versions of ourselves in a way that is similar to how quantum particles are connected and react when the other is influenced? And that maybe since a particle that you think should be here can be detected somewhere else, that our consciousness can be somewhere else too? Wait, I just confused myself," Jenson said, scowling.

"Yeah, that's basically what I'm saying, but there's more. Recently, it's been discovered that there are anomalies in maps of radiation left over from the Big Bang which may be evidence of other universes and their effect on our universe. In the instant after the Big Bang, our universe was small enough to behave like a subatomic particle, which allows for the possibility that it could become entangled with other universes during that time. Therefore, our universe may be connected with and influenced by other universes. Now, throw in the concept of remote viewing, and the ability of our minds to gather information from others' minds, and you should see where I'm going with this," Don smiled as he finished yet another beer.

"Everything's connected," Jenson said as he tried to wrap his mind around such a concept. "How can you even fathom these ideas after the amount of alcohol you've just ingested?" he asked in amazement.

"It makes it all seem a little less crazy, Jennie," Don replied simply.

"Please stop calling me Jennie," Jenson requested.

"Can't. You've become 'Jennie' to me now."

"Fine, Donnie."

"I've been called worse."

Jenson gave up on the name game. "I still don't quite get what's happening to me when I dream of other worlds. You've given me the science-y bullshit, now tell me plainly what is going on."

"Here's what I think. In your sleep, your consciousness sometimes takes a little trip. I like to call it 'dream jumping.' You are still you in your bed sleeping, but you've connected with someone somewhere else, usually a Level One parallel version of you because that is what is most like you. Well, other than Level Three versions, but I am fairly certain we aren't able to 'visit' Level Three parallel universes. Anyway, these versions of you may even share consciousness with you on some level, like you are all part of one general consciousness…like the branches coming off of a tree, if you will. Or maybe like an ant colony, where all organisms operate as with one mind. Those are fascinating, aren't they?"

"Anyway…"

"So you jump into that person, and your consciousness connects and takes over. Sometimes you are able to transfer some of their knowledge to your own mind, like in your apocalyptic dream, but sometimes not. And you are able to control them and be them until your consciousness is summoned back to your original body. Have you had dreams where you wake up into another dream before waking up to this world? Of course you have, everyone has. I think that may be your mind jumping from one parallel universe into a different one. And in the case of your dream with that woman, you and the Kristine from this world managed to jump into the same universe and interact. The chances of that happening, and of you then meeting up with that person later in this world, seems ridiculously unlikely. I'd be surprised to ever learn of that happening again in my lifetime."

"How can our consciousness travel so far and still maintain its memories? Aren't memories part of your brain functions? How can consciousness operate without the physical brain?"

"I like to think of our consciousness as a flash drive, in a sense – a more compact component where information can be copied and then carried elsewhere while the information still remains on the hard drive, or your brain. You could even think about your consciousness as a laser or x-ray when it is being transferred – the wavelength of a laser beam is microscopic, and an x-ray even smaller yet, which means you can compress lots of information onto its wave pattern. When your consciousness enters another body, that information can then be uploaded to that body's brain, but perhaps only temporarily."

"So the people you jump into, do they remember anything?"

"It depends. I think that events where people do things they don't remember, cases of temporary insanity, possessions, maybe even some sleep walking cases, can possibly be attributed to someone from a parallel universe jumping into someone from this world. The jumpers think they're dreaming, they aren't fully aware of what is going on, and they do crazy things. Then when they return to their own worlds, the person who was being controlled is left to deal with the consequences. Sometimes, though, I think people do remember, but they feel that they 'lost control' of themselves."

"Then I probably got Jamie killed in the apocalyptic dream. I felt a horrible pain in my back right before I woke up from that dream. I think Andrea, or Natalie, stabbed me…or Jamie. Jesus. What if I hadn't woken up before Jamie died with my mind controlling his body?"

"I'm sure you still would've returned to your body. Perhaps when he died, his mind just went somewhere else too. Maybe consciousness doesn't really die, but becomes part of the Akashic record."

"What the hell is that, anyway? I've read a little about it, but I have a hard time wrapping my brain around it."

"It is where all of the information and knowledge of the universe is stored. I think it could be a real thing, and I want to find it. Ramanujan, whom I read about extensively after my first dream jumping experience, claimed that it was where his formulas came from, that he was somehow able to collect information from it through a goddess. I don't think it is a parallel universe, though, but rather a dimension. Again, not a matter of distance, but of dimension."

"I read a little about him as well when I was researching alternate realities and dreams. I have a hard time imagining a dimension that is nothing but knowledge and information."

"Can you imagine time as a dimension? In Einstein's special theory of relativity, time is considered a fourth dimension. Maybe information is its own dimension. What is consciousness, really? Where do our ideas come from? Our brains are magnificent organs, but lots of living creatures have brains. Yet they don't seem to have ideas the way we do, don't seem to have the level of consciousness we do. Why is that? I think it's because our brains are connected to something bigger, and I think it's the Akashic record. Or God, if you want to call it that. Or whatever it may be. And I think, given the right circumstances, we can tap into it, and we do it all the time without even knowing it. I want to be able to consciously 'visit' it, to not just pick up what randomly comes to me, but to seek out specific knowledge from it. Don't think of it as a place, but as a higher level of consciousness. The ultimate internet."

Jenson felt like the conversation was veering off course. He was incredibly skeptical of this Akashic record, and he felt a little insane even talking about it.

"I have another question about the dream jumping. We discussed what you think would happen if the parallel version of me died while I was controlling him, but what do you think would happen if your own body died while you were visiting a parallel universe? Would your consciousness stay there? And what happens to the consciousness of the person you take over, for that matter?" Jenson wondered.

"I've pondered that myself. I suppose it's possible that you could stay, but more likely I think there is some kind of tether on your consciousness that keeps you connected to your body. If your body dies, I would think your consciousness would be affected in some way. Not to say it would die, as I said earlier, but I think it would follow the same course as the consciousness of someone who was 'present' when they died.

And as for the mind of the person you take over, I have no idea. I'm inclined to think that it stays with the body, but is suppressed. That's what makes sense to me."

"None of this makes sense."

"Yet it makes perfect sense. Otherwise you wouldn't still be here talking to me."

Jenson took a drink of his water for the first time since sitting down. "There's a girl I met when dream jumping, and she's been in two of my dreams. Is there something drawing me to her? She was my roommate in one dream, and I think she was my girlfriend in the other one. Yet I've never seen a woman who looked like her in this world. I definitely would've remembered if I had."

"I don't know. She's apparently been in the life of the other versions of you, so maybe it is just a matter of the decisions you made, the path you took in your life. A version of her may very well exist on Earth, but it would be exceedingly hard to find her. She could be anywhere. She could be dead. Maybe she was never born because her parents didn't meet in this world. Who knows?" Don started putting on his jacket.

"Wait, are you leaving?"

"I intended to, yes. I could sit and talk about this topic all night, and have many times before, but not tonight. I have some things I have to take care of at home. A very hungry cat, first and foremost."

"I still have a lot of questions, and I didn't even get to talk to you about participating in your studies! Are you still doing studies?" Jenson asked as Don stood.

"Not at the moment, but it doesn't mean I wouldn't like to. After all the criticism my paper received, I lost my funding for it. Right now I'm working on something else, but I won't bore you with the details. If something comes up, I'll let you know. I've got your number. Good chat." Don held out his hand. Jenson shook it, but he wasn't ready to end the conversation for good.

"Can we meet again? I still have a lot of questions. I brought a whole list with me."

"You can call or email me. Now that I know who you are, I won't send your emails to spam. Have a safe trip home, Jennie." With that, Don threw some money on the table for the server and walked away.

Jenson stood there, dumbfounded. The information Don had dumped on him was swirling around in a hectic whirlwind in his brain, and he needed time to think through it. What was he supposed to do now? What was he to do with all of this information? He had thought Don wanted to meet with him to see if he was a suitable subject for his studies, but apparently that was not the case. Did Don summon him here simply so he could chat about dream jumping with someone who wouldn't think he was crazy? Given Don's personality, he couldn't rule out that possibility. Jenson needed some direction, though. He had some answers now, but what was it that he truly wanted to do with that information?

He wanted to find Andrea. That was it, wasn't it? He didn't just want to know who she was, or why he kept running into her in his dreams. He wanted to find her, to spend time with her. Was that even possible? Could he find a way to guide his consciousness to a parallel universe in which his alternate self was close to her? He wondered what his feelings for Andrea meant for his relationship with Maggie. He was dealing with an unusual moral dilemma. Was trying to pursue a woman he met in his dreams, a woman who may not even exist in this world, a form of cheating? Was it any different than simply fantasizing and having dreams about someone else? He loved Maggie, and he had no plans to leave her, but he still felt that the goals of this whole endeavor may be putting him on shaky moral grounds.

On the other hand, Jenson was truly excited about the prospect of exploring parallel universes and learning all that he could about this amazing phenomenon of dream jumping. It was something that he was certain the rest of the world wasn't ready to accept, but he was also certain that it was real. He thought it to be akin to discovering that vampires were real.

Well, for all I know, they just might be real somewhere else, he thought to himself as he remembered the "demons" in his Kristine experience.

When Jenson arrived home later that evening, he was dismayed to discover that Maggie's dinner guests were still at the apartment. He had been hoping they'd be gone by now. When he walked through the door, Maggie called to him from the living room.

"There are leftovers in the fridge if you are hungry." And that was it. She hadn't even come into the kitchen to greet him or ask him how his meeting went. He shouldn't be surprised.

He fixed himself a plate and microwaved his dinner. As he sat at the table, eating alone while Maggie and her guests chatted away in the living room, he felt like an outcast. Of course, even if he were in the living room with them, he would still be an outcast. He didn't fit in with Maggie and her friends. He always had been and always would be the outcast. He thought he had accepted that a long time ago, but recently he had begun to realize that he shouldn't have to accept it. Even if Maggie's friends didn't like him, she should at least try to make him feel welcome in the group. He should be able to count on her to stand by him when her friends threw snide remarks his way, rather than just stand to the side and pretend nothing had happened. She never made an effort to defend him, or to even acknowledge that any of her friends were being asses. He was always the ass. She had him almost believing it, too.

After putting his plate in the dishwasher, Jenson walked into the living room. Immediately, Dick stood up.

"Well, I suppose it's time for us to be heading out. It was a lovely dinner, Maggie," Dick said. As he and Heather walked past Jenson on their way to the kitchen to leave, Dick nodded his head toward Jenson indifferently. "Jenson," he regarded him.

"I hate that guy." Jenson blurted once Maggie returned to the living room after seeing her guests out.

"I'm aware." She sat down on the couch and turned on the television, saying not another word to him.

He sat down next to her. "Are you going to ask me about my meeting with Dr. Wesson?"

"I didn't figure I'd have to. I thought you'd be readily volunteering the details."

"Don't you want to know what I found out?"

"Just spill it already. Why make it so dramatic?" Maggie snapped.

"What the hell, Maggie?"

"Well, jeez. You come in here, don't say a word to anyone which made everyone uncomfortable, then get mad at me when I don't ask you how your day was the second my guests leave? I didn't hear you asking me how my day was, either. You can be so selfish, Jenson." Maggie still hadn't looked at him once.

Jenson was flabbergasted. *He* was selfish? He had no words. He had been excited to tell Maggie about his conversation with Don, but now he was just angry. He could argue in this endless circle with her all night, and it would resolve nothing. It would just add more resentment to their relationship. He shook his head and stood.

"Unbelievable." He started to walk toward the bathroom.

"Don't you dare walk away from me," Maggie threatened. Jenson turned, and she was looking at him with fury in her eyes. "You have embarrassed me twice now in front of Heather and Dick. What do you have to say for yourself?"

"Well, Maggie, I didn't exactly feel welcome to join your little party. My dinner was in the fridge. That was all I got from you when I walked in the door. So I ate my dinner, and the second I walked into the living room, Dick announced that it was time for them to go. That's not exactly behavior that screams, 'Hey, let's be buddies! Come hang out with us!'"

"He and Heather felt uncomfortable because you came in and didn't say one word! They thought you were mad that they were here! Of course they left!"

"But only when I came into the room. They seemed perfectly chatty and happy while I was in the kitchen. They certainly didn't sound uncomfortable until I walked into the living room. They don't like me, and I am certain there is nothing I can do to change that. I will never be good enough for them to consider me their friend."

"Don't you ever stop to think about me?" Maggie exclaimed. "Can't you just *try*, for *me*? No, it doesn't cross your mind to think of anyone but yourself. You just want to go play mad scientist with a stranger and forget all about our life here and what is expected of you. I need more than that, Jenson. A lot more."

"What do you want me to do then? Change who I am so I fit in with your friends? Stop being interested in things that interest me? Live the life that *you* want me to live instead of the life *I* want to live? Please, tell me, dear, what is it that I should be doing differently?"

"I'm not asking you to change who you are. I just want you to make an effort to get along with the people close to me. I want you to understand the difference between a wild goose chase and a legitimate interest. I want you to be a man that I could marry some day, and not a kid chasing butterflies. I want this to work, but I don't see how that is going to happen if you continue following the course you're on."

Jenson felt both heartbroken and enraged. "Chasing butterflies? Is that how you see me? I'm a kid chasing butterflies? I get the distinct feeling that you are giving me an ultimatum. Are you going to leave me over my interest in a *legitimate* phenomenon and my disinterest in befriending Dick Gillespie? If so, I think that says a lot more about you than it does about me." He sat down on the couch, as his legs were feeling weak.

Maggie looked shocked. "Oh really? What exactly would that say about me?"

"So it is an ultimatum, then?"

"I never said that. I just said I don't see how it will work if you don't stop the bullshit. I didn't say I was leaving."

"I don't think my interests are bullshit. I was glad I met with Dr. Wesson tonight, and I plan to meet with him again if I can. If you ask me, the only bullshit going on is Heather and Dick treating me like I'm subhuman, and you allowing it and asking me to be ok with it. No, *expecting* me to be ok with it." Jenson was trying his best to keep from yelling.

"All I want is for you to be civil. That's all. They are good people, and if they treat you any differently than they treat me, it's because you've given them reason to. Either you don't talk to them, or you speak rudely to them. I can't entirely blame thcm for thinking you're an ass," Maggie said.

"I treat people the same way they treat me. I gave them a chance, and they've looked down their noses at me from the day I met them. I tried to be nice, yet the snarky remarks and condescending demeanor continued. I'm done trying to be nice to them. If you want to hang out with them, go ahead. Just don't drag me along. I'm sure they'd appreciate that as well."

"Fine. Apparently you *want* to be excluded. Don't blame me next time you don't feel 'welcome' in my group of friends. This is on you."

"Excellent. Thank you. So am I allowed to indulge in my dream 'bullshit' still, or am I supposed to exclude myself from that as well?" Jenson asked with sarcasm in his voice.

"What are you planning to do with it, anyway? What exactly is your goal with this whole thing? Just to find answers? To perform studies? To become a science guinea pig? I don't want this consuming your life, yet it seems to be doing just that. What happened to actively seeking exposure as an artist? You used to spend your time looking for new customers, trying to collaborate with businesses, signing up for art shows. You have done none of that since the day you discovered you'd had an odd dream. If this obsession continues much longer, then I don't see how you will have time to become the artist I thought we both wanted you to become."

"You're right, I have put my art on the backburner. But it is temporary. I worked my ass off to get my paintings done early so I would have a little time to myself to learn about what is going on with my dreams. It doesn't mean that I've given up on my art. I still have the same career goals I had before. I just have *another* interest now. Earlier you said you supported me, and now I get the feeling that that's not the case. So what is it? Are you going to allow me to pursue this until my art show or not?"

Maggie sighed heavily. "Whether or not I support this new interest in dreams isn't going to change anything, is it? It's just going to breed more contempt between us if I say no, but

I'm afraid if I say yes, that you'll think I'm saying that I'm ok with you quitting art. I don't want either of those things."

"How many times do I have to tell you that I'm not quitting art? Call it a brief hiatus, if you will. That's all it is. You think I want to be broke my whole life? To have nothing to contribute? No, of course I don't want that. I will continue to paint and try to pick up new clients. That isn't going to change. I just need to be able to do other things that interest me, too. I don't think it is the fact that I'm doing something unrelated to art that is bothering you, but the fact that it is something you find absurd and crazy."

"I'm not going to lie; I do find it absurd and crazy. But I guess it doesn't matter, does it? It doesn't matter what I say, because you are going to do what you want to do. I'm just trying to be the voice of reason, and if it falls on deaf ears, so be it. At least I tried." With that, Maggie stood up and left the room.

Jenson had a feeling that Maggie was preparing him for a break up.

Chapter 7

Jenson didn't know how he was supposed to feel. He loved Maggie, but she made him miserable more often than not. If she kicked him out, he would have nowhere to go. He had no real friends anymore, as most of them had stopped talking to him shortly after he had started dating Maggie. None of them could stand her, and she couldn't stand them. He had done what he thought was the proper thing to do in such a situation - he had chosen his love over his friends. Maggie had taken the opposite approach, and now it was ruining their relationship. He wondered if there was any way to repair the damage that had been done without losing his self integrity in the process. He decided to go to her.

He walked into the bedroom as she was climbing into bed. She glanced at him, then shut the lamp off, bathing the room in darkness. He found his way to the bed and sat down.

"Maggie, what are we doing? Why are we always fighting? I don't want to fight anymore. I love you tremendously. Don't you still love me?"

"Of course I do. If I didn't love you, I wouldn't fight with you. I wouldn't worry about the choices you make. I wouldn't worry about you fitting in with my friends. If I didn't love you, why would I even care what you did? I do love you, and I do care. That's why I get angry when I can't make things work perfectly for us. Right now, things are far from perfect, and it is making me insane."

"Love isn't perfect. We are not perfect. But that's ok. How boring would things be if we were perfect all the time? It's the curveballs in the relationship that test how strong we can be, and I know we are stronger than this. I don't want to control who your friends are, and I don't want you to control what interests I take up in my free time. That's what this boils down to, doesn't it? We need to just let each other be happy, even if we don't understand why something makes the other happy," Jenson reasoned.

Maggie rolled over to face Jenson. His eyes had adjusted to the dark, and he could see that she appeared to be smiling. "I definitely don't understand why chasing butterflies makes you happy, but if it does, chase away, I guess," she teased. "Just please don't chase away my friends, because they do make me happy."

"Deal. Just don't make me hang out with them, because they definitely do not make me happy. So are we friends again?"

"Come here, buddy," Maggie said, and she pulled Jenson down into the bed.

***

Jenson woke up on the couch. He sat up and looked out the window behind him. It was sunny and…snowy. When had it snowed? Leaves were still falling from the trees last he knew. He went to the window and stared at the yard before him. He wasn't in his apartment anymore. Realization hit him. He had dream jumped again. Only this time, he was fully aware of himself and of the fact that he wasn't in his normal home. Was his mind already getting better at this? He wandered around, trying to gather anything he could from the brain he had taken over, but its memories were closed up and locked from him. He only had his own.

He found a bathroom, and looked in a mirror. He looked strange. It was still him, but he had longer hair and a goatee, and he was chubbier. He lifted his shirt and looked at his pudgy gut.

"Aw, man, that sucks."

"What sucks?"

Jenson was startled and pulled his shirt down quickly, embarrassed. There was a woman standing in the doorway, and he recognized Andrea instantly. She had short black hair and glasses, but it was still Andrea.

"Nothing," he said awkwardly. "Just thinking that I really should get to the gym more often."

Andrea laughed. "I can't imagine you anywhere near a gym. But hey, if you want to try it, I'd go with you. I wouldn't mind losing a few pounds myself."

Jenson looked at her perfect body and scoffed. "Nonsense. You are absolutely beautiful exactly as you are."

Andrea smiled at him and walked off. "Lunch is ready. Can you get Jeffrey up from his nap for me?"

Jenson froze. Did he have a son in this world? He walked down the hall until he found a bedroom that was obviously a nursery. He entered quietly and approached the crib against the wall. He looked inside, and there was a beautiful little sleeping boy, probably less than a year old. Jenson was awestricken. He recognized the long little eyelashes and the cute little ears. They were the same as his, only miniaturized. This was his child. He gently lifted the sleeping baby from the crib and cradled him in his arms. His knees felt weak, but his heart was full of pride. Jeffrey started to squirm and fuss, and Jenson didn't know what to do. He had never held a baby before, let alone tried to console an angry one. He quickly brought Jeffrey out of the room and found the kitchen.

"Oh, is my big boy mad we woke him up?" Andrea said sweetly as she took the baby from Jenson. "Were you having happy little dreams?"

Jenson watched as Andrea calmed the baby and strapped him into his highchair. When Jeffrey had stopped crying, Jenson could see that, though he had Jenson's long eyelashes, Jeffrey had Andrea's big brown eyes. He was absolutely breathtaking.

Jenson sat down at the table as Andrea brought him a plate of food. He glanced over at the clock on the oven and noticed that it was nearly noon. He thought about Don's question of time in relation to parallel universes. Was this world not in the same time as his? Or was it that linear time was the same, but something else was different and caused the time of this world to be different in relation to the earth's orbit around the sun? His brain wanted to shut down just trying to comprehend it.

"Did you take the garbage to the street yet?" Andrea asked him.

"Um, I don't remember," he answered honestly.

"Here, feed Jeffrey. I've got another bag to throw out, so I'll check for you." She pulled the bag out of the garbage can in the kitchen and walked out the back door.

He moved to the seat next to Jeffrey's highchair. He scooped up a spoonful of the weird mash Andrea had put on the highchair tray and brought it to Jeffrey's mouth. He laughed at how eagerly the little boy opened his mouth for the food, like a little fish. Jeffrey looked at Jenson as he mushed the food around in his mouth, and after he swallowed, he said, "Dada dada dada."

Jenson felt his eyes welling with tears. He continued to feed the baby, trying to keep it together until Andrea returned. As soon as she came back and took over the feeding, he excused himself to the bathroom.

He closed the bathroom door and sat on the floor. He let some of the tears fall, and dried them with his sleeve. He couldn't believe how happy he felt. It was overwhelming. He wondered how long he could stay here. Why couldn't he have this in his world? A beautiful home, a happy wife, a happy baby…a happy life. Why did parallel Jenson get all this, but he didn't? What had he done wrong? Could he have this in his world someday? He desperately hoped so, but he didn't know if this was a life he could ever have with Maggie. Maggie didn't want children, and before now, he had thought he didn't either.

He suddenly felt guilty. He was depriving parallel Jenson of this wonderful experience. Parallel Jenson was the one who had earned it, yet here he was, enjoying it for him. What if that was the first time Jeffrey had said "Dada" and parallel Jenson didn't get to hear it? He needed to go home. He needed to let this happy family be happy together. He was just an intruder. But how did he make himself leave? Could he make himself wake up? Jenson wondered if falling asleep in this world would bring him back to himself. It would also make it easier on parallel Jenson if he weren't thrust back into control while his body was awake. He left the bathroom after making sure his tears were all dried.

"I'm going to lay down for a bit," he called to the kitchen as he went back to the living room. "I'm just feeling really tired today."

He lay down on the couch and closed his eyes.

***

Jenson heard the alarm clock beeping. He opened his eyes. He was home. The realization of this made him feel both relieved and disappointed. As Maggie shut off the alarm and headed to the bathroom, he lay in bed and thought about the life he had briefly experienced while he slumbered. How could he continue to dream jump if he couldn't get past feeling guilty for taking over someone else's life? Now that he understood what was happening, or at least what Don thought was happening, he couldn't help but feel like an unwelcome intruder. He had probably even gotten Jamie killed in the apocalyptic world. If he hadn't jumped into Jamie's world, Jamie might still be alive. He knew, though, that he couldn't stop dream jumping. At this point, it wasn't something he could control.

He remembered how quickly he had realized he'd jumped in his dream last night. Did that mean he was getting better at it? When it happens again, will he realize it just as quickly as he had this time? What exactly would he do with that knowledge if he did? He needed a game plan. What was the point in jumping into these parallel versions of himself if there was nothing useful he could learn from it? He had thought the only point was to see Andrea, but now he knew he needed a greater purpose. Jumping into other people just to experience their life did nothing to improve his own life or to further the knowledge about the phenomenon. He needed to talk to Don again.

Jenson rose from bed, feeling troubled. He and Maggie seemed to be on the right track again, but he knew that could change in an instant. While she showered, he composed an email to Don.

Don,

Are you there Don? It's me, Jennie. It happened again. I dream jumped last night, and I realized it as soon as I awoke as a different me. Does that mean I'm getting better at dream jumping? I know the jump had to have happened sometime in the middle of the night, but in the parallel world, it was noon. And it was winter. How is that possible? I think I may have even been a little older, too. The woman I keep meeting in these parallel worlds, Andrea, was there too, and I think she was my wife. We even had a son. It was wonderful and happy, but I felt guilty for intruding. Is there an easy way to make myself return to my own world if I wish to do so? I was able to go back to sleep in the parallel world, and then I awoke in my own bed again. Is that typical? How long is it possible to stay in these parallel worlds? Are you limited to the amount of time you are asleep? I would think that would be the case, but I honestly haven't got a clue.

Also, I had a question about language. How is it possible that all these worlds speak English? It seems like there would be different languages that have arisen.

Finally, I'm starting to wonder what I should be doing when I find myself in another world. Is there anything I can do to help gather information to better understand this phenomenon, or to figure out how to better control it?

I look forward to your response. Thanks for meeting with me yesterday. It was an eye-opening experience, and I hope we can meet again sometime soon.

Jenson gave Don his phone number again and signed off. He was just closing his laptop when Maggie emerged from the bathroom, all dolled up for a Saturday at home.

"What are you doing up already?" Maggie inquired. "Normally you sleep in until at least ten on Saturday."

"I was emailing Dr. Wesson. I dream jumped again last night, and it brought up more questions I wanted him to address."

"Dream jumped?"

"That's what Don calls it when someone travels to another world in their sleep."

"How do you know it wasn't just a vivid dream?" Maggie asked, sounding skeptical.

"It's just different. I knew right away that I wasn't dreaming. I was aware of myself just as I am aware of myself right now. I looked at myself in the mirror. I controlled myself completely. It was nothing like the normal dreams I have," Jenson explained.

"Where did you go?"

He hesitated. He didn't want to tell her about Andrea, but he supposed he could tell her he was living with someone. It wasn't as though he could control the fact that he kept jumping to worlds that Andrea inhabited, but he still felt that it was something that wouldn't please Maggie.

"It was similar to this world, except the version of me in that world had a wife and a baby. And I was chubby."

"A wife? Did she look like me?"

"Um, no, not really," Jenson said vaguely.

Maggie furrowed her brow. "Hm." Then she went into the kitchen without another word.

Jenson followed her into the kitchen. He tried to direct the conversation away from the other woman, as he sensed she was bothered by it. "Can I tell you what Don told me about dream jumping now? I would really like to be able to talk to you about it, even if it is a little crazy."

Maggie whirled around and looked at him accusingly. "Is that what you want?"

"Of course! I would love for you to be involved in this-"

"No, I mean a wife and a baby," she interrupted. "A wife that isn't me, and a baby that isn't mine." Maggie was angry.

Before Jenson could answer, she said, "Tell me about the baby. Did you hold it? Did it look like you? Did it look like her?"

"Wait, what just happened?" Jenson said, holding his hands up defensively. "Of course I don't want a wife that isn't you. And I thought that I didn't want kids, but after holding that baby, seeing myself in its features, hearing it call me 'Dada'…I don't know, it made me wonder if maybe it was something I did want after all. But with you, of course!"

When Maggie started crying, Jenson tried to give her a hug. She pushed him away, as usual.

"What's wrong, Maggie?" he asked, perplexed.

"I can't have kids!" she shouted.

He stared at her as she sat at the table and sobbed into her hands. "You mean-"

"I mean I am not physically able to have children. I never told you because I didn't think it was an issue for us. But now…now what? Now you want kids because you had a dream you had a baby?"

"I'm sorry. It's ok, Maggie. You know, if there ever comes a time when we do want children, we can always adopt. I didn't mean to upset you. How was I to know?"

"What if I don't want to adopt? I thought we didn't want kids, Jenson. I don't understand how one little dream can change that for you. And if a dream can change your opinion on that subject, does that mean one can change your opinion of me? Are you going to fall in love with some other person in a dream and then decide you don't love me anymore?"

"That's crazy. I meet lots of new people in real life, yet you don't see me falling in love and changing my mind about you. Why should an alternate world be any different?"

"Why was it different with the baby? You see babies all the time, but you never once thought you wanted one until you dreamed about it. Excuse me, dream *jumped*," Maggie added mockingly.

"Listen, I'm truly sorry about the whole baby issue. Just forget I said it. If I can't have kids with you, then I don't want kids. End of story. So please, don't be upset anymore." He stood behind her and wrapped his arms around her. He felt her body stiffen, so he left her alone. He knew she didn't like being comforted or touched in any way when she was upset, and this situation was no different. He went into the living room to wait for her to compose herself in her own time.

He wondered why Maggie hadn't told him about her infertility before now. They had been together for three years, and they had even discussed how they didn't think kids were right for them. To Jenson, it seemed like that would've been the time for her to tell him she couldn't actually have kids. He felt like it was something she had purposely kept secret from him, but why? Did she think he would've left her if he knew? She'd said that she didn't tell him because she didn't think it was an issue for them since they didn't want kids, but it seemed to him like it still would've been something that should've been revealed in the three years they'd been together.

The more he thought about it, the more he realized that he really didn't know much about Maggie's past. She liked to talk about herself, and she spent a lot of time doing so, but it was always in regard to what was currently going on in her life. She never talked about places she'd been, her childhood, her past loves, or anything too personal. He knew her entire academic history, her career history, and everything that had gone on in her friends' lives, but nothing about her. He'd met her parents only once, as they spent most of their time overseas on business trips and vacations, and even then, her past never came up. He talked about his past with her all the time, and he was certain she'd heard every silly childhood story he had to tell. He'd told her about his past girlfriends, his college days, and all the major events that made him who he was today. He knew nothing about how Maggie's experiences made her the way she was, though. Perhaps that was why he sometimes had such a difficult time understanding her opinions and feelings.

Maggie came into the living room and sat down next to him. Other than the black smear of mascara under her left eye, she exhibited no signs that anything had been bothering her. She flipped through the channels on the television.

"Anything you want to watch?" she asked.

Jenson wasn't going to let her just brush this off and forget about it. He didn't want to fight, but he wanted her to start dealing with her emotions and problems instead of just sweeping them under the rug.

"We should talk about this. You were obviously upset a few minutes ago, but now that you've had time to collect your thoughts, I want to talk about why you were so upset." Jenson tried to be calm and open to her.

Maggie gave him a sideways glance, then returned her attention to the television.

"Please, Maggie. We need to stop bottling things. Let it out. Tell me why you got so angry when I brought up my dream." He called it a dream only because he knew that was the term with which she was comfortable. He would've preferred to call it an "experience."

She ran her hand through her hair and exhaled loudly. "I don't know why I got so upset. I guess it just bothered me to hear you talking so happily about having a child of your own and knowing that I can never give you that. I was avoiding having the conversation about my inability to have children because I was afraid I might find out that it was a deal breaker for you. I see it as my failure as a woman, and a major flaw that I can't fix. It's something I don't like to talk about if I don't have to."

"Thank you for sharing that with me. I wish you would do that more often. I think we'd have fewer explosive arguments if we would just be more open with each other and talk about things calmly rather than waiting for our feelings to simmer so long that they boil up into anger. Your inability to have children is not a failure. It happens. I still love you, and knowing we can't have kids doesn't change that in the slightest."

Maggie nodded, but continued to stare at the television.

Jenson continued, "You know, I was thinking that it would be nice to hear you talk about some of the experiences you have had in your life. Things that happened before you met me. I haven't heard much about the Maggie of the past."

"There isn't much to tell. You know where I grew up and went to school and college, what I studied, what jobs I've had. I can't think of anything I haven't told you."

"I want more than that. I want stories, life-changing experiences, your first love, your first heartbreak…something more personal than where you went to school."

Maggie continued to avoid looking at Jenson while she answered. "I don't have any stories that stand out as interesting. I was the preppy kid in school. I didn't drink or party or do anything crazy. I've always been the rational minded individual I am today. I didn't go to clubs in college, or attend any wild frat or sorority parties. My life has not been wild and crazy or tragic and heartbreaking. I had boyfriends here and there, but they were never serious. I have experienced no great first love or heartbreak. Really, I guess you would be my first love. So you can see, I haven't told you stories about my life because there are no stories to tell."

Jenson had a hard time swallowing what she'd just said. She was basically telling him that she'd never experienced "life." She'd had no great joys, no great disappointments, and no great loves? He had his answer, then. She was the way she was because she expected her life to have no adventure, no complications, only stability and perfection, and it upset her to have uncertainties and any possibility for failure. She was against his pursuit for knowledge in dream jumping because it was outside her comfort zone, and his involvement in it brought about uncertainties and the possibility of failure in other aspects of his life. In truth, Maggie shouldn't be with someone like him. She should be with someone who has a stable job and no sense of adventure. He began to wonder how long Maggie could be content with someone like him. He loved a good adventure, and he had chosen a career path that was about as uncertain and unstable as it gets.

He asked, "What do you love about me? In all honesty, I don't understand what a successful, business-minded woman of your stature sees in someone like me. I'm not overly successful, I don't have a secure job, I'm not wildly intelligent, and I seem to annoy you more often than not. What is it that makes you love me?"

She was quiet for a moment. She finally looked at him, and said, "I love that you are everything I can't be. You are

98

comfortable with taking risks. You dive into things head first, without worrying about whether or not you've made a mistake. You are fun and adventurous. You don't feel a need to control everything. And yes, sometimes those things drive me crazy, but I need someone like you in my life. You are the yin to my yang. When everything goes to hell, I know that you'll still have a clear head and you'll help to keep me sane. Your ability to thrive in the midst of chaos is what I love most about you. That, and you're not so hard to look at, either," she added with a slight smile.

"I thought you hated those qualities in me. Considering the arguments we have, I thought you wanted me to be more like you. More career driven and focused on the future."

"You should know by now that I feel a need to control everything in my life. I know I try to control you and make you more like me, but when it comes right down to it, I need you to be just the way you are. It sounds stupid, I know. I have a hard time understanding it, but I know it's true," she said.

"You love me for being adventurous, but it drives you crazy at the same time. That is hard to understand, but I'll take it. As long as you love me, I guess it doesn't matter why."

Later that afternoon, Jenson checked his email. He didn't know if Don would respond to him over the weekend, but he was still hopeful. When he saw he had a message from Donald Wesson in his inbox, he quickly opened it.

Jennie,

Are you there, Jennie? It's me, Don. Nice Judy Blume reference. You had some excellent questions, and I'm glad none of them were about menstruation. I'm surprised you were able to understand your situation so quickly in your last dream jump. I would take that to mean your mind must be getting more adept to the dream jumping experience. As for the time difference, I have to assume Einstein's theory of relativity has something to do with it. I think I mentioned that when we met. Time may be moving more quickly there relative to here. Have you heard of time dilation and the Twin Paradox? Probably not, so let me give you the gist. One twin gets on a train that travels close to the speed of light, while the other twin waits at the station. While a short period of time passes for the twin on the train, when he returns to the station, the awaiting twin has aged considerably. Time moved more slowly for the twin who had accelerated away from the waiting twin. Also, gravity can affect space and time. GPS satellites have to be adjusted to a different time than our clocks on earth to compensate for the effects of general relativity. The thing to keep in mind is that time is relative. I studied one subject who claimed to have been in a dream jump for over a week, yet his brain only exhibited the patterns congruent with dream jumping for a total of 34 minutes. The only answer I have for this is to assume that time was moving more quickly for him in the parallel world.

When it comes to leaving a parallel world, I have yet to find an easy way to escape back to yourself. Only one study subject was able to do this, and she claimed that all she had to do was will herself back to her own body. She could not explain precisely how she did this. Going back to sleep seemed to work for you last time, but I wouldn't expect that to always be the case. The subject who was "gone" for a week had slept in that time without returning. He just kept waking up in the same world. Again, I don't understand how this was possible other than to assume time was moving at a different pace than it does here.

You asked about language. It could be possible that these people aren't all speaking English. You understand it to be English because that is your native tongue, but in actuality, it may just be that the brain you've jumped into is understanding the language that is spoken and translating it into your thoughts as English. I had a Korean-speaking subject who claimed that the language spoken in the worlds he visited was Korean. I think it is just how we perceive it.

Now, as far as what you should be doing in these parallel universes, I think that's more a question for you. What do you want to gain from the experience? What do you want to do with this knowledge? You mentioned a girl that you wanted to find. Perhaps that is what you should be doing. It is possible, though not likely, that if this girl seems to be as connected to you as you think she is, that she might be dream jumping into the women you are meeting in your dream jumps. You had that experience with the Kristine woman, so I suppose it could happen again. I seriously doubt it, but as a scientist I have to think that anything is possible. My goals when I dream jump are to find a way to access Akashic record, so I've been trying to focus on controlling where I jump to. I haven't had much success, but it doesn't mean it can't be controlled. I am intrigued by your abilities and how quickly you've been able to gain some control over your dream jumps. I wonder if it is possible that you are subconsciously controlling where you jump to, that you are seeking out this girl without even knowing it. Just something to think about. Good luck, Jennie.   –Don

Only when Jenson had finished reading the email did he realize that Maggie was standing behind him, reading over his shoulder.

Chapter 8

He quickly closed the laptop, pretending that he still hadn't noticed Maggie's presence. He stood up from his chair and started to walk to the kitchen.

"Jenson." Maggie said quietly.

He stopped midstride. "Yes?" He slowly turned toward her. She had a scowl on her face.

"What was Dr. Wesson talking about when he said there was a girl you wanted to find?"

Jenson's heart jumped into his throat and he couldn't speak. He didn't know what to say. He briefly considered lying, but he didn't know how much she had read before he closed his laptop. He tried to remain calm to keep his cheeks from flushing, and he told her as much of the truth as he felt necessary.

"There's a woman who keeps showing up when I dream jump. It's driving me crazy that I don't know who she is, and I wondered if maybe she was a real person and if it was possible that she was a dream jumper too, like Kristine," he divulged. A partial truth was not necessarily a lie, he told himself.

Maggie just scowled at him. "Was she your wife in the dream you had last night?"

"…Yes."

"What the hell, Jenson?! This is getting weird. Why haven't you told me about her? Why do you want to find her?"

She was obviously angry at that point, and he understood that she had a right to be.

"You never wanted to talk about the dream jumping, and I didn't think it was important until she kept showing up. I want to find her because I want to know if she's dream jumping too! It isn't weird, it's just another possible lead to figuring out this whole thing," Jenson reasoned.

"Is she pretty?"

"No!" Jenson lied. "I'm not interested in her in the way you seem to be thinking I am."

Maggie walked up and stood in front of him, looking him straight in the eye. "It is incredibly weird, especially since you never breathed a word of it to me. You seemed eager to tell me every other little detail of your dream jumping experiences and what you've learned about it from Dr. Wesson, so I find it very odd indeed that you would keep that part of it from me. What do you do with this girl in these dreams? Is she always your wife? Are you attracted to her? If you do find her, what then?" Maggie interrogated him.

"No, she was only my wife in that last dream jump. No, I'm not attracted to her. I just want to know what connection I share with her that brings us together in these other worlds. I have no interest in her sexually, Maggie. Calm down."

"Don't tell me to calm down. This is not normal, Jenson! It doesn't feel right to me, and I've learned that when something doesn't feel right, then it probably isn't. I think you like her, and you want to find her because you want to know if she's a viable option to you if you and I don't work out. That is what I think. And I want you to stop immediately," Maggie demanded.

"I can't stop dream jumping. I can't control it. It just happens. I don't know how many times I have to tell you this, but I'm not giving up on learning more about dream jumping. It's an amazing phenomenon, and the more we can learn about it, the better."

"Better for whom, exactly? Better for you and for Dr. Wesson, maybe, but I fail to see how it is better for me or anyone else. I don't even understand how it can be real! I think it is all a coincidence and you idiots are just looking for some kind of meaning in pointless dreams. I want this to stop, and I won't ask again," she declared.

"Idiots? *Idiots*? You think I'm an idiot?!" Jenson was shocked. "Wow. Thank you for that, Maggie."

"I don't mean you are an idiot, I just meant that this whole thing is idiotic! And having some weird dream affair with another woman and thinking it's real and not telling me about it? Thank you for *that*, Jenson. You sit there on the couch and tell me about how we need to be open with each other, yet the whole time you've been keeping this weird little secret from me. It isn't normal, and it isn't right. As a matter of fact, I think maybe you should go."

Jenson took a step back. "I should go? Where the hell should I go? Are you kicking me out?"

Maggie's expression grew cold. "I don't care where you go. I'm thinking Hell, maybe, but whatever. I'm not kicking you out permanently, but I don't want to look at you right now. You are making me sick."

A sharp pain shot through Jenson's chest. He went to the bedroom and grabbed his luggage bags and started throwing his belongings haphazardly into it. He had no idea where he was supposed to go, but he needed to figure it out quickly. Maggie had suggested he go to Hell, but he felt very strongly that he was already there.

Once he had packed all the clothes he could fit, he went into the bathroom and grabbed his toothbrush and other toiletries. As he carried his luggage into the kitchen to get his coat, he saw Maggie just sitting on the couch, watching television as though it were any other lazy Saturday. She didn't even acknowledge his presence. He put on his coat and hat, tied his shoes, and then just stood there. He stared at her for a minute, looking for any sign of emotion on Maggie's face, but she continued to watch the television with a blank expression. No anger, no sadness, nothing. He walked through the living room to grab his laptop, and then he left without looking back.

To Jenson's dismay, he discovered it was snowing outside. He hated Michigan's weather. He walked to his car and threw the luggage in the trunk. He dug out the ice scraper, intending to brush the snow off his car before leaving. He started the car to allow it to warm up, and brushed the snow off the windshield. As he walked around to the back of the car and started brushing snow off the back window, a pickup truck pulled into the parking lot. The driver was going entirely too fast for the slick conditions, and when Jenson looked up, he saw the grill of the truck careening toward him. He saw a bright flash of light.

He suddenly found himself somewhere else. His vision was hazy for a moment, but he could feel his body moving. When he could finally see clearly, he recognized the house he was in as the house he had visited the previous night. He was sitting on the couch with Andrea, and Jeffrey was in his lap, giggling at a noisy, colorful toy in his little hands. Jenson and Andrea were both laughing with the little boy, and everyone was happy. He realized that it wasn't he who was laughing, exactly, but the body in which he inhabited. He wasn't in control of it. It seemed like he was just along for the ride, but he felt everything the body felt, and he felt the appropriate emotions that the body should be feeling. He felt happy and peaceful. His body leaned over and kissed Andrea lightly on the lips, and he felt himself smile. He put the baby onto the floor and watched him crawl away to a large toy box in the corner of the room. As he sat and watched television with Andrea's head rested on his shoulder, he became less aware of the fact that he wasn't controlling this body. He just allowed his mind to flow with it, and it began to feel natural. He and Andrea were watching a movie that Jenson had never seen or even heard of, but he recognized one of the actors from some of the blockbuster films he'd seen at home.

When Jeffrey started fussing, he got up and prepared a bottle of formula for him. He'd never prepared a bottle before, but his body seemed to know exactly what to do, like he'd done it hundreds of times before. He brought it out to Andrea, and she fed the baby and put him down for a nap in his crib. When she returned to the living room, she lay down on the couch with Jenson and they continued to watch the movie. He felt content.

"That was such a good movie!" Andrea said when it was over.

"I know, I'm glad Rory let us borrow it," he responded. "What time are we supposed to go over there tonight?" he asked, and Jenson somehow knew that he and Andrea had plans to go visit their friends Rory and Janet. He could even picture their faces. He remembered things about them that he couldn't possibly know. He knew what their house looked like, and even how to get there.

"We've got a couple hours, yet. My mom won't be here to watch Jeffrey until about eight."

"So, we've got a couple hours to kill, then..." he said as he ran his hand over Andrea's perfect behind.

"Well, when you put it that way, how can I say no?" Andrea said with a giggle. They went to the bedroom and made love, and Jenson experienced the encounter as though it were truly him.

Afterward, he was lying on his back with Andrea nestled in beside him, her head on his chest, and he was gently running his fingers through her hair. He couldn't remember a time when he'd been more at ease. He inhaled the lovely scent of her hair, and he realized that it had become a familiar scent to him. It was the same in every world. He wondered how that was possible.

At that moment, he suddenly remembered Maggie. He remembered the fight. As he remembered seeing the truck coming at him, it felt like it was something that had happened ages ago. Then he began to feel strangely numb. He felt so tired that he couldn't keep his eyes open, and he drifted to sleep.

***

"He's under my insurance," Jenson could hear Maggie saying, but she sounded far away. He opened his eyes, and instantly was blinded by the bright lights of a hospital room. He felt a dull ache throughout his entire body. He tried to sit up, but there was a stabbing pain in his right side when he moved.

"No, sweetie, you can't be moving around yet," a tall, blond haired nurse in blue floral scrubs said to him as she rushed to his side. "You have several broken ribs and a fractured pelvis.

You got incredibly lucky, but you'll still be out of commission for a while."

"Did that truck hit me?" Jenson asked, his voice barely a whisper.

He then saw Maggie approach the hospital bed. "It grazed you, but they think most of the damage was done when you hit the ground. You're lucky to be alive. If that truck had hit at a slightly different angle, it would've pinned you between it and your car, and you might've been killed. God, Jenson, I'm so sorry this happened," she said. Her eyes were reddened, but she still looked fairly well composed, as usual.

"I need to talk to Don," Jenson whispered. "Something happened when the truck hit me. I need to tell him, because I think it may be important."

Maggie's face took on a look of absolute disgust. "Really, Jenson? You almost die, and the first thing you want to do is talk to Dr. Wesson? I've been a nervous wreck for the past several hours hoping that you would be ok, feeling guilty about making you leave, and you want to dive right back into the one thing that drove us apart in the first place?" Maggie closed her eyes and inhaled deeply, trying to calm herself. She continued in a less agitated voice, "I think maybe you should just rest for a while, and we'll deal with the Dr. Wesson thing later. Nothing is as important right now as you getting better. Now, I've got to go to the front desk to give them our insurance information, but I'll be back soon. Just rest." She touched her lips to his forehead and left the room.

He lay helplessly in the hospital bed while nurses poked and prodded him. He wished there were some way he could talk to Don. He had dream jumped while awake, and he knew that had to be something of great importance. If he hadn't already known about dream jumping, and hadn't already visited the world he went to today, he would've thought he'd had a near-death experience or experienced Heaven. But this dream jump was different. He didn't control the body he jumped into. He was just *there*. He wanted to know if that had happened to anyone else Don had studied.

He thought about Andrea. Her name must've been Andrea in the world he visited, because it seemed like he would've figured it out had it been different. He knew Rory and Janet, and how to prepare a baby's bottle, so it seems like he would've known his wife's name. How had he known all those things, though? When he dream jumped before, he carried his own memories and was only once able to pick up slight clues from the brain he'd taken over. In this jump, he knew everything that parallel Jenson knew. He was pretty sure his name was Jenson, as well. Or was it? Perhaps names weren't always the same, but were instead "translated" just as language might be translated for his consciousness to understand. He wondered if he would ever be able to wrap his mind around the true nature of what was going on.

A long time passed before Maggie returned. Jenson was just beginning to doze off when she walked into the room.

"This hospital visit is going to cost us a small fortune," she complained. "The health care system is such a scam anymore. Did you know that an individual aspirin is like $4.00 here? And they also charge you a fee for the nurse to 'dispense' it to you! Absolutely ridiculous!" She grabbed the television remote off of Jenson's bed and sat down in the only chair in the room.

Jenson said nothing as he stared at her, watching her flip through channels, wondering if she was more worried about his well-being or the financial hit they were about to take. He was already feeling angry with her, and she'd only been in the room for about 10 seconds.

"You know, Jenson," she said after selecting a show on the television, "you're damn lucky I wasn't kicking you out for good when you left the apartment today! Could you imagine having to take on this financial burden by yourself? Oh, and don't think that I've forgotten why I kicked you out in the first place. Being in an accident doesn't get you out of the doghouse."

Jenson could hear the beeps on his heart rate monitor taking on an allegro tempo as his anger with Maggie's inconsiderate behavior intensified. He was afraid to open his mouth for fear of what might come out. He closed his eyes and took several slow, deep breaths to try to calm his nerves. Then, just when he was starting to regain his cool, Maggie took a step over the line.

"Are you trying to fall asleep so you can dream jump and visit your other girlfriend?" she asked snidely, glaring at him.

"You know what, Maggie? Your behavior is abominable. You're being spiteful and selfish, and I'm sick of it. But that is you. That is who you are. I figured it out a long time ago, but I've been lying to myself, trying to make myself believe that there is a truly good person underneath that layer of ice. I've tried to find her, but now I'm pretty sure she doesn't exist. I'm tired of being the constant focus of your negativity. So I'm done. I'm out. I fold," Jenson declared, wishing he could produce more effective gestures in his injured state to demonstrate his exasperation.

Maggie's face was stone cold for a moment after Jenson's rant. Then her nostrils began to flare, and her jaw clenched. Her eyes widened in a disbelieving rage. She stood up from her chair and threw the television remote at Jenson's face, making impact.

"Well, look who put his big boy pants on today. You feel good about this? You want to throw everything away after all I've done for you? You're a selfish child. Go ahead. Throw your little tantrum. But when it's all over, and you realize your mistake, I'll be long gone, having moved on to bigger and better things. Your belongings will be on the sidewalk before the night is over, so I would suggest sending someone to gather them up. Have a nice, shitty life, Jenson." She whirled around and stormed out of the room.

Jenson felt a flood of emotions wash over him. It was over? He had meant to end it, but now that he had, he felt remorse and uncertainty. Had he been too rash? He fought the urge to call out to her. *No, let her go. This is for the best,* he told himself. He sat in a stupor for several minutes, unsure of himself, unsure of his actions, unsure of his future. He needed a new plan, but the pain medication coursing through his veins muddled his mind, and he was having a hard time focusing on figuring out what he needed to do next. The only thing he knew for sure was that he needed some help.

Jenson pressed the button on his bed that called for the nurse. When she came, he asked her to help him make a phone call. She handed him the receiver and she dialed the numbers he recited to her.

"Mom, I need your help," he said when his mother answered the call.

"Jenson, sweetie, where on earth are you calling from? You sound terrible!"

"I'm in the hospital. I was in an accident. Maggie is gone. I don't know what to do. Please, I hate to ask this, but can you come down here and help me figure this out? I'm kind of lost right now."

"Oh my God, you were in an accident?! Maggie is dead?! Oh my God, Jenson!"

"No, no, she's not dead. She's just gone. She left. We split up. She said she was going to throw all my stuff out on the sidewalk tonight and that I needed to have someone go and get it."

"Oh! Oh my, what a peach. Ok...yes, yes I can come right now. Are you ok? How bad is it?"

"I broke some ribs and fractured my pelvis. I got grazed by a truck in the parking lot. I probably also have a smashed up car I need to report. I have no idea if Maggie took care of any of that before she left. I just...I don't know where to start."

"I'm coming. If I leave now, I can be there in a few hours. Hang in there, sweetie."

Jenson woke up to his mother's voice. He must have fallen asleep after he got off the phone.

"Jenson, I'm here. Are you awake?" she asked in a gentle voice.

"I'm awake. Thanks for coming."

"I'm your mother. It's my job to take care of you when things fall apart. How are you feeling?"

"Broken, in every way imaginable," he answered.

"Poor fella. I made a call to the police station, and they said that the incident has been reported, but they wouldn't tell me any more than that. I imagine that someone will be questioning you at some point. I'll call your insurance company for you tomorrow, so we can get the car taken care of."

"I don't know what to do about my stuff out on the sidewalk at the apartment."

"James is going to go get it. I just hope she doesn't decide to damage things while she's at it," Carla worried.

"Me too. I've got several thousand dollars' worth of paintings in that apartment. If she does destroy anything, then I guess I'll have something else to report to the police when they question me."

"That's the spirit. So what happened? You had told me she was giving you grief about the dream jumping thing."

Jenson told her about the fights they'd had recently, and about finally telling her off. It felt good to be able to finally complain about Maggie without feeling badly about it.

"Well, I can't say that I'm surprised," Carla admitted. "I never much liked that girl. I know she helped you out a lot by supporting your art, but she always acted like it was more of a favor to you than an act of love. I know it hurts now, but later on, you will be glad you got rid of her."

"I know it is for the best, but I still feel like I made a mistake. I know she was awful, but for some reason, I loved her anyway. It's going to be hard to let those feelings go."

"I know, but you will. Someone is going to come along and make you realize that Maggie was just an infatuation."

Jenson sighed. "I was with her for three years. She seemed so wonderful for the first six months, but then I started to see the real Maggie. I loved her even though she made me miserable. I stayed because I thought that it was enough, that my love for her would make her worth my time. I thought maybe she would change, or that things would get better once I found success as an artist. But it never got better. The better I did with my art, the more apparent it became that it still wasn't good enough. I'm realizing now that it was never going to be good enough. This break up is the best thing for both of us. She will be happier with someone more like her – conservative-minded, wealthy, well-educated – and I will be happier with someone more like me – adventurous, curious, and down-to-earth."

"People don't often change. That's a big mistake a lot of people make, thinking that the one they love will change for them. You need to find someone you love as they are, not someone you need to change before they can be worth your love," Carla advised.

The phone in the room started to ring. Carla answered it, and Jenson surmised from the conversation that it was James on the other line.

After hanging up, Carla said, "That was James. He has your stuff, and it all seems to be intact. Maggie was still hauling things out when he arrived, so she let him gather the rest from the apartment himself. He's coming down here so we can figure out together what to do with all of it. Do you know where you want to go when they release you from the hospital?"

"I don't have anywhere to go. I have no friends around here. I know a lot of people through the art business, but no one I know well enough to move in with. I don't even have any real money of my own right now. Any money I ever made went into Maggie's account, so I don't even know what money is mine and what's hers. I guess it's all hers now. I won't have anything until my art show, and that's over a month away. I might have to find myself a nice cardboard box and start stocking up on newspapers," Jenson said.

"Nonsense, you can move back home for a while. It's not like you have anything tying you to this city other than Maggie. You are an artist. You can work anywhere."

"I know, but I want to be close enough to U of M to continue working with Dr. Wesson. I have some important things I need to discuss with him, and, well, he's easier to speak to in person than over the phone. I can't abandon the study of dream jumping."

"What about James? He lives alone, since Craig just moved out and there's plenty of room for you in his house. And he only lives thirty minutes from U of M. I know he would be glad to take you in."

"I can't ask my brother to house and feed me for a month without compensation. I'm not an asshole."

"You can pay him back after your gallery show. Trust me, he can handle it financially. I'll talk to him. I know he wouldn't mind at all."

Jenson wondered how James would feel about his mother making such offers on his behalf. Knowing James, who was a fairly laid-back and kind individual, he probably wouldn't mind much, but would likely feel better about it if he were making the offer himself.

When James arrived, he immediately began making jokes, as was his way.

"Jeez, Jenson. I know they make signs to warn drivers, but you really need to stop chasing balls out into the street," James teased.

"I know, but I distract so easily," Jenson said. He tried to laugh, but when he did, it sent a sharp pain through his entire torso.

"Don't make him laugh, he has broken ribs!" Carla scolded.

"But they always say that laughter is the best medicine! Oh well, I suppose you can't really trust alternative medicine anyway. Hocus pocus voodoo for hippies," James said.

"Thanks for picking up my stuff for me," Jenson said.

"No problem. It was worth it just to see that wonderful Maggie. She's so nice. And pleasant. It really is such a shame that you dumped her. She's so great!" James replied facetiously.

"James!" Carla chided.

"But seriously, dude, you made the right move. She's just terrible. Kudos."

"Yeah, I know it is. I just wish it *felt* like the right move. Now I have nothing."

"Except a bunch of shit in the back of my car. There's always that." James pointed out. "What should I do with it, anyway?"

Carla said, "We were discussing that. Jenson doesn't have anywhere to stay for the time being."

"You can stay with me, if you want," James offered.

"I don't have any money for rent or food," Jenson replied.

"Just do a painting for me. We'll call it even. What do you charge for a painting, anyway? Like seven hundred, a grand?" James asked.

"Depends on what it is. I've sold a few for three grand, even."

"Wow! How can you be broke?! Oh, that's right. Maggie," James said. "Well, for a three thousand dollar painting, I think I can house you and buy you some food. But only off the dollar menu. One cheese burger a day," he joked.

"Deal."

"Cool. So I'll just take your stuff back to my house then. Hope you feel better soon, bro."

***

Jenson spent four days in the hospital. His mother came to visit him every day, as she had taken a week off of work and was staying in a nearby hotel in order to help him get his life straightened out while he was incapacitated. She was his only visitor. He had hoped that Maggie would at least check in on him once, thinking that perhaps she still cared for him enough to be concerned for his well-being, but she did not. She didn't even call him. Apparently, she was absolutely done with him after all. Jenson struggled with the knowledge that she could so easily let him go. It hurt him deeply. He knew he was the one who had called it quits, but he hadn't expected it to be so final. After three years, she seemed quite alright with walking away and never looking back. He wished he could be so cold.

In the four days he was laid up, he was dying to talk to Dr. Wesson about his odd dream jump. However, he had been informed that his cell phone had been destroyed in the accident, and with it, Don's contact information. He had no idea what he had done with the paper that Maggie had given him with Don's U of M number, either. He had to wait until he was released from the hospital and had access to his email before he could contact him. In the meantime, he decided to write down everything he wanted to tell Dr. Wesson.

Don,

I have had quite a week! I had something very strange happen to me, and I'd like to get your thoughts on it. In the parking lot of my apartment complex, I was hit by a truck while cleaning snow from my car. I looked up, saw the grill of the truck coming at me, and my vision was suddenly flooded with a bright flash of white. In an instant, I was somewhere else. It was the world I had visited in my last dream jump, but this time I wasn't in control of my parallel self. I was just in his head, experiencing everything he did, everything he felt. I knew things that he knew, and had his memories. How is that possible that I was able to be in his mind with him without him knowing? I felt like it was a one-way street as far as information being transferred. I received everything from him, but I am certain he was unaware of my presence and he received none of the knowledge I possessed.

When it came to an end, I started to feel very tired, like I couldn't possibly stay awake any longer. I don't think it was because he was tired, but because I was slipping back into my own body. When I returned, I was in the hospital. And I now realize that I can't remember all the things I knew when I was in that body. It's like I only had access to the memories and knowledge while I was in the body, but once I left it, the knowledge and memories didn't all come with me. The whole experience was very strange. Pleasant, but strange. Have you ever heard of anyone who was able to dream jump suddenly from an awake, alert state? It has me wondering if this is what near-death experiences actually are. They could just be dream jumps into another world. Perhaps Heaven and Hell are just other worlds in a parallel universe. If I died, I would consider that world to be my Heaven anyway.

I also have had a lot of strange dreams during my stay in the hospital, but I can't be sure if any of them were dream jumps. The pain medication has fogged up my brain, and I have a hard time remembering the details of the dreams. I just know they've been weird. It makes me wonder if certain medications would make one more susceptible to experiencing a dream jump. I don't know, but it's a thought. Let me know what you think. I would like to meet with you again sometime once I'm healed, when you have the time. And also, I lost your phone number when my phone was destroyed in the accident, so could you please include it in your response so I may call you again? Thanks!

When Jenson was finally released from the hospital, James picked him up and he had a long and painful ride to James's house. He spent much of the ride learning how to use the new smart phone his mother had bought for him to replace his broken one. Once he had it figured out, he accessed his email and tediously composed his letter to Don from the phone. It would have been quicker and easier to do it from his laptop when he arrived at James's house, but he was too anxious to wait.

That evening, James ordered a pizza and listened to Jenson's tales of dream jumping. He hadn't spoken to James since the weekend of their grandfather's birthday party, so most of Jenson's stories were new to James, and he seemed to be intrigued by them.

"I wonder if any of my dreams have actually been dream jumps," James said. "I've had a lot that seem to fit the bill – realistic, strangers that I somehow seem to know, blacking out and waking up in places and wondering how I got there – no, wait. That's just when I drink," he laughed.

"Yeah, that's probably not it," Jenson agreed, trying not to laugh. He wondered how long it would be before laughing and sneezing no longer hurt. It was going to be a painful stay at James's house.

"So, if you are visiting parallel universes, does that mean that the people you encounter are aliens? Would they be considered that? They aren't from Earth as we know it, so I would think you could call them aliens. Which means you banged an alien. And also, you are a body snatcher," James pointed out.

"I guess I hadn't thought of it that way, but I suppose you could be right. And so eloquently put, by the way."

"Class, through and through," James stated, sitting a little taller as he took a drink of his beer. "Well, I have to work tomorrow, so I should get to bed. The guest bedroom is all set up for you. You need anything before I turn in?"

"No, I should be fine. I can hobble to bed on my own."

"Alright. I'll see you tomorrow. Don't bring any alien chicks home with you, because I don't know how I feel about that yet," James jested.

***

Jenson woke up to the alarm clock beeping, and he lay in bed until he heard Maggie get up and shut it off. He felt troubled about a dream jump he had had that night, and he felt he needed to email Dr. Wesson about it. As he climbed out of bed, he noticed that, again, he was not in control of himself. His body walked out to the living room and sat down at the laptop while Maggie showered. He started to compose an email to Dr. Wesson, and he recognized the words he was writing as words he had already written…because it was Saturday. Again.

Chapter 9

He experienced the fight with Maggie over her infertility all over again. He knew what she was about to say, and how he would respond. After reading Don's email, he knew Maggie had read it over his shoulder. As the Jenson of the past argued with Maggie about Andrea, Jenson's present consciousness tried to make sense of what was going on. How had he gone into the past? Briefly, he entertained the idea that perhaps this wasn't the past, but the present, and the only reason he knew what was going to happen was because he had dream jumped into the future and brought those experiences back with him. But he knew that wasn't the case, since he wasn't in control of himself. It had to be the past...didn't it? Past or present, he knew he needed to somehow warn himself of the impending danger in the parking lot.

He tried to focus his energy on remembering the accident, hoping that if he thought about it hard enough, that the past Jenson would be able to pick up those thoughts. As past Jenson walked to his car and grabbed the ice scraper, present Jenson was screaming in his head to stop what he was doing. He put all of his will power into trying to take control of the body in which he inhabited. In the final moment before Jenson knew the truck would hit him, he felt himself jump up onto the car and scramble to the roof. For a brief second, he had control. He turned his head in time to see the truck collide with the car, and the jostling of the collision sent him rolling down the front of the car and onto the sidewalk.

"Oh my God, are you ok?!" the man from the truck shouted as he ran to his aid.

Jenson couldn't feel his body, and his first thought was, *I'm paralyzed! I made it worse by reacting!* But then he heard himself respond, "Yeah, I'm ok," as his body sat up. He was no longer in control. Past Jenson stood slowly, with the help of the man from the truck, and he brushed himself off.

***

"Hey Jenson," James whispered.

Jenson opened his eyes, and there was a face only inches from his own. He startled and reflexively struck his hand at it, and smacked James right in the face.

James jumped back and started laughing hysterically, holding his cheek. "You smacked me, like a girl!"

"Dammit, James! You ass!" Jenson reproached him. He inhaled sharply as he felt the pain from moving his arm so quickly.

When James was able to calm his laughter, he said, "Ah, you should've seen your face. That was great. Anyway, I just wanted to see if you needed anything before I left for work."

"Some Xanax, maybe, if this is what I have to look forward to while living with you. Christ. You are such an ass. I hope you need an icepack for that," Jenson replied.

"Nah, you slap like a little girly man. It was worth it. I'll bring some dinner when I get home from work. I expect all the dishes to be washed and my laundry to be done by the time I get home," James teased as he left the room.

After he heard James leave the house, Jenson slowly climbed out of bed, cursing and moaning from the pain. He grabbed his pain medication off of the nightstand and hobbled to the kitchen for a glass of water. He stood at the sink, leaning against it for support for several minutes after swallowing his pills. Scooter, James's German Sheppard-Husky mix, came wandering into the kitchen and sat down in front of Jenson, looking at him quizzically as if to say *why are you still here?*

"Just you and me today, Scooter. Get used to it. You're going to be my guide dog while I recuperate. Can you do that?"

Scooter wagged her big fluffy tail and cocked her head to the side, ears erect. *Sure! What's my first task?*

Jenson patted her giant head and limped past her. He went to the living room and carefully lowered himself onto the couch. It was only after he sat down that he realized the remote to the television was sitting on the armrest of the chair on the other side of the living room. It was less than 10 feet away, but it might as well have been in Hong Kong.

"Great," he said to himself. He contemplated just taking a nap instead of trying to get back up. As he sat there, staring at the remote that was so close, yet so far away, he started thinking about Maggie. He wondered what she was doing right at that moment. She was working, of course. He wondered if she was thinking of him, as he was of her, or if she had conveniently erased him from her thoughts and moved on. She hadn't tried to contact him once at the hospital. It was clear to him that she was done with him, but he had a hard time accepting that this was absolutely the end of their relationship. He still had a strong attachment to her that confused him. When they were together, she made him miserable. Shouldn't he be happy that it was over, that he no longer had to suffer her constant scrutiny? Was what he still felt for her actually love, or just an unwillingness to let go of the familiarity of her presence in his life? There was a time, not so long ago, that he truly believed he was in love with Maggie, but now that he could analyze the situation from the outside, he wasn't so sure. He knew she was a horrible woman, but she must have had enough goodness about her to make him want to be with her, didn't she?

The dream jump from the previous night suddenly rushed back to him. In the chaos of the morning, he had completely forgotten about it until now. He remembered how confused he had been in the beginning of that experience. Briefly, he hadn't known what was past and what was present. If he were to dream jump enough times, night after night, into different "times" of his life, would he actually begin to lose sight of what was his own life and what was another world? The thought scared him. He began to wonder if what he was doing was going to become dangerous to his own psyche. Would it be possible for him to forget who he was?

He needed to talk to Don. He knew, given his current condition, that he hadn't actually time-travelled. If he had, wouldn't he have woken up to a different situation than the current one since he had changed his past? He did change the outcome for that particular version of himself, though. If he hadn't jumped, that Jenson would've likely been hit by the truck as well. He had actively forced his will upon the other Jenson and made him move out of the way, thus changing the course of that Jenson's life. That Jenson was probably still with Maggie.

If he dream jumped into that Jenson again, he could be with Maggie again.

Did he want that?

Jenson's phone started ringing from the bedroom. He tediously lifted himself from the couch like a broken old man and limped to the bedroom as quickly as his aching body would allow. By the time he was halfway to his room, the phone stopped ringing. When he finally reached it, he saw he had a missed call from his mother. He dialed her number.

"How are you faring today?" his mother asked.

"I hurt everywhere. I didn't realize just how effective the drugs at the hospital were until I didn't have them anymore. I wish I had somebody here to help me around."

"My poor baby. What about the crutches they gave you at the hospital?"

"I'm better off without them. They rub on my ribs when I try to use them, and that's worse than if I just hobble along on my own."

"Do you need me to take some more time off work to come and help?"

"No, I'll survive, but thanks." After Jenson convinced his mother that he would be just fine on his own, he ended the call and returned to the couch with his phone. He remembered to grab the remote before he sat down this time.

Jenson checked his email on his phone after settling into a somewhat comfortable position on the couch. He was pleased to see he had a response from Don.

Jennie, my boy! What bad luck! But what an extraordinary experience you gained from it. I have not yet had a case where someone jumped while fully awake, and it does make an interesting case for NDEs (near-death experiences) being a dream jumping type of occurrence. I've entertained that idea myself, but when people describe glowing beings summoning them to come with them, it makes me wonder what kind of a parallel universe they would have jumped to. Perhaps our idea of Heaven and Hell is just another universe, as you hypothesized, just one vastly different from our own. It is something to think about.

As for your particular experience with being present inside someone else's mind yet not being in control of the body, I have had this happen myself, as well as several subjects from my studies. I call it "shadowing." It is an odd feeling, is it not? It is not my preferred type of jump. It is interesting how you can access all of their memories and everything they know, but I have also discovered that when you return, you lose most of that knowledge. I have tried to find a way to retain that knowledge through the jump back to myself, but I haven't been able to accomplish this. The only time I can return with knowledge from the brain of my parallel self is when I experience a jump in which I am in control of the body. It may have something to do with the type of connection achieved with each type of jump. Maybe a shadowing dream jump doesn't connect your consciousness as strongly with your parallel self as a first-person jump, and thus you don't retain the information to which you had access. It's like looking at a video on the internet versus downloading the video to your computer. If you lose the internet connection, you can't watch the video again unless you were able to download it.

You asked about drugs influencing your dream jumping abilities. This is something I have not been able to test. It was in my agenda when I was doing studies, but I lost my funding before I had a chance to experiment with it. I believe that it might be possible for different types of drugs to affect the quality and frequency of dream jumps, considering the effect some drugs seem to have on consciousness. Think about all the stories of people who go under anesthesia for surgery, then claim to have been in the room, watching their surgery as it happened. I would not be surprised to find that those types of drugs help our consciousness to free itself from our physical bodies and travel. In fact, I find it very likely. But again, I have not tested it and do not wish to test it on myself. I don't know if those drugs would make it any easier to travel to another universe, though, but they definitely seem to be able to separate the mind from the body.

Good luck with the recovery, Jennie. I'm sure I'll be chatting with you soon.

Don signed off and included both his office and cell phone numbers. Jenson immediately dialed Don's office number.

"Hey, Don, it's Jenson," Jenson said when Don answered.

"You sound like shit," Don greeted him.

"Thank you, I'm well aware of that. It isn't easy to talk when you have broken ribs."

"Then why did you call me? You do realize that you have to talk when you call someone, correct?"

"Yes, I am aware. I called because I had another dream jump last night and I wanted to get your thoughts on it."

Silence.

"Are you there?"

"Yes, where else would I be?"

"Ok, I just...anyway, I jumped into a past version of myself. I woke up into a Jenson who was experiencing the day that I had my accident. It was a shadowing jump. I knew everything that was going to happen, including the accident. Everything happened exactly as it had for me on that day, right up until the accident. I tried my hardest to warn the past version

123

of myself about the truck in the parking lot, but none of it was getting through. At the very last second before I knew the truck was going to hit me, I was able to gain control of the body and I jumped up onto the car and avoided getting hit by the truck. But as soon as I was able to accomplish what I wanted to, I fell back into a shadowing state. I don't even know for sure at what moment it happened. All I know is that I was suddenly no longer in control again. The past version of myself rolled off the front of my car and then stood up, apparently unharmed. That was when I woke up."

"Interesting. You were able to exert control over the body from a shadowing state. I've never done that," Don said.

"I was really confused at the beginning of the dream jump. I didn't know if I was actually in the past, or if that was the present and what I had experienced before had been a dream jump to the future. If I hadn't been shadowing, I don't know if I would've been able to tell the difference, and that thought scares me a little bit."

"I imagine it would...being lost in time."

"Could that happen? I've been thinking about it today, and I am starting to worry that if this jumping to past and future versions of myself were to continue, I might start to forget what was truly the present."

"That would be troublesome. But you know that you weren't really in the past, right? You were in a parallel universe that was behind our time. When you returned, you realized this, did you not?"

"Yes, of course, especially considering I still had all my broken bones. But you see, if this were to happen enough times, back to back, with first-person jumps every time, I don't know if I would be able to trust that one particular 'waking world' was the correct one for the time I'm supposed to be in."

"Yes, I do understand what you are worried about. However, this jump was the first jump you've ever had to a different time of a life like your own. I find it very unlikely that you will continue to jump to so many similar versions of yourself in different times that you would become confused. It would be exceedingly interesting, though, if it were to happen," Don said.

"No it wouldn't! It would be terrifying!"

"Come now, Jennie! Where's your sense of adventure?"

"I'm sorry, I forgot for a moment that I was talking to a crazy person."

"I'm not sure how you could forget that. I pretty much always keep that on the table."

"I've noticed," Jenson replied. He sighed. "I don't know what I'm doing. I have this amazing ability to visit other worlds, the past, and maybe even the future, but I don't know what I'm supposed to do with it. There has to be some purpose to it, right?"

"Probably not. The only purpose in anything is what you perceive the purpose to be. I don't think there's any grand scheme of things in which you have a plan set out for you that you have to follow. I know what my purpose is for you, and that is simply to gain knowledge from your experiences. My purpose for my own ability is to find a way to access the Akashic record and gain the knowledge of the universes. Ultimately, though, what you do with your ability is up to you. Didn't you want to find a girl?" Don inquired.

"Yeah, I did. But now I don't know. I just broke up with my long-time girlfriend, though, and it has left me a bit confused about all that."

"Well, it'll come to you eventually. Or maybe it won't. I don't know. I've got work to do."

"Alright, I guess I'll let you know if I have any more interesting jumps."

"Later, tater," Don said as he ended the call.

Jenson laughed at Don's closing line, and instantly regretted it as a sharp pain shot through his body. Don's personality had confounded and annoyed Jenson at first, but the more he got to know him, the more he actually enjoyed his delightfully eccentric quirks.

As Jenson lay on the couch, staring at the television, he began to ponder Don's mystical Akashic record. To him, it was an incomprehensible concept. Even if such a dimension did exist as a plane of infinite knowledge, would a human mind be able to understand all the knowledge available? He looked over at Scooter, her enormous body curled up into a fluffy black ball on the floor next to the couch, and thought about the limitations of her canine brain. He could never teach Scooter trigonometry, or make her understand the quantum mechanics of subatomic particles. She was incapable of such complicated cognitive functions. What reason was there to believe that the human mind wasn't similarly limited in its ability to understand certain information? In all likelihood, there is a vast wealth of knowledge available to us that we just can't grasp, regardless of where we look or how it is presented to us. We humans like to think of ourselves as having an unprecedented level of intelligence, but all we have to compare ourselves to are other earth-bound organisms. In terms of all living organisms in all of the universes, however, we may only be mildly intelligent. There might exist beings that would consider us to be at the same level of intelligence as we consider dogs to be. On a cosmic scale, Jenson thought, we probably aren't nearly as smart as we think we are.

Jenson started changing the channels on the television, trying to find something that would hold his attention long enough to keep his mind distracted. His brain needed a break, but he was afraid that if he stopped contemplating cosmic queries, he would start thinking about Maggie. He tried several different television shows, but nothing could keep him interested. Maggie started to take over his thoughts, and it made his chest hurt. Exasperated with himself, he picked up his smart phone and dialed her number. Maybe if he talked to her, he would feel better.

"Can I help you?" Maggie answered the phone, sounding irritated.

Her voice, even dripping with contempt, caused a feeling of familiarity and contentedness to wash over him.

"I just wanted to see how you were doing. I haven't talked to you since you left the hospital," Jenson said quietly.

"I am doing as well as can be expected. I suppose you want me to ask how you are doing, so how are you doing?"

"Not so good. I'm out of the hospital now, staying at James's house. I feel like I've been hit by a truck," Jenson said with a smile.

Maggie didn't laugh. "I suppose you do."

"...so how's work going?" Jenson said after a long silence on the line.

"Why are you calling me? You broke it off, so I don't understand what this is," Maggie said curtly.

"I miss you. I wanted to hear your voice. Isn't that understandable?"

"Oh God, not the 'I miss you' line. Spare me the bullshit. I think that our breakup was a good thing for us. I was angry about it at first, but now I see that it was necessary. You and I are no longer compatible, plain and simple. I'm happier now without you. I trust you will feel the same way once you've moved on. Remember, this was your decision. Live with it." Maggie hung up.

A few seconds later, as Jenson was putting down his phone, he received a text. It was from Maggie.

And don't call me again.

He stared at it, finally realizing that it was truly over. There was no getting back with Maggie. It was time for him to accept it. His chest was tight and it ached. As he was about to delete the text, he changed his mind. He would keep it on his phone and look at it every time he thought he missed her in order to remind himself that he needed to move on. She was as unobtainable to him as was Andrea.

Andrea.

He hadn't thought of Andrea much since his breakup with Maggie. He had spent so much of his time recently obsessing over Maggie that Andrea had been pushed out of his thoughts almost completely. Now that Maggie was out of the picture, didn't that mean that he could put all of his efforts into finding the mystery woman that had so quickly and powerfully captured his attention? She was special to him, of this there was no doubt, so why was he still trying to hold on to a woman whom he was certain he would've someday grown to despise? He needed to refocus and find the resolve he once had. He needed to try to find Andrea. He closed his eyes, intending to take a nap and begin his search throughout the universes. Instead, he had a hellish nightmare.

Jenson was at his ten-year class reunion. He recognized all the faces around him as those of his classmates. He was attending with Maggie, but Andrea was there as well. He sat down at a table and began to talk to Andrea when Maggie was out of the room.

After talking for a while, Andrea said, "Jenson, why didn't we ever date? You know I had the biggest crush on you in high school."

Jenson was surprised. "Really? Why didn't I know this?!"

Maggie walked up behind him. "What difference does it make now? Why would you even say that, Andrea?" Maggie said with a glare. "He's happily married, so back off, skank."

"Wow," Andrea said, her eyes widening. "I didn't mean to start anything, I'm sorry."

"Yes you did. Don't talk to him again," Maggie growled as she grabbed Jenson's arm and dragged him away from the table.

Jenson looked back and saw a hurt expression on Andrea's face as she watched him walk away. He felt badly, but he didn't know what to do.

One of his old friends, Aaron, approached him and wanted him to look at some pictures on his phone of his new house. Jenson looked at the phone screen as Aaron scrolled through pictures of well-designed rooms and landscaping. Then, when the pictures of the house ended, Aaron started scrolling through strange pictures of people standing in one particular room of the house, clad in costumes.

Aaron starting scrolling more quickly. "There's a video on here I want you to see too, but I think it's at the end," he said. The pictures Jenson was seeing were odd. There would be a few pictures of costumed guests, then a picture of the empty room. Then there would be pictures of another group of people in costumes, followed by another picture of the empty room. There were several groups of these photos on Aaron's phone, but Aaron gave no explanation.

"I guess the video got deleted. Oh well. It was nice talking to you!" Aaron said as he simply walked away.

Jenson felt deeply bothered by the pictures he had seen. He knew there was something significant about them, like a bad omen, but he didn't understand it.

"Jenson!" he heard someone call to him. It was another old friend, Ashley. "Hey! Could you do me a favor and get everyone to gather in this room? I need to make an announcement," she said. Jenson obliged and began directing classmates to join him in the banquet room.

When everyone was present, Ashley called their attention. She stood in front of the group, and opened her mouth. Jenson was horrified when it opened much wider than any human mouth should open, and it distorted her face into a grotesque appearance. Suddenly, a strange sound like rushing wind came from her throat and a powerful vacuum force began sucking people into her mouth, like a black hole. As they were sucked in, they were also compressed until they appeared to be only the size of toy soldiers by the time they reached her mouth. Terrified, Jenson grabbed Maggie and ran down the nearest stairway. Somehow he knew that Andrea would be down there, and he felt the need to protect her.

When he and Maggie reached the basement of the building, they found Andrea sitting on a couch, crying. He grabbed her arm, wondering why she was crying but not having time to ask, and pulled her and Maggie with him as he ran through the basement hallways, looking for an exit.

"We need to get away from other people," Jenson said urgently. Inexplicably, he suddenly knew what was going on. "Ashley isn't the only one of these Suckers. They've amassed an army," he said. He knew what Aaron's pictures meant now. The few Suckers that had invaded Earth had lured people belonging to obscure fetish groups into Aaron's house, and the pictures of the empty room were the evidence that all the people in the room had been sucked in. Jenson knew that they had somehow been transformed into Suckers themselves. He didn't know how he knew, but he knew.

Jenson, Andrea, and Maggie found their way outside, and it was then that Jenson discovered they were in the middle of a busy city. It would be next to impossible for them to find seclusion.

"We need to look for any kind of woods or a park, anything without people!" Jenson said. "If we stay away from people, the Suckers aren't as likely to look for us or waste their energy sucking in only three people."

As they ran through the streets, Jenson saw Ashley ahead of them, walking toward them. He ducked into an alley and cut through to a different street. When they rounded the next corner, Aaron was there, waiting for them. They turned and ran away from him as Aaron's mouth began to open, and they ran into the nearest building. It was an apartment complex. Jenson saw an apartment door was ajar, so he pulled Andrea and Maggie with him into the apartment.

Inside, they encountered a couple who were somehow already aware of the situation. They had hiding places built into their apartment, and they took Andrea and put her in their best hiding place. Before they had time to hide Jenson and Maggie, however, Aaron and Ashley walked into the room. Jenson and Maggie fled to a back room and climbed out the window. Jenson feared for Andrea, and hoped she would be safe in her hiding place.

"Look, woods!" Maggie exclaimed, pointing to an overgrown wooded area behind a building. They ran to it. It was a marshy wetland, and Maggie and Jenson frantically searched for a place to hide in the brush. They found an area of especially thick, tall grasses, and ducked down into it. Then they waited.

Jenson's heart pounded as he heard someone moving through the brush, toward them. The swishing of tall grass against legs grew louder and louder, until he was certain their pursuer would walk right into them. Then it stopped. Everything was silent except for the sound of blood rushing in Jenson's ears.

He heard an eerie whistling, and it sounded close. He couldn't see anything through the brush, but he knew someone had to be standing only a few feet from them. He then heard what sounded like more people walking through the brush toward Maggie and him, but as they got closer, they also stopped.

Then Maggie sneezed.

The footsteps all rushed at them at once. Jenson and Maggie jumped up and ran, and Jenson felt a tug on the back of his shirt. He pulled free and looked back in time to see his shirt slipping from the grip of an angry-looking white-haired man in a uniform. He was surrounded by several other people in similar uniforms, and they were all watching Jenson and Maggie flee. They did not pursue them.

Over and over, Jenson and Maggie found a place to hide, and Jenson waited with his heart in his throat. Over and over, they were discovered and had to run for their lives. Jenson was sick with worry for Andrea, and it bothered him deeply that he had just left her behind. After a while, Jenson was certain his heart and his nerves could withstand no more. When they found a large abandoned greenhouse, they hid inside.

Outside the greenhouse, Jenson could see what appeared to be a large construction area. There was an enormous structure standing in the middle of the site that appeared to be a machine, yet organic. It was somehow alive. It looked like a steel tower covered in wet, black skin, and at the top was a huge skull-like head, covered in the same substance. He watched as a Sucker climbed the living tower all the way to the top. It approached a large hole in the back of the skull-like head and began to expel all of the people it had sucked in into the back of the head. All the people that went in appeared to be dead. They passed through the skull and then slid out of the mouth, encased in a viscous material. When they hit the ground at the bottom of the tower, they stood up, alive, and transformed. This was how the Suckers were creating more soldiers. Jenson felt sick. He was at the limit of his horror, and he was shaking. He wondered if Andrea had suffered such a fate, and his heart felt like it was trying to pump thumb tacks through his veins.

With pure terror as his only driving force left, Jenson sought a place to hide. He climbed under a pile of discarded burlap bags, and held his hand out to Maggie for her to join him. She looked down at him and smiled. Her face suddenly became menacing, and she laughed loudly.

"I'm tired of this game. You trusted me so completely, but didn't you ever think that maybe I was part of this? You're such an idiot." She opened her mouth impossibly wide, and he felt a helpless desperation overtake him as he was pulled toward her. As he accepted his fate and slipped into the dark, cavernous pit within Maggie, he thought only of Andrea.

Jenson woke with a start. His heart was pounding still from the nightmare. He remembered every horrible detail vividly, and his emotions were still strong. Though he was certain it wasn't a dream jump, that it was purely his mind's own sick creation, it felt real enough that it might as well have been one.

"I know Maggie was the wrong woman," he said to himself. "I didn't need a nightmare to tell me that."

Chapter 10

"What are you yammering on about?" James called from the kitchen.

Jenson looked up at the clock on the wall. It was already 5:30 pm. He had slept the entire day away. "Sorry, I didn't know you were home. You should've woke me up. I was having a bad dream."

"I didn't want to get slapped again. Can you come to the table to eat, or do you want me to bring your dinner over there?" James asked considerately.

"I don't think I can sit comfortably at the table."

"Ok, princess. I'll bring it to you."

Jenson sat up slowly. "Could you bring me my pills, too?"

"Damn, demanding, aren't we? You want me to bring you your tiara, too?"

When James handed Jenson his plate of fried chicken and placed his pills and a soda on the coffee table in front of the couch, Jenson said, "Thank you, Jeeves. Your services are greatly appreciated."

James bowed to him and sat down in a nearby chair with his own plate of food. "So did you sleep all day?"

"Mostly. I tried calling Maggie today, but – "

"What? Why the hell would you do that?" James said disapprovingly.

"I know, I know. Don't worry, though, because she definitely set me straight. It's over. I get it."

James sighed. "I'm sorry you had to finally realize what a terrible person she is. But it was going to happen sooner or later. Just be glad that you figured it out now, before vows were exchanged. Trust me, you will look back on this and thank your lucky stars for having the balls to stand up to her and get rid of her."

"I'm pretty sure of that as well. I'm just having a hard time adjusting. It's like my heart hasn't realized what my brain knew a long time ago."

Conversations about feelings seemed to make James uncomfortable, so James quickly changed the subject. "So, this nightmare you had, was it a dream jump?"

"No, just a plain old regular nightmare. But the dream you woke me up from this morning was a jump. Thank you for that, by the way. My shoulder has been killing me today from slapping you."

"Serves you right, you violent asshole. Where were you, in a Victorian era world, slapping people with your pansy white gloves?"

Jenson ignored James's teasing and told him about the dream jump and his initial confusion regarding his place in time. "I'm getting a little freaked out about the idea of not knowing where I am supposed to be. I'm afraid I might end up in a situation where I can't figure out if I am in the world I'm supposed to be in."

"But when you dream jump, don't you always know you are in a dream jump? I mean, you figured it out pretty quickly at the beginning of that last one, even if you were confused for a second."

"Yes, but what if I had been in control in that dream jump, and it had lasted a lot longer? Don told me about someone who was in a dream jump for what seemed like a week to the jumper. What if this is a jump, and I'm actually at home, sleeping in bed next to Maggie right now?" Jenson pondered.

"You had a dream jump, which was obviously a jump, then woke up from it to this world. Isn't that proof enough? You knew your condition before, and everything in this world coincides with your memories of the world you've always known, so it must be the right one," James reasoned.

"You'd think that, but what if I'm just drawing from the memories already stored in this body, which makes me think that I remember things happening even though they didn't directly happen to *me*?"

"Whoa, calm down. You are in the right world! Look at you, getting all crazy on your meds," James said lightheartedly, smiling and shaking his head.

"Ok, I do believe I'm in the right world right now, but do you see what I'm getting at? Do you see how things could get weird pretty quickly if all the conditions were right?"

"I get it, but I wouldn't worry about it. You want me to write 'This is the right world' on the message board on the fridge for you, so if you get confused you can just check it?" James said, not being serious.

"I know you are joking, but that still wouldn't necessarily work because obviously, given my last dream jump, I'm not the only Jenson who is jumping. Who's to say there aren't multiple universes where this conversation is happening, or has happened, or is about to happen? If all of those versions of you did write that on the fridge, then it wouldn't be much help to me, now would it?"

"Guess you're screwed, brother. Do you think you could stop dream jumping if you wanted to? If things got too confusing for you, would you be able to quit?"

"I can't control it. It just happens…and that's what has me so worried."

"You know, Jenson, does it really matter what world you are in if you *feel* like you are in the right one?"

This thought had never occurred to him. If everything felt right and normal to him, did it really matter which world he inhabited? He was stumped. "Well, I guess my biggest concern is being aware of all of my jumps and feeling like I don't belong in any of the worlds I am in. If that happens, what then?"

"I don't know. But if you are so certain you are in the right one right now, I wouldn't be spending too much time worrying about whether you are correct. I'm more worried about how crazy you are making yourself just by over-thinking it. Perhaps you are the one who needs to be slapped."

***

Jenson's body healed slowly over the next several weeks, but his mind seemed to be deteriorating. His obsession with getting caught in a strange time loop of dream jumps intensified as he spent his days recuperating on the couch. He couldn't keep his mind off of it by working because it was uncomfortable for him to sit upright in a chair at a table and paint for any length of time. He no longer had Maggie to fight with as a distraction, and James was gone at work most days. He was alone with his thoughts a large portion of the time.

The fact that he hadn't had a single dream jump since the day he slapped James was also weighing on his mind. He began to wonder if he had been dream jumping, but had somehow become unaware of it happening. Was he always waking up as the Jenson he should be? He seemed to be, but his paranoia made him constantly second-guess himself. He had stopped sharing his concerns with James, as he could tell James was starting to seriously worry about Jenson's mental health and even tried to talk Jenson into seeing a therapist. He didn't need a therapist. He needed to have a dream jump that he could acknowledge was a jump, and when he returned, maybe then he would be certain that he was where he was supposed to be. It just wasn't happening, though.

Jenson had spent so much time focusing on his obsession that he almost forgot about his art show. Before he knew it, the gallery manager was calling him, wondering when he was going to get set up. He had James help him gather all of his paintings into his new (used) vehicle, and Carla met him at the gallery to help him set up.

"Thanks, Mom. I know this was a long drive for you. I've never had to set this up by myself. Maggie always used to help me," Jenson said as he and his mother carried his paintings into the building. The manager had already put up the displays, and he was there to help them with placement. After several hours, the setup was complete.

"Jenson, your work is so beautiful," Carla gushed as she wandered around the gallery, looking at all of his work finally displayed properly. "It never ceases to amaze me."

"Thanks. Now let's just hope everyone who comes to the show agrees with you. I'm ready to finally have some cash of my own. I need to get my own place and quit mooching off of James."

"Oh, you know he doesn't mind one bit. He's happy to have been able to help you out in your time of need. Plus, he's really looking forward to the painting you are going to do for him."

"I know, but he needs to settle on one idea. He keeps pitching me a new idea for his painting every day. Yesterday, he wanted a painting of battling dragons. The day before that, he wanted a painting of the Andromeda galaxy. I won't even bother to tell you what he wanted before that," Jenson said with a chuckle, remembering James's insistence that the painting had to be of himself in Viking attire, fighting a bull, to signify his ambitious nature and "grabbing the bull by the horns."

"Whatever it is, I'm sure it will be perfect," Carla said as she hugged Jenson goodbye. "I'll see you tomorrow at the show. Good luck, honey."

Jenson drove back to James's house, and for once was not plagued with worries of dream jumping. He was excited for his show, and he was starting to feel like his old self. He hoped his paintings would do well. He'd gone home from gallery shows in the past with thousands of dollars in revenue. If he were to do that well this time, he would be able to regain his independence. What a wonderful feeling that would be, not having to rely on anyone.

He began to wonder where he wanted to start searching for an apartment. Did he want to stay near James, or did he want to go back to Grand River, where he lived with Maggie? He liked where James lived, but it wasn't home to him. He could go anywhere he wanted, but where was that, exactly? Where was "home?" Suddenly, he began to feel lost. His obsession with dream jumps returned in an instant, and he wondered if he was truly a man without a place – or time, or world – to call home. He tried to shut such thoughts out of his mind. He wanted to allow himself to feel content, to feel rooted, but he couldn't. He didn't know where he belonged in this world, or any world, for that matter. He felt like a ship adrift at sea, and he needed to find a safe harbor. No, not just a safe harbor; he needed an anchor. He needed something to attach himself to, or somewhere he could always go to feel safe and content.

Maybe it wasn't "something" or "somewhere" he needed, but "someone." Could Andrea be the anchor he needed keep him from losing himself? Is this why he was always so drawn to her? When he thought about it, he realized that every time he had encountered her, he was content when he was near her. She felt like home. It didn't matter where he was when he was with her because *she* was all he needed to have a certain measure of peace. If he could find her in this world, or find a way to stay with her in another world, maybe he would find his true home.

The next morning, Jenson felt strange when he awoke. His brain felt foggy, and he had a hard time remembering what day it was. As he climbed out of bed and walked out into the hallway toward the bathroom, James called to him from the kitchen.

"What time is your show today?"

He remembered then that it was the day of his art exhibit. "Um, four o'clock, I think," he replied, his memory still hazy.

As he showered, his thoughts became clearer, and he started to feel more alert. However, something still felt odd. He couldn't place his finger on what it was that was nagging at him until he started to dry off. He looked at his towel after drying his face, and noticed that it was an unfamiliar towel. It wasn't the same blue towel he had used yesterday. This towel was green and white. He didn't own a green and white towel.

When he came out of the bathroom, he asked James if he had switched out his towel.

"No," James replied, giving him a strange look. "I haven't touched your towel. I damn sure didn't wash it, either, if that's what you're asking."

Jenson went back to his room, knowing now that something was definitely amiss. He looked through his clothes. Sure enough, his wardrobe was slightly different. Most of it was the same, but there were a few pairs of pants and some dressier clothes that he hadn't seen before.

He was in a dream jump.

His heart began to race, and he felt like he was on the verge of a panic attack. Had he not noticed those subtle differences, he wouldn't have known he had jumped because everything was so similar to how it was supposed to be in his world. He felt like his fears were becoming reality. He needed to calm himself down.

He reasoned with himself. *I noticed the differences, though. I'm not confused. I know I'm in a dream jump now, so why am I panicking?*

Jenson took several deep breaths, and thought about how he should proceed. He decided to just go through the day to see how it went. When he returned to his own world, maybe he would return with some knowledge of the future. Granted, things weren't exactly the same here, but it appeared that his life was moving along the same trajectory in this world as his own. If he did well at this show, then it might mean he would do well at the show in his own universe. If not, he might be able to make some minor changes to make sure that it does. Regardless, he knew he could gain some knowledge from this experience and use it to try to improve the outcome of his show when he returned. He felt calm again.

Jenson spent the day trying to find the abnormalities in the world he currently inhabited. James had a girlfriend in this world, who was planning to attend his art show later that day with James. Jenson had a feeling that the version of himself he inhabited had met James's girlfriend and that he really liked her, because when James spoke of her, Jenson didn't feel like she was a stranger. He had a distinct feeling of fondness for her, and happiness for James for finding such a catch.

Other than James having a girlfriend, the differences in this world were very minor. James's fridge was a different color, but the same style. His dog, Scooter, had two blue eyes in this world instead of having the heterochromia trait. Jenson noticed that his toenails seemed to have been cut recently, which he hadn't done in his own world (though probably needed to). As he took mental notes of all the differences, he became more aware that, though this world was very similar to his own, it would be exceedingly unlikely that he would've been confused into thinking he was in the right world. He may have thought he was home at first, but there were enough cues to clue him in on the fact that he was elsewhere. This knowledge comforted him, and his fear of being lost in different worlds and different times abated slightly. He still had concerns about the possibility of it happening, but he was less certain that it *was* going to happen.

Jenson, James, and James's girlfriend, Brianna, all rode together in Jenson's car to the art exhibit. When they arrived, Carla was waiting for them at the entrance.

"You're late!" she chided. "You're not supposed to be late for your own show!"

They hurried inside, and Jenson was overwhelmed at the number of visitors strolling about, talking in low voices to each other, critiquing his work. He surveyed the room, trying to ascertain whether people seemed to be enjoying his art or not. It appeared that most of the faces were pleased, which gave him hope that he might make a few sales tonight.

The manager spotted Jenson and rushed over to him. "Ladies and gentlemen," the manager addressed the room in a booming voice, "thank you for coming out tonight. This is Mr. Thorne." Jenson bowed his head slightly. "He's the artist responsible for the wonderful artwork you see before you. Please feel free to approach him with whatever questions or comments you may have about his work. Thank you, and don't forget there are refreshments and coffee available."

The manager then turned to Jenson. "Quite a turnout tonight, hey? I've been hearing nothing but good things from visitors so far."

"That's great! This is already a lot more people than I was expecting. I'm hoping we do well tonight," he said honestly.

He wandered around the room, making small talk with the visitors, and hearing a lot of the same comments and questions he hears at every show.

I have a [insert relative] who paints. (I don't really care.)

I wish I could paint, but I can't even draw a stick-figure. (If everyone could paint, it wouldn't be such a special talent.)

Do you do custom orders, because I have a [insert item] I would like to have painted. (Not interested, because you'll likely be displeased when my vision and your vision don't match up precisely)

How long does it take you to complete a painting? (Depends on the painting.)

You must be a very patient person. (Not necessarily.)

Don't you have a painting up at [insert business]? (That isn't my painting.)

Wow, that's a lot of money for a painting. Would you take less? (It's a lot of work. No.)

Though he appreciated their interest, he sometimes wished that people would think about their comments and questions before opening their mouths. He assumed that they didn't go up to every cashier or bank teller and announce to them that they had a relative who was also a cashier or bank teller. He was especially irritated when people scoffed at prices and tried to finagle. Did they go into the supermarket and finagle with the cashier about the price of tomatoes? Why should the price on his work be negotiable? If you want it, buy it. If you don't, enjoy looking at it and move along.

"Jenson, dear," Carla whispered to him. "You are starting to make a face. Don't look so irritable."

"Sorry," he whispered in reply. "I had forgotten how ignorant some people can be. I guess I'm out of practice with dealing with the public."

"These people are the ones who are potentially going to put money in your pocket, so don't scare them off with that grimace."

Jenson plastered a smile onto his face and took another look around the room. His eyes fell upon a woman across the room with her back toward him. She was wearing a knee-length damask patterned dress, and she had a lovely figure and long dark hair. There was something familiar about that woman. She started to turn around, and he saw her profile.

His heart almost stopped. It was Andrea.

He started to walk toward her, but halted when he saw her link her arm through the arm of a well-dressed gentleman standing next to her. He badly wanted to approach her, but he didn't know what to say. He knew her fairly well through his dream jumps, but to her, he was a random stranger. He couldn't just walk up to her and say, "Hey, do I know you from somewhere?" He figured the man she was with wouldn't appreciate it either. So what was he to do?

He stood awkwardly in the middle of the room, staring at Andrea. When she glanced over and caught eyes with him, he quickly looked away, embarrassed. He began to meander through the visitors, indirectly heading her way. He wasn't sure what he would do when he got close to her, but he felt a strong urge to be near her. As he got closer, however, a woman with a young child stepped in front of him.

"You are the artist, aren't you?" she asked, touching his arm lightly.

"I am."

"You do amazing work! These paintings are beautiful," she said. Jenson watched her young boy run off toward one of his paintings. As the woman talked to him, he saw the kid reach up, standing on his tiptoes, and start running his hands over his most expensive piece.

He interrupted her, "Ma'am, is that your child?" He gestured toward the boy, who had started bouncing his hands off of the canvas. He was trying to maintain his composure, though he was mentally screaming at the kid.

"Bartholomew! Stop that this instant!" She called to the boy, much less sternly than Jenson would've hoped. The boy looked at her and continued smacking the painting.

"I'm so sorry," she said, but didn't move to stop the child.

"That piece is worth $2500. If he damages it, I do expect that you will reimburse me for that amount," Jenson said calmly.

The woman took off and grabbed the boy, pulling him away from the painting. Jenson followed her and inspected the painting, making sure that the woman saw him doing so.

"It appears to be unharmed. I would appreciate it if he didn't touch anything from this point onward. I'm sure you understand," Jenson said condescendingly.

"Yes, of course," the woman replied sheepishly and quickly guided the boy away from him.

Jenson never understood why people would bring their children to such shows and then allow them to run amok. He was not above yelling at other people's children, and had done so in the past, but he didn't want to make a scene when Andrea was around.

He looked over to where Andrea had been, but she was no longer there. He scanned the room, but he didn't see her. He walked to the entrance, and saw her just as she was walking out the door with her companion. He wanted to chase after her, but he knew he'd missed his chance to speak with her. His heart sank. He returned to the showroom, feeling sullen. He avoided speaking with anyone other than family for the rest of the evening.

Once all the visitors had left and the show was over, he walked around the room. He saw red tags under several of his paintings, which meant they had been sold. He mentally added up the total sales, accounting for the commission owed to the manager, and came up with $12,000. It was the most he had ever made in one night. He was elated, until he remembered that he was still in a dream jump. These earnings weren't actually his. Again, he was overwhelmed with disappointment.

As he drove home with James and Brianna, he didn't have much to say. He was lost in his own thoughts, wondering if

143

the Jenson of this world would be able to remember today. He wondered if it were possible that his body was going through the same day in his own universe, with a different version of himself at the helm. How strange that would be, to wake up and find that he'd missed an entire day of his life. He did it to other versions of himself, so he supposed he couldn't be upset if one of them did it to him.

He thought about Andrea's presence at the exhibit. If she showed up at this show, in this world, and this world seemed to closely mirror his own, did that mean that it was possible that she would show up at his show in his own world? He desperately hoped he would wake up to find that he hadn't missed his art show. If he saw her there, in his own world, he would definitely approach her whether or not she was alone. If he didn't, he might not get another chance. He would have to seize the opportunity to find out who she was, even if it meant making a fool of himself. His determination was suddenly stronger than ever.

When he returned to James's house, he retired to his bedroom for the night. He needed to get back to his own world. He lay in bed, waiting to fall asleep, but sleep was eluding him. He had begun to worry that he would wake up to find that he'd missed his show, that someone had taken the experience from him. If that happened, and he had no memory of the day, then he would be no closer to finding Andrea, and he wouldn't even know if she had been at his show. At this rate, he was never going to fall asleep.

He tried to think of something else in order to calm his nerves, but his mind kept returning to dream jumping. He suddenly thought of a new scenario that brought him anxiety. What if he jumped directly into another dream jump? If that happened, and he then returned to his own body after the second jump, would he remember this jump, or would the experience be lost? He was slowly becoming convinced that this was what was going to happen. As he finally grew tired, he tried his hardest to think about returning to his own body, but his mind was still focused on the fear that he would jump somewhere else instead.

***

144

The phone was ringing loudly in his ear. Jenson reached over to grab it off the nightstand, but a pain in his side stopped him short. His eyes shot open. He was instantly aware that he wasn't in his own universe. He was still feeling the pain of his accident quite intensely, but that shouldn't have been the case in his world. He was somewhere in the recent past. He carefully sat up and looked around as the phone continued to ring. Everything looked to be in place. He picked up his phone and saw that he had missed a call from his brother, Pete. He then knew where, or when, he was. It was a day he had experienced two weeks ago. He slowly climbed out of bed and walked out to the living room, looking for any subtle differences from the world he knew. Surprisingly, he could find none. He looked in the bathroom. It was the same, right down to the towels. He checked the kitchen. "You are in the right world!" was written on the dry erase board on the fridge, just as it had been in his own world (ironic, now, but still not funny). Scooter came into the kitchen, toenails clicking on the tile, and Jenson saw that she had one blue and one brown eye, as she was supposed to. She sniffed him carefully, as though she could tell something was amiss with him. She looked up at him and whined, as was her way of "talking."

"Yeah, I know," he said to her. "I think it's weird too."

James came out of his office, singing his own little song about everything he was doing. "Going to the bathroom, gotta take a piss, going to the bathroom, walking like this," he sang as he strolled into the bathroom and shut the door. Jenson remembered James singing that, except he had been in bed, talking to Pete on the phone when it had happened two weeks ago. How could everything be so exactly the same? Maybe he needed to rethink his assertion that he would find differences in every world that would let him know he wasn't home.

He waited for James outside the bathroom door.

"Wah, shit!" James exclaimed in surprise when he opened the door to find Jenson standing there, waiting for him. "I thought you were still sleeping!"

"Remember that conversation we had a while back when I said I was afraid I would lose myself in my dream jumps?"

"Yeah, that's why I wrote that dandy note for you on the fridge! What, did something happen?"

"I'd say. I'm not in the right world right now."

"Yeah, you are."

"No, I assure you I am not. I'm supposed to be two weeks ahead of this. I was supposed to wake up to the day of my art show. I already experienced today."

James furrowed his brow. "Seriously? Are you sure?"

"Absolutely positive. I knew I was in a dream jump as soon as I woke up. I'm not the same Jenson you talked to yesterday."

James started laughing, out of shock rather than humor. "So, did you come back to stop the robots from taking over the Earth?"

"Not funny."

"I know, but I had to. Wow, this is awkward, isn't it? What are we supposed to do? Does anything exciting happen today?" James asked.

"I don't know. I've already changed the course of the day with my own actions. I was supposed to still be in bed, talking to Pete on the phone, but I'm not. This conversation didn't happen, obviously, in my own universe. Oh, and by the way, I told you that note on the fridge wouldn't work."

"I didn't honestly think it would. But I didn't think this was going to happen, either. I'm at a bit of a loss as to what to do right now. Do we just go about our day?"

"I guess. But I do have a message I want you to give to the Jenson who's supposed to be here, when he returns. Tell him to look for Andrea at the art show. I assume that this Jenson had talked about Andrea, right?" he asked.

"Yes indeed. I will tell him. Did you find her?"

"Not exactly. It's complicated. Just tell him that. I don't know if she will show up or not, but in one of the future worlds I visited, she was there. It means she might show up in this world too, I think."

"So where is the Jenson that's supposed to be you right now? The one who is supposed to be here?" James wanted to know.

"I have no idea. He might be here in my head with me, but I have no way of knowing."

"Maybe he's you right now, experiencing the future," James suggested.

"I hope not," Jenson replied simply.

"Why?"

"Because that would mean that I would've missed the art exhibit and missed my opportunity to talk to Andrea in my own world."

"Maybe he's talking to her right now. Maybe when you get back, you'll find out that you got her number."

Jenson nodded his head. "Well, then I guess that wouldn't be too bad, would it? But I was hoping to be able to experience it myself."

He and James stood in the hallway, an awkward silence hanging in the air.

"Ok, good chat, spaceman from the future. I think I'm going to get back to work on my new app, because I doubt a future version of myself is going to come back here and finish it for me."

"I'm going to go back to bed and try to sleep. I need to get back to my own world. I don't want to waste my time living a day I've already experienced and end up missing a day I haven't," Jenson said.

"Oh, hey," James said as Jenson started to walk away. "Maybe you should call that scientist you've been talking to about your dream jumps. I bet he'd find it pretty cool to be able to talk to a dream jumping Jenson in the midst of a jump."

Jenson was intrigued. "Wow, why didn't I think of that?! That's a great idea!"

He went into his room, found Don's office number in his phone, and called it.

"Dr. Wesson," Don answered.

"Hey, Don, it's Jenson...well, sort of," he said ambiguously.

"How are you, Sort-of-Jenson?" Don replied, without even a hint of mocking in his tone. "I haven't heard from you in a while. You don't sound as rough as you did the last time we spoke."

"I'm doing alright, despite the fact that I'm in a dream jump to a past universe right now."

"You're in a dream jump…right now? Splendid! How far back is this from where you are supposed to be?" Don sounded interested. He was oddly accepting of the situation.

"I'm two weeks behind where I should be, and I jumped here directly from a world that was slightly ahead of my own time."

"You don't sound confused, so I take that to mean that you are well aware that you aren't in your own world and are thus not lost in time, as you've feared would happen. Or at least, that's what the Jenson of this universe was afraid would happen."

"Sort of…"

"You are a fan of the phrase 'sort of' today. Tell me about what has happened. Exactly what has happened, not sort of what happened."

"It was the Friday night before my art show when I jumped, but I wasn't immediately aware that I had dream jumped when I woke up because it was Saturday, as it should have been. Something felt a little off, but I couldn't figure out what it was. It wasn't until I noticed that the towels in the bathroom were unfamiliar that I understood what had happened. I was panicked at first, because I thought it meant my fears of being lost in time were coming true. But I went about my day anyway, and discovered many minor differences in the world I had jumped to. Seeing those little differences and being able to understand that they were abnormal compared to my own world made me feel a little less anxious about ever being 'lost.'"

"What kind of differences?" Don wanted to know.

Jenson told him all that he could remember, then described his day to Don. "I went to my gallery show this evening, and when I was there, I saw Andrea, the girl I've been looking for. But I hesitated, because I didn't know how to approach her, and she left before I had a chance to speak with her. I went to bed that night, hoping to wake up in my own world on Saturday morning. As I tried to fall asleep, though, I started worrying that I had missed my own art show, that a different version of me had jumped into my body and that I would wake up on Sunday and miss the chance to meet the Andrea of my world. Then I started to worry that I wouldn't wake up in my own world at all, but instead wake into another dream jump. I was afraid if that happened, then when I did finally return to myself, I would forget the first jump, and not know to be looking for Andrea at my art show."

"You worry excessively."

"Yeah, I hear that a lot. Apparently all that worrying wasn't unfounded, though, because here I am, two weeks in the past after jumping directly from my previous dream jump."

"You obviously haven't forgotten the previous jump, though. What makes you think you'll forget it when you return?" Don inquired.

"Haven't you ever had multiple dreams in one night, and when you wake up, you know you had multiple dreams but can only recall the last one?"

"Oh, I get what you mean. These aren't just dreams, though. They are experiences, and they seem to imprint themselves much more strongly than a regular dream. I have no doubt you will remember both jumps when you return to your own body. However, I can't say that it isn't possible that you may have missed Saturday. You caused one of your future selves to miss Saturday, so who's to say one of your other selves didn't take you out for a spin while you were away? Hell, he could've been a Jenson from a completely different world and made a total ass of himself in your stead, leaving you with a lot of explaining to do when you return."

"That is comforting, thank you," Jenson replied sarcastically, feeling anxiety welling up within him. It was becoming a too-familiar feeling for him. "God, what if I'm away for more than a day?"

"You don't have to call me God, you can just call me Don. I'll allow it."

"What?"

"Nevermind, Jennie. You need to stop worrying so much about it and focusing your thoughts on it. There's a saying that goes something like, 'Whether you believe you can or you can't, you are right.' Have you heard that saying?"

"Everyone has heard that saying."

"I think that's what's happening with you."

"How so? I don't follow," Jenson said, perplexed.

"You were so certain that you were going to start time jumping, and you did. You were so certain that you would jump from one dream jump to another, and you did. Get it now?"

Realization set in. "I'm causing it."

"Bingo."

Chapter 11

"It seems, Jennie my boy, that you are starting to figure out how to control your dream jumps, to some extent," Don explained. "I can't say I'm not a little jealous."

"But I'm not going where I want to go!" Jenson exclaimed.

"No, it seems your fears are strongly outweighing your desires. Instead of being so consumed with the fear that you are going to keep jumping around until you completely miss your own Saturday, make the assertion, in your mind, that you will be returning to your own world. Have confidence that you will go where you want to go. Be the ball, Jennie. Be the ball."

"Are we having a little league pep talk?"

"You're in the big leagues, now, Jennie."

"Please stop."

"If you build it, he will come," Don whispered.

"Seriously. Stop."

"Does this world have any differences?" Don asked, changing the subject without warning, as was his way. "You said the last one had a few differences, but most of it was the same. What about this one?"

"Oddly, I haven't found anything different in this world except that it is behind where I'm supposed to be. I was hoping you might be a little less crazy in this world, but no dice.

Everything seems to be identical except for my actions. This is definitely not how my day went when I experienced it two weeks ago."

"It makes you wonder how much you have altered the course of different universes just by visiting them, doesn't it?"

"It certainly does."

"I'm glad you called. It has been immensely interesting to be able to talk to the Jennie from another world. It hadn't occurred to me that we could have this experience, but I'm pleased that we did. You should leave a note for this Jenson to have him call me when he returns. I'm interested to know if he remembers any of this, or if he jumped somewhere else while you were here. This should be fascinating."

"I wish I could find out, too."

"I'll let you know if you ever come back. I imagine that someday, perhaps soon, you will be able to direct your jumps more accurately. When that happens, come back to this world and get a hold of me."

"That's a big ten-four. I'm looking forward to it."

When Jenson got off the phone, he felt more at ease than he had in weeks. He was exerting control over his jumps without even realizing it, which meant that it was possible that he could hone his skills enough to be able to go wherever he wanted. It also meant that, if he was able to master this skill, he would no longer have to worry about becoming lost in different versions of his world. He sat in his bed and composed an email to himself (rather, his parallel self) from his phone, letting the Jenson of this universe know what had transpired today, before climbing under the covers and closing his eyes for a nap. As he started to doze off, he couldn't help but think, *There's no place like home. There's no place like home. There's no place like home.*

Jenson felt an odd jolt, then awoke to the sound of a woman's voice. It sounded like Andrea, and she was casually telling him about her day as though they were having a chat over a cup of coffee. However, he was unable to see, and unable to move. He could feel her hand holding onto his, and he tried to focus all of his energy on that external stimulus. He didn't understand what was happening, but he knew he needed to somehow pull himself out of this suffocating darkness, to make himself move. He sought out any kind of information from this body's memories, thinking that perhaps he was in an oddly deep shadowing state, but he found nothing. He was alone in this body. He had no memories to help him understand his condition. It felt like he had jumped into an empty shell.

As he focused on the feeling of Andrea's hand, he tried to draw the ability to feel to the rest of his arm, attempting to urge his nervous system into action. It wasn't working. He couldn't feel what his body was supposed to be feeling, other than his hand. He just felt *heavy*. In a fit of frustration, he started screaming in his head. No words were in the screams, just primal screams of anger, confusion, and hopelessness. He suddenly felt a dull ache in his chest, which quickly began to intensify. He was grateful for the pain, however, because it was *something*. He screamed louder in his head, and the ache began to spread. Was he pulling himself out of this, or just giving himself a heart attack? He didn't care. He already knew that he would rather die than live in this unfeeling darkness, so he would be satisfied with the outcome of either scenario.

In the midst of his pain and screaming, he felt the light brush of fingers across his forehead. The ache in his chest instantly shot to his brain and exploded through the rest of his body as though he had been electrocuted. He was flung bolt upright, a horrifying scream tearing from his throat.

He fell back onto the bed he was lying in, quickly overtaken by overwhelming weakness. He heard a woman screaming. He looked around, blinking rapidly as his eyes adjusted to the light in the room. It felt like these eyes hadn't been used in a very long time, as it was incredibly difficult to focus. After a few moments, his vision began to clear, and the woman who was screaming had stopped. He finally looked upon her. It was Andrea, just as he thought. But she looked unwell. She was too thin, her hair was dull, and her face appeared to have fine lines from stress in the middle of her forehead, the corners of her eyes, and around her mouth. She looked as though she hadn't been taking care of herself as well as she should.

"Oh my God. My God. You...you...you're awake!?" she said in disbelief, her words muffled under her hands which were covering her mouth. "I can't believe it. I can't believe you woke up!" In sudden elation, she ran to him and threw her arms around him, sobbing tears of joy. "I have missed you so much..."

Jenson tried to hug her back, but he felt weak, his arms feeble. When he tried to speak, it sounded like he had a throat full of gravel.

"Just relax, let me get a nurse! Don't go back to sleep!" Andrea instructed excitedly as she ran from the room, yelling, "Nurse! Nurse!"

She returned quickly with a short, middle-aged, dark haired nurse in pink scrubs. The woman had a dark complexion and wire-framed glasses of a prescription that made her eyes look too small. She stopped when she entered the room and stared at Jenson.

"Well, I'll be damned," the nurse said in a rich, pleasing voice. She approached the bed and began taking his vitals and checking his monitors. "Can you tell me your name, hun?" the nurse asked him.

He cleared his throat, then attempted to speak. "My name is Jenson Thorne," he said with a hoarse, cruddy voice.

She stopped what she was doing and looked at him, a worried expression on her face. She then looked at Andrea. Andrea walked up to him and grabbed his hand. "Do you know who I am?" she asked.

"Andrea?" he guessed.

Tears began to fall from her eyes once again, though this time it appeared they were tears of sadness. "No, honey. I'm Maggie. I'm your wife. And you are Jeffrey. Jeffrey Tyson. Do you remember anything?"

Jenson didn't know how to answer. Yes, he remembered everything about himself, but he knew nothing about the person he had jumped into. How was he to explain that to them? He decided to be vague.

"I remember things, but...I don't know if they really happened or not."

"I'll go get the doctor," the nurse said.

Andrea – or, Maggie – stopped the nurse as she started to leave. "Is this normal?" she asked her.

"It's normal for some confusion or amnesia when someone wakes from a coma, but I've never heard of anyone claiming a false identity. The doctor should have more answers for you."

Maggie looked at him again, and the look of joy on her face had been replaced with deep concern. "Jeffrey, what do you remember? Where did you come up with the name Jenson Thorne?"

"I don't know how to explain it to you," he answered honestly. He wasn't sure what he should tell her. If he tried to explain everything to her or the doctor, they might think he had brain damage, or was psychologically unwell. Perhaps he should just pretend that he remembered nothing. It might be safer that way. He didn't want to land himself, or the guy he'd taken over, in the nuthouse.

"Try," Maggie urged.

"I think I dreamed a lot while I was unconscious. That must be it. I don't remember anything about this real life, though."

"Maybe once you are awake for a while it will come back to you," Maggie said hopefully.

Jenson just nodded. He wondered how long he would be in this world. He was never in one place for more than a day, so he assumed that once he fell asleep again, he would leave. What would happen to this body when he left, though? Would it go back into a coma, or would its original inhabitant return? When he'd jumped into this body, he'd had the distinct feeling that it had been "empty" for quite some time. Where was Jeffrey's consciousness?

When the doctor came in, he gave Jenson a medical assessment and asked him a few questions about his life. Jenson pretended to know nothing.

"Do you know where you live?" the doctor asked.

"No."

"Do you know what country you are in?"

155

"United States?"

"Do you know who your parents are?"

"No."

"Do you have any children?"

"I don't know."

"Are you married?"

"I've been informed I'm married to Maggie."

"Do you remember her?"

"Kind of. I recognize her face. I feel like I know her, but I don't seem to know anything about her."

The doctor's questions continued for several minutes. At the end, he said, "Mr. Tyson, I think you are suffering from amnesia brought on by the accident and the coma. It may be temporary, but sometimes the memory never comes back. Luckily, I don't think you have any serious brain damage that will interfere with your day-to-day life, but we will run some tests to be sure. It's rather odd how well you are doing right now. It's almost like you were never unconscious."

"How long have I been unconscious? How did I end up this way?" Jenson asked.

The doctor looked at Maggie, allowing her to answer.

"Honey, you've been in a coma for three years. You were hit by a truck in the parking lot at our old apartment building."

Jenson didn't know how to respond. He wondered if it had been a similar event as the one that put him in the hospital in his own world. The parallels were eerie in this universe. Everything was so different, yet it seemed that there were smatterings of similarities among this world and the others he visited, including his own. The connectedness of it all bothered him slightly, but he couldn't put his finger on exactly why it bothered him yet. He couldn't wait to get out of this world.

He had an eventful day. He was put through brain scans, x-rays, and several other tests while Maggie waited. Finally, he was returned to his room to rest. When the doctor and nurses had left, Maggie sat in a chair at his bedside, holding his hand.

"These tests are going to cost us a fortune, I imagine," he said, remembering ex-Maggie's comments from when he was in the hospital in his own world.

"Why would it cost us anything?" Maggie asked, her brows furrowed.

"It won't?" Jenson realized that the healthcare system must be run differently in this world. "Are we under a universal healthcare system now?"

"Universal healthcare? I don't know what that means. Healthcare has been free for as long as I can remember. Why on earth would we have to pay to be healthy? That would be so unfair. No, hospitals are run on tax money, just like any other public service."

"That's what universal healthcare is, or at least what my understanding of it is."

"Oh. I've never heard it called that."

"I'm sorry I don't remember anything. It must be very hard for you to deal with this," Jenson said sympathetically.

"It was harder for me to deal with you being gone. Now that I have you back, I feel like I can deal with anything."

"Can you tell me about yourself? About us? Maybe if you talk about our life, I'll start to remember," he lied. He just wanted to know more about her, about the kind of life they had before the accident. "Do we have any kids?" he asked with a smile.

Maggie's face contorted into a pained grimace, and she started to cry. "Oh, Jeffrey, you really don't remember anything, do you?" She got up and left the room quickly, and he could hear her loud sobs from the hallway. He didn't know if she was upset with him for not remembering their children, or if something had happened to them. He felt horrible for bringing it up so cheerily. He tried to climb out of his bed, but his leg muscles were weak from years of inactivity. He collapsed onto the floor. He tried to squirm across the floor, but he was stopped by all of the wires and tubes attached to his body. He started pulling them out. He needed to go to her. He needed to comfort her. His monitors started beeping loudly as they were detached from him, and Maggie ran into the room, alarmed.

"My God, Jeffrey, what are you doing!?" she exclaimed as she ran to him. She grabbed his arms and helped him to his feet. His knees shook under his weight as she assisted him back into his bed. "You can't just pull all this stuff out!" she reprimanded.

"You were in pain. I wanted to hold you."

The tears fell once more. "Oh, Jeffrey." She climbed up onto the hospital bed with him and curled up next to him.

"Please tell me what's wrong," he implored.

She looked up into his eyes, and the pain he saw was unbearable. "I envy you for not having to remember it. When you fell into a coma three years ago, I was so mad at you for leaving me to deal with this pain alone. But then I began to see it as a blessing to you, since you no longer had to feel the heartbreak. It had weighed so heavily on you. I realized the coma was God's way of giving you relief from it. I don't want to be the one to bring back that horrible pain for you. Please, don't try to remember it. I will bear the burden for us both. You've been given a second chance at happiness, and maybe with your happiness, I will find mine once again as well."

Jenson was silent. He had tears in his eyes and an ache in his chest. Something exceedingly horrible must have happened. They must have lost a child or children. He didn't want Maggie to have to be alone in her pain, but he was afraid that when he fell asleep tonight, he would be leaving her alone again. He didn't want this woman to have her last shred of hope ripped away from her so abruptly. It broke his heart to try to comprehend the damage it would do to her if he left now. He needed to stay, at least for a while. He had to find a way to keep from jumping back. He was suddenly unconcerned with missing his Saturday in his own world. He had his "Andrea" here and now, and she needed him.

Doctors and nurses rushed into the room, responding to the alarms from the monitors. Maggie moved from the hospital bed and the doctors and nurses reattached him to the monitors. He lied and told them that he accidentally ripped some of them out in his sleep. When they left, Maggie returned to the bed and rested her head on his chest. Within a few minutes, he could tell she had fallen asleep. He stroked her hair gently, and inhaled the familiar scent of it. It was the same in every world he visited. He matched his breathing with her slow, easy breaths, and hoped that if he held her tightly enough tonight, that it would somehow keep his mind tethered to her as he slept.

When Jenson awoke the next morning, he was afraid to open his eyes. He didn't know where he would be. He didn't feel Maggie in his arms, but he still felt like he was in a hospital bed. Slowly, he lifted his lids…and breathed a sigh of relief. He was still there. He looked around for Maggie, but she wasn't in the room. As he lay there, alone, he began to wonder what he looked like. This body was much thinner than the one he was used to, but his hands looked the same to him. He ran his hands over his face and through his hair, but he couldn't tell by touch if it was the face he knew. He looked around for something reflective. He noticed a breakfast tray next to his bed, and there was an applesauce container with a foil lid. He grabbed it and opened it, accidentally tearing it in half. He licked the applesauce off the back of it and held the larger piece up to his face. The reflection was warped from the flimsy material, but he could tell that the face of this body looked relatively similar to his. His eyes looked more sunken, and his complexion more sallow, but he assumed that would change as his health returned.

He thought about what Maggie had told him last night, about the great heartbreak they had suffered. Rather, the heartbreak she and Jeffrey had suffered. He felt guilty about deceiving her, making her believe that he *was* Jeffrey, but what else could he do? She needed him right now. He knew he would have to tell her eventually that he was not Jeffrey, but, when, and how? If he continued this lie too long, she would think he'd suddenly lost his mind when he did tell her. Even if she did believe him, then she would be hurt that he'd been lying to her. But, if he told her too soon, she would likely close herself off from him and suffer even more. He needed to tell her before he left this world, though. He needed to find a way to warn her that he would be leaving and that the real Jeffrey might not come back to replace him. It would be painful, but, in his mind, it was necessary. She needed to know.

Maggie strolled into the room, already looking less haggard than the woman he had seen yesterday. She had a container of pudding and a cup of apple juice.

"I got you something from the cafeteria. I figured it'd be better than the rubbery eggs and dry toast they'd be bringing you."

"Thank you. I didn't realize how hungry I was until now."

"You've been tube-fed for three years. I thought you deserved something with actual flavor as your first breakfast back."

Jenson ate the pudding and drank the juice. Later that morning, he went to physical therapy to work on rebuilding his muscles. The PT commended him on how quickly he was regaining his strength. After physical therapy, his doctor met with him and told him that all of his tests had come back normal. The doctor couldn't believe Jenson's recovery. It was unheard of for someone to seem so unaffected after three years in a coma. If everything continued to improve, he would be going home in days rather than weeks. Jenson hoped he could keep himself in this world long enough to go home with Maggie and spend some time with her in the comfort of their own home. He didn't want to reveal anything to her until they were out of the hospital.

In talking to Maggie, he discovered that she was an accountant, and that he had been a wildlife biologist before the accident. She'd commented on him returning to work someday, but he didn't have the heart to tell her that it would be impossible since he didn't know enough about biology now to perform such a job. He learned that they lived in Michigan, but in the Upper Peninsula, not the Lower Peninsula he was used to.

"Do I have any family?" he asked her, wondering if there was a reason that she had been his only visitor thus far.

"Yes, you have three brothers, and both parents."

"Why haven't they come to see me? Are we not close?"

"Oh, it's not that they don't want to see you! I spoke on the phone with your parents the very morning after you woke up, while you were having your tests, and when I told them that you were experiencing a lot of confusion and memory loss, we decided to slowly ease you back into your life. We didn't want to overwhelm you right off the bat. When you are ready, they will be overjoyed to come see you. Your mother was so happy you woke up that she was crying. Do you want to see them?"

"Yes, I would like that very much. Do they live far away?"

"Your parents live just down the road from us. Your brothers live downstate, but I know they would make the trip immediately if you were ready to see them."

"What are their names?"

"Your mom's name is Janet. Your dad is Gerald. Your brothers are Jake, John, and Jordan."

"What are they like?" Jenson was curious if they had personalities like the brothers he knew.

"Jake is the oldest. He lives on a farm, and he likes to work on his tractors and cars in his spare time. He's a nice guy, but he's also not afraid to tell you exactly what he thinks about something. Pretty much an open book, whether you like it or not," she said with a laugh. "John is the second oldest, older than you. He is very likeable, and very funny. He's kind of known for his antics. He likes his guns, hunting, and his dogs. He's married and has a couple of kids. Jordan is the youngest. He's into computers and technology. He's very charismatic, and hilarious. He's the type of person who could get into a fight with someone and in the end have the other person buying him a beer. Needless to say, there is never a dull moment when your brothers are around."

"What about my parents? Are they nice?"

"Very. Your parents have been a tremendous help through all of this. They are very supportive, hard-working people. You were close to all of them before the accident, and I hope you can become close to them again, even if your memory never returns. They love you, and I know they will do whatever is needed of them to help you through this."

His family here sounded exactly like his family in his own world. He knew he would get along swimmingly with them.

"If my parents could come tomorrow, I would like to see them."

"I'll call them and let them know!" Maggie replied. She was in good spirits today, and it made him feel happy. He wondered how long it had been since she'd felt this upbeat.

That night, as he drifted off to sleep, he again tried to focus all of his energy on remaining in this world, and tried to keep all thoughts of his own world from his mind. He had been doing this every night as he fell asleep, and it had worked thus far.

In the morning, he was still Jeffrey. He went through his physical therapy, and when he returned to his room, walking slowly with Maggie's assistance, his mother and father were there waiting for him.

"Oh, my Jeffie!" his mother exclaimed as she rushed to him. She hugged him carefully, but tightly, and kissed his cheeks all over. Then his father hugged him. Gerald and Maggie helped him to his bed.

"Thank you for coming," Jenson said, smiling.

"I was basically standing at the door, just waiting for Maggie to call me and let me know you wanted to see us. I can't even express how happy I am that you finally woke up…" Janet began to cry.

Jenson held out his hand and grasped hers. She looked very much like his mother from his world. Her hair was a different color, and she was slightly heavier, but her face looked the same. His father, other than looking a little older, looked the same as well. The familiarity comforted him.

He visited with his parents for several hours, and they told him stories of his childhood. Some of the stories were of experiences he never had in his own childhood, but most of them shared similarities to his own. He enjoyed hearing about the life of Jeffrey.

Over the next week, Jenson remained in this new world. He became stronger, and was able to walk on his own for short distances. He bonded with Maggie, discovering that she seemed to be everything he hoped she would be when he knew her as Andrea. She was strong, caring, funny, and loved him deeply. He knew it was a love that he himself had not earned, but he accepted it anyway and loved her back as though he'd been in love with her all his life.

Finally, after a week and a half in the hospital, Jenson was released. Maggie had brought him a heavy winter coat, a hat, gloves, and a sturdy pair of boots. As he donned the winter attire, he wondered if he would be able to support the weight of it all on his way to the car. He was still in a weakened state.

"Do I really need all of this?" he asked. "I mean, how bad can it be outside?"

"We live in the U.P. It's negative temps outside. You need to bundle up," Maggie assured him.

A nurse brought him to the entrance in a wheelchair, in accordance with the hospital's policy. He looked out the big glass doors and windows of the entranceway and stared, mouth agape. He'd never seen so much snow in all his life. The parking lot had huge banks of snow piled up along its perimeters, and more snow was falling from the sky. Some of the cars were so completely covered in snow that you could hardly tell that there was a car beneath it all.

"I'm going to walk out there, slip, break my face, and have to be rushed right back in here," Jenson jested.

"It's ok, I'll make sure you don't fall. Let's just go very slowly," Maggie said, tightening her grasp on his arm as he stood up from the wheelchair. "I've brought the car up front so you don't have to walk very far."

When the doors opened for them, he was greeted with a blast of icy air, and it bit his face. If he could've rushed to the car to get out of that bitter cold, he would have. Instead, he had to gingerly shuffle his way across the icy pavement, grimacing against the wind. Maggie opened the car door for him, and helped him lower himself into it. He'd never been so grateful for seat warmers as he was at that very moment.

Maggie carefully drove them home. He had lived in Michigan all his life, but he'd never been to the U.P., and he wondered how anyone could drive so calmly in such inclement weather. He thought he'd seen tough winters in the Lower Peninsula, but this was something else entirely. She pulled into their driveway, which appeared to have been recently cleared of snow.

"That was nice of your dad to snowblow the driveway for us. I thought I'd have to do it after we got home."

"You can run a snowblower?"

"Of course, silly. You have to know something like that living here."

"You're a cool lady," Jenson said with a smile.

Maggie laughed. "The coolest. Let's get you inside."

Jenson looked up at the house, leaning against the porch rail for support, while Maggie went on ahead and unlocked the door for him. It was an expansive log home, and it was beautiful. He surmised that they must be fairly well-off to afford such a home. Maggie returned and helped him up onto the porch and brought him inside. He was even more impressed by the interior. It was clean, modern, and open. The kitchen appliances were shiny and new looking. There was a bear-skin rug hanging on the wall over the fireplace. The television was huge, and the furniture in the living room looked cozy.

"Welcome to your new home. This is the first time you've seen it. I bought it about a year ago, two years after your accident. I hope you like it. I wanted to wait for you to wake up before I went house shopping, but…" Maggie's voice trailed off, not wanting to finish the sentence.

"It's ok. You couldn't wait for me forever. You had no way of knowing if I ever would wake up."

"I would've waited for you forever, though. Maybe not in buying a house, but in other aspects of my life. I could never love another man but you. You are my one true love, and for that, I would've waited for you until the end of time."

Jenson was flooded with guilt. He was touched by her sentiments, but he wasn't the one she'd been waiting for. He needed to tell her…but later. He didn't want to ruin this moment for her. He needed to tell her soon, though. Especially before she tried to become more intimate with him.

"Let me make you something to eat. I went shopping this morning while you were in physical therapy and bought all of your favorite foods." She went into the kitchen and opened a cupboard. She pulled out a bag of pork rinds and made the bag dance around in the air in front of her. "Remember these? You *love* pork rinds."

Jenson liked pork rinds, but he didn't love them. For her, though, he pretended like he'd seen nothing more glorious than that bag of pork rinds.

"Oh, man, pork rinds sound amazing!"

She opened the bag and brought it to him. "You remember pork rinds, but not your own wife?" she said teasingly. "I see how it is." She smiled at him and handed him the bag. She helped him walk to the couch and he sat down. He sank into the fluffy cushiness and sighed contentedly. "I'll go make you some bacon pancakes. If you want, I'll even sing the song while I make them."

Jenson laughed. "Please do. I don't know what song you are referring to, but I imagine it'll be entertaining." He sat on the couch and ate pork rinds, and soon he heard Maggie singing a song about making bacon pancakes in the kitchen. He chuckled to himself. He loved this woman.

He started thinking about how he was going to bring up the topic of his true identity. It was a conversation that he didn't want to have. The purpose of the conversation was to prepare her for the fact that he would be leaving, and that her Jeffrey might not return when he did. But the longer he was with her, the more time he spent with her, the more his conviction that he *wanted* to leave wavered. He was happy. If he had his choice of worlds, he was beginning to feel that this world would be the one, not his own. Could he stay if he wanted? Forever?

It was still a lie, even if he did. He still would never be the Jeffrey that she had fallen in love with. He was Jenson. Regardless of what body he was in, he was still Jenson. He remembered a conversation he'd had with James, in which James had asked him if it mattered what world he was in, as long as it felt right and he was happy. At the time, he hadn't been sure if that was true or not. Now, however, he was ready to believe that it didn't matter. In this world, unlike all the others, he'd taken an empty body. He hadn't seemed to displace anyone's consciousness. He wasn't exactly stealing this life from anyone, so would it be wrong if he stayed? He felt like he'd be hurting more people if he left than if he stayed.

He started to wonder about his life in his own world. Was someone controlling him right now? Was he still sleeping soundly in his bed? What if his body was empty, in a coma like this one had been? Don had mentioned that he thought that people's minds were somehow tethered to their original bodies. If that were true, then what did that mean for him here? Did that mean that he *couldn't* stay, even if he wanted to?

He was getting ahead of himself. Instead of thinking about how wonderful it would be to stay here forever, he should be thinking about whether or not Maggie would want him to stay here forever once she knew that he wasn't the real Jeffrey. If it was possible for him to stay, she needed to be part of the decision. She might rather not have him around if he wasn't Jeffrey, and he couldn't go on deceiving her this way just to ensure her continued love for him. If he stayed, he needed her to love *him,* as Jenson, not as a memory of her husband.

Maggie came into the living room, holding a plate piled high with oblong pancakes smothered in maple syrup. She had the most wonderful smile on her face. He hated to do what he was about to do. He took the plate from her.

"Maggie, sit down. There's something I need to tell you."

Chapter 12

Maggie sat down in a chair adjacent to the couch. Worry lined her face. Jenson looked at the plate of pancakes. He wasn't sure what to do with them. He wanted to eat them, as it would be rude to have her go to the trouble of making them and for him to not eat them, but at the same time, he felt it would also be rude to sit there and stuff his face while he told her he wasn't really Jeffrey. He decided to take one bite, then leave the plate sitting in his lap while he revealed his story to her.

He used the fork he was given to cut a small piece from a pancake. There was a slice of bacon inside of the pancake, hence the name bacon pancakes. He ate it, and if he hadn't been feeling so anxious about what he was about to tell her, he would've realized that it was the best pancake he'd ever eaten. He looked at her as he chewed and swallowed. She was staring at him, waiting apprehensively for him to speak.

"Jeffrey, what do you have to tell me?" she asked impatiently.

"I don't know how to explain this, but I will do the best I can. I'm not Jeffrey. I really am Jenson Thorne. I know it sounds crazy, but it's true."

Maggie gave a short, nervous laugh. "Is this some kind of weird joke that I'm just not understanding? You are kidding, right?"

Jenson shook his head slowly. "I'm not kidding. I'm not trying to be funny. Before I woke up from a coma in this world, I had a life-"

Maggie interrupted him. "In *this world?* What are you talking about?"

"Bear with me. It's going to be confusing, weird, and frankly, unbelievable. But I swear to you that this is the truth. I had a life in a different universe. I am not from this Earth, but an Earth that is very similar to this one. I discovered a few months ago that I was able to perform a strange feat when I slept. I could transfer my consciousness to the bodies of parallel versions of myself in parallel universes. I have visited several different worlds this way. It's called 'dream jumping.' It sounds crazy, I know. I don't belong here, but I've been staying here because I was happy here with you, and I wanted you to be happy. Also, I didn't want to leave in case Jeffrey didn't return to his body. I didn't want you to be left all alone again." He was silent to allow her time to process his words.

She stared at him, wide-eyed, and disbelieving. "I don't know where you came up with this story, but it's bullshit. I think you are still confused from your coma. Maybe your brain has concocted some crazy story to try to cope with your amnesia, but there is no way that you aren't Jeffrey."

"I assure you that I am Jenson, not Jeffrey. I can tell you my whole life, if you'd like. I remember everything about it. I don't remember Jeffrey's life because I didn't live Jeffrey's life. I was never Jeffrey. His consciousness seems to be somewhere else. When I jumped into this body, I could tell it was empty. Jeffrey isn't here, and I don't know where he is." He set the plate of pancakes on the coffee table in front of him and waited for her response.

"What about this makes sense to you? You used to say that the simplest solution was always the best solution. To me, the simplest solution is that you have created memories of a life for yourself since you can't remember your own. You may believe that these memories are real, but I know they aren't. I know you, Jeffrey, and you are most definitely Jeffrey."

"How can I prove to you that I'm not Jeffrey? I know nothing about Jeffrey other than what you've told me. He was a biologist, yet I know very little about biology. I was an artist in my own world. Did Jeffrey paint?"

"No, you didn't paint. You weren't into art at all. Stop referring to 'Jeffrey' as though it isn't you."

"I can paint something for you. Do you have paint? I will show you!"

"We don't have art supplies. You didn't paint, and I don't either."

"If you got some paints and brushes, I could show you that I can paint. I used to sell my art as a living in my own world. I can tell you all about art, the terminology, techniques, whatever you want to know! If Jeffrey wasn't into art, would he know those things? Would he know what scumbling was, or perspective, or gesso, or color theory? Bring me a pencil and paper, and I will sketch for you. I'll show you I'm an artist, not a biologist."

"Jeffrey, you are starting to scare me."

"I don't mean to scare you. I'm not insane. I'm just trying to tell you that the world you know is not exactly as cut and dried as you might think it to be. Had Jeffrey studied physics at all? Did he understand relativity or quantum entanglement or the multiverse theory?"

"I don't know. You were always into biology, but I suppose you may have had some background in physics. I know you had physics in high school, and probably at least a course or two in college. I think it's very possible that you already knew these things before your coma. You may have even had an art class in college or high school, too. You must have known these things already. That's the only explanation."

"I don't think that explains it. I can tell you all about my world, and I'm sure there will be differences from this one. For example, remember when I was talking about how expensive the hospital visit would be, and you didn't understand why I would think that? That's because universal healthcare doesn't exist in America in my world. We have to buy insurance and pay a premium, and even then a stay in the hospital can end up costing you hundreds of thousands of dollars. I had gotten hit by a truck in my world, too, several weeks ago, and I broke my ribs and fractured my pelvis. I still hadn't gotten the bills for it yet, but I know I'm going to be in a mountain of debt from it when I get back."

"I wish you would stop talking like you are returning to this imaginary world! You aren't! You are Jeffrey, not Jenson!" Maggie shouted in anger. She grabbed the plate of pancakes off the coffee table. "Fine. If you aren't Jeffrey, you can't have these. I made these for Jeffrey." She stormed off to the kitchen.

Jenson put his face in his hands. He knew this wouldn't go well. He felt horrible for ruining her happiness, but he would've felt worse if he'd continued lying to her. He needed to find a way to make her listen, to make her believe him. He slowly rose from the couch and shuffled his way to the kitchen. He found Maggie leaning over the sink, crying into her hands. He grabbed a stool from the bar in the kitchen and sat down, feeling too weak to stand for any length of time.

"Maggie, let me tell you about my world." He talked about current events, the president, popular television shows and movies, social media, and politics. The entire time he talked, she stood at the sink with her back to him. When he made mention of the year 2014, she turned around and looked at him. Her eyes were red and her cheeks tear-streaked.

"It's 2012."

"Not where I'm from."

She stared at him. He couldn't read her face. It wasn't exactly blank, but he could tell she was guarded. "Where did you come up with all of this?"

"I lived it. That is what is going on in my life, in my world. Is it anything like this world?"

"Some of it. But…some of the things you talked about are things that happened when you were in a coma."

"See? How could I have known those things if I were truly Jeffrey?"

Maggie contemplated. "Maybe you were hearing things on the television in your room while you were in a coma. I watched a lot of TV when I was sitting there with you. Maybe

170

your brain was still processing the information you were hearing even though you were unconscious."

"Then what about the rest of it, the things that haven't happened here?"

"I think it's something your brain created on its own. What if you just had a long, elaborate dream while you were in a coma, and all of these memories you have now are from that dream? You can have a pretty long, crazy dream in one night's worth of sleeping, and you were 'sleeping' for three years. Don't you think that it's possible that these memories were all created by your own imagination? That you were incorporating things you were hearing and things you remembered from your life into an entirely new life and identity?"

Her words gave Jenson pause. He had been absolutely convinced that his world was real…but was it? Was it possible that it had all been in his head?

"Bring me some paper and a pencil. Please." Jenson needed to test his artistic abilities. He was beginning to doubt himself now.

"Not so sure of your imaginary world anymore?" Maggie asked smugly as she dug out some paper from a drawer. She handed him a pencil from a jar on the counter and put the paper down in front of him at the bar.

"I'll tell you in a few minutes." He began to sketch a picture of one of his favorite paintings from his most recent art show. He remembered it clearly and was able to quickly produce an exquisite pencil sketch of it. He doubted himself less when he was finished. He held it up for Maggie, who was watching him draw.

"How did you do that?" she asked.

"I'm an artist. This is a drawing of one of the paintings I did for my art show."

"The accident must have done something to your brain that improved your artistic ability."

Jenson sighed. "Are you serious?"

"It's easier for me to believe that than it is for me to believe that you are a man from another universe."

Jenson let the paper fall from his hands and watched it float back onto the counter. He slowly stood from the stool and shuffled back to the living room. He flopped onto the couch, feeling defeated. He didn't know who he was anymore. He was Jenson Jeffrey, the artistic biologist who knew nothing about biology.

Maggie came into the living room a few minutes later and sat in the chair near him. "Can I ask you something?" she wanted to know.

"Anything."

"Do you love me?"

"I do," he replied without hesitation.

"If you were truly someone else, then why would you love me?"

"Because you are an amazing woman, and you've been an amazing woman in every world I've visited you in."

She paused and smiled briefly. Then her smile wavered. "Why did you call me Andrea when you first woke up?"

"Because your name was usually Andrea when I was with you. Once it was Natalie, but I always thought of you as Andrea."

"When I told you my name was Maggie, you made a weird face. Was it just because you thought my name would be Andrea?"

"My ex-girlfriend's name was Maggie."

"Oh." Maggie looked surprised. "You had a girlfriend in your dream?"

"If you want to call it a dream, then yes, I had a girlfriend in my dream. Her name was Maggie. She was cold, controlling, superficial, and pretty much the opposite of everything I've found you to be. We broke up right after I got hit by the truck. We had been together three years." Jenson wondered if it was a coincidence that he'd been in a coma for three years here and dating ex-Maggie for three years in his own world. He probably would've been better off being in a coma.

Maggie didn't miss the coincidence either. "That seems odd. You were in a bad relationship for three years, then got hit by a truck. In reality, you got hit by a truck, then went into a coma for three years. Maybe your brain was equating your ex-girlfriend to your coma. You ended it with her after three years, not long before you woke up from a three-year coma. I see enough of a similarity there to still believe that this other world is your imagination."

He had to admit that it was odd. He was bothered by how much he was beginning to doubt that his entire life had existed the way he remembered it. It was the only life he knew – how could it not be real? He thought about his dream jumping, and how he continued to seek out "Andrea" every time he jumped. He had begun to obsess over her in his other life. He had wondered what his connection was with her and why he always visited her in his jumps. Was this his answer? Was it because his own world wasn't real, and that he was simply trying to find his way back to this one so he could be with her once again? If that were true, then why was she always "Andrea" to him, and not "Maggie"?

He was in love with this woman, but he couldn't explain how it was possible. It was love at first sight when he'd seen her in his second dream jump. He'd felt like he knew her, but he'd always assumed it was because the person he'd jumped into had known her. Perhaps the real reason he fell so quickly and inexplicably in love with her was because he truly was Jeffrey, and had shared a life with her. Perhaps he had been in love with her all along. He had been so worried that he would lose himself in his dream jumps that he'd never considered that he might have already been lost to begin with.

It seemed crazy to him. He preferred the dream jumping explanation to the false memories one, simply because he hated the idea that the only life he remembered had been a lie. If it hadn't been real, though, and if he *was* Jeffrey, then that meant that he could stay in this world for as long as he lived, without complication. He strongly desired to remain in this world with Maggie, but he needed to know what was real, who he was, and where he had come from before he could allow himself to become too comfortable in this life with her. He felt that he belonged here, but he still had no answer as to *why*.

"Jeffrey?" Maggie said, startling him from his thoughts.

He realized he'd been sitting in silence for a long time. "Sorry, I was lost in my thoughts."

"You've been lost in your thoughts for three years. It's time to come back to the real world."

"That's easier said than done when you don't know what the real world is."

"I know you are confused, but trust me when I tell you that I know you are Jeffrey, and I know that this is the real world."

"I understand that you are completely convinced of that, but I'm not. You haven't experienced what I have, or at least what I seem to have experienced. If you had, you wouldn't be so certain either."

"I believe what makes the most sense to me. And honestly, this dream world jumping-"

"Dream jumping."

"Ok, this *dream jumping* sounds about as logical as brushing your teeth and then taste-testing oranges. It just doesn't make sense."

"How can you make that decision before I've even explained it to you? If I tell you about it, will you hear me out and keep an open mind?" Jenson requested.

Maggie sat back in her chair and folded her hands in her lap. "Fair enough. I'll try to be as open-minded as I can about it, but I'm going to warn you that I carry a strong bias already."

Jenson smiled. "I am keenly aware of that." He told her about his first dream jump, with Kristine, and about meeting her at the gas station, and about his subsequent research on remote viewing and separation of the mind from the body. He talked about his dream jump where he first met her, and about the apocalypse world. He told her about finding Don's paper, and about contacting him. She appeared to be intrigued when he tried to explain Don's hypotheses regarding the phenomenon, though he was sure he was over-simplifying it. He described the difference between a shadowing jump and a first-person jump. When he started to tell her about his jump to the world with the baby, he decided to leave out the part about them having a child. He knew it would be painful to her. He also left out the baby when he told her about his jump after being hit by the truck. He shared with her his worries he'd had about becoming lost in his dream jumps. He told her that he'd started to jump from world to world, to different times in relation to his own world, and how he had been afraid he would miss his opportunity to meet her in his own world at his art show. Finally, he described to her what it felt like to wake up from Jeffrey's coma.

By the time he had finished his story, he was pleased to see how captivated Maggie had been by it. She was staring at him in wide-eyed wonderment. They sat in silence as she contemplated the implications presented by the information she'd received.

She broke the silence with, "I understand your confusion."

"But?" He expected her to have a "logical" explanation for his story.

"But nothing. I understand your confusion. I would be confused too, if I had experienced that. Actually, I am confused as well. That's a remarkable story."

"So am I Jenson or am I Jeffrey?"

"…I don't know. I don't know who you are," she replied, looking bewildered.

"That makes two of us. I think the only way I can truly know who I am is to find out if dream jumping is real. If it is, it corroborates the theory that I am Jenson. If it isn't real, then I must be Jeffrey, right?"

"I don't know. What if you were Jeffrey to begin with, and you dream jumped when you got hit by the truck three years ago, and you jumped into Jenson? What if, when that happened, your consciousness jumped as it did when you got hit in the other world, but the trauma of the incident caused you to jump without your memories. Maybe it happened so suddenly that only the core of your consciousness was able to jump, losing all of your knowledge and memories. Then when you jumped into Jenson, your consciousness accessed all of Jenson's memories and, since it had no memories to work from, you *became* Jenson without even realizing that anything had happened? Think about it. If you lost everything in your mind, then had it replaced with an entire lifetime of different memories, you would never know the difference. You would think you had always been the person whose memories you stole. Maybe that's why you were able to dream jump so freely once you realized it was happening, because you'd done it before. For all you know, many of the dreams you had as Jenson might've been dream jumps, but you didn't know it at the time until you met Kristine."

Jenson felt like his brain had exploded. He remembered Don talking about the idea of consciousness as a laser or x-ray. Was it possible that his consciousness could have left his body without any of his "information" being imprinted on its "wave pattern"?

Maggie added, "And maybe that's why, when you learned about dream jumping, you started subconsciously seeking out versions of me when you travelled. Maybe you were trying to find your way back to me, back to your own body, even though you didn't understand why you were doing it. Your consciousness might've still shared a connection with your real body."

"If all of this happened to be true, then what would've become of the 'real' Jenson? Would our consciousnesses have become *one* since we essentially became the same person? Or did I just steal his memories and his body? Where would he have gone? Would he be stuck in a shadowing state, or would he go somewhere else? What is he doing now that I'm gone? And for that matter, if I *am* Jenson, then what is going on with my body back home without me in it?" He paused for a moment, feeling overwhelmed. He buried his face in his hands. "Who the hell am I?!" he shouted in exasperation.

He felt a gentle touch on his shoulder.

"It will be ok. Calm down," Maggie said in a soft, soothing voice.

"Will I ever know who I am?" he asked even though he knew Maggie didn't have the answer.

"Maybe, maybe not. But you know what? Maybe it doesn't matter who you are on paper. Maybe it doesn't matter where you came from, or whether the past you remember is really yours or not. You are you. Will finding out your true identity make you change who you are inside? Will it make you change your personality? If you are Jeffrey, will you act differently than if you are Jenson? I don't think so. I'm not trying to play down the importance of discovering what is truly going on here, but in the meantime, I want you to worry less about who you are, and just be *you*."

Her words resonated with him. She hadn't been able to tell that he *wasn't* Jeffrey, so it seemed true that, regardless of whether he was Jenson or Jeffrey, he was still basically the same person. Their knowledge and talents were different, but their personalities were the same. Who he was did matter to him, but he agreed that knowing who he was wouldn't change anything about the kind of man he had become.

He took a deep, calming breath. "Ok. Let's take this one step at a time. First, I think we should start looking into dream jumping and see if we can find a version of Donald Wesson here. It might be a dead end, but it wouldn't hurt to try to find him."

"I agree. In the meantime, is it ok if I continue to call you Jeffrey? I know you tend to think of yourself as Jenson, but given the circumstances, I think it would be better if we referred to you as Jeffrey."

"That's fine. I'm already starting to get used to it. I'll just think of it as a nickname for now. Hell, Don used to call me Jennie. By comparison, I like Jeffrey better," Jenson admitted. Maggie smiled at him, and he found all the comfort he needed in that smile. He wondered if she still had feelings for him even though she now knew that he might not be the man she fell in love with. He looked like her husband and acted like him, so it wasn't so hard to believe it was possible. He wanted to ask her, but thought better of it.

"Where do we start looking?" Maggie asked.

"The almighty internet, of course."

Maggie went to the kitchen and returned with a laptop for him. "You can use this. I'll use the tablet."

They sat in the living room and browsed the internet in silence. Jenson realized that the search engine he typically used didn't exist in this world. The one he was using now took a few minutes to figure out, but once he did, he found it to be much more efficient and useful than his old one. He searched "dream jumping," but the results he found were about some kind of extreme bungee jumping. He then tried "dreams, parallel universe." An abundance of blogs and articles came up on the screen. He read through several of them, and his hopes rose. Theories existed in this world, too, regarding mind travel to alternate realities or parallel universes. He found a few blogs from people who claimed to dream jump (though they all had a different name for it), but only one of them appeared to be legitimate. From his own dream jumping experiences, he could tell that the others were either mistaken or outright lying. One of them claimed that she could go to the past and change her current life by altering events. He called bullshit on that one. Another one claimed that every story that was ever created by mankind existed in its own, very real universe. The blogger asserted that simply creating the story in one's mind would make it exist in another realm, and that he was able to visit all of these worlds. The blogger tried to relate it to the premise of quantum theory that observation affects reality, and took it a step further by saying that it must mean that observing something in your mind, something you created, made it reality. Even Jenson, with his incredibly limited knowledge of quantum physics, knew it was malarkey.

"Well, I see a lot of theories suggesting its possibility," Jenson remarked.

"Yeah, but unfortunately, a lot of it is nonsense. I mean, you can find a lot of articles, stories and blogs on the internet about magic crystals and vampires and fairies, but it doesn't make them true. It's still hard to say if this is real or not."

"I found a blog by a guy who claims to be able to dream jump. It appears to be the real deal. He calls it a 'mind holiday.' I think he's from the U.K. His experiences are congruent to the types of things I've experienced while in a dream jump. He talks about shadowing, or as he calls it, 'stalking,' and how the bodies he takes 'holiday' in all seem to look a lot like him. He doesn't seem to have first-person jumps though."

"It still doesn't make it real. We need something concrete," Maggie said.

"We need Don," Jenson replied. He searched the internet for Dr. Donald Wesson, and wasn't surprised when none of the results were the Don he was seeking. "These aren't the Dons you're looking for," he quipped, his hand gliding through the air in front of his face. He was surprised when Maggie laughed. "You understood that reference?"

"Of course. We have that movie here, too. It's a sci-fi classic."

"Actually, I'm more surprised by the fact that you understood and laughed at the joke than I am that the film exists here. I knew I liked you for a reason...nerd."

Maggie laughed out loud. "You think you're the first person to call me a nerd? I'm an accountant. I do math for a living. 'Nerd' is all I do."

Jenson and Maggie spent the next hour looking for some version of Don in this world. Jenson tried looking up studies and papers relating to dream jumping, but without a database from which to search peer-reviewed journal articles, he came up empty-handed. He needed access to a library or college database. He then started browsing through all of Michigan's college and university web pages, trying to find faculty members who looked like Don. Again, he found nothing.

"I need to make dinner," Maggie announced. She grinned at Jenson, and in an odd, froggy voice, she said, "Hungry, I am!" He chuckled, understanding her call-back to the movie he had referenced earlier.

"Make food you must!" he replied as she walked away.

He closed the laptop and took a break from his disappointing research. He was beginning to think that finding a parallel version of Don was going to be impossible. For all he knew, the Don in this world might not be a physicist. He probably had a different name and could be anywhere, doing anything. He might not even exist at all here. Jenson was starting to think that the only way he could determine if dream jumping was real was to do it. If he could dream jump, he would have a definitive answer. It wouldn't tell him if he was Jeffrey or not, but it would at least be a step in the right direction. It would be *something*.

When Maggie brought him a TV tray and a heaping plate of spaghetti, he shared his thoughts with her regarding the matter. She looked worried.

"But if you do jump, you might not come back," she said uneasily.

"…I know. But I have to. I think it's the only way we're going to get answers."

"Answers for you, maybe. If you leave and don't return…I don't know if it's worth it. I can't lose you again."

"You lost Jeffrey. I might not be Jeffrey. I could just be a stranger in Jeffrey's body."

"I'd rather have you here with me, not knowing if you are Jeffrey or Jenson, than have to be alone again. That may sound selfish and horrible, especially if you aren't Jeffrey, but I don't care. That's how I feel, and feelings don't have to be rational." Maggie's eyes were welling up with tears.

"I don't want to leave you, Maggie. I really don't. But if dream jumping is real, then I'm fairly certain that it's going to happen to me eventually anyway. I'd rather be ready for it, trying to control it, than to have it happen by surprise. In my opinion, this is the only solution."

"And what if you don't wake up? How long am I supposed to wait for you to come back? When will I know if you're returning or not?"

"I don't have an answer for that. My dream jumps never used to last for more than the night, but that seems to have changed. Don once told me about someone who had jumped for what seemed like a week to the jumper, but it didn't last more than half an hour for his body in his own world. Time passes differently from one world to the next…which probably also means that it's possible for a jump that seemed like a day to the jumper could pass as a week in his own world. There's just no way of knowing how long you will be gone when you jump."

"I don't like this."

"I know. I'm sorry, Maggie."

They ate their dinner quietly. Well, relatively quietly. Jenson noticed that when Maggie chewed, her jaw clicked. Every time she took a bite, he heard *click, click, click*. It sounded like she was eating a marble, and it was more grating on his frayed nerves than nails on a chalkboard.

"Can we turn something on TV?" he asked, hoping for some background noise to drown out the irritating jaw click.

Maggie grabbed a nearby remote and turned on the television. She skimmed through the station guide until she found a show that appealed to her. Jenson was pleased to find it was a show with which he seemed familiar.

"Oh, I like this episode," he said. "This is the one where Cooper takes up the Bongo drums."

Maggie gave him a skeptical look. "This is a new episode."

"I'm telling you, I've seen it before." He started telling her everything that was about to happen, and every time, save for one incident, he was correct. It was almost exactly as he remembered the show from his own world.

When the show concluded, Maggie was amazed. "I don't think I need any more convincing that something incredibly odd is happening here. This show wasn't created until after you'd gone into a coma, yet you knew all the characters. I know I've never watched this in the hospital room because the hospital TV doesn't carry this channel. If dream jumping isn't real, then something else equally peculiar has happened to you."

"Dream jumping *is* real. I'm certain of it now. I didn't create these memories with my imagination. Everything I remember has happened…somewhere." Jenson felt some of his confidence returning. The memories he had were real, but whether they were truly his or someone else's remained to be discovered.

"This is amazing," Maggie said. "Terrifying, weird, and amazing. Do you think other people dream jump? I mean, obviously some people must if that scientist in your other world was able to study it, but maybe it happens to a lot of people who don't realize it. Maybe everybody dream jumps. I wonder if I've ever done it."

"Do you remember your dreams?"

"Not usually. Only once in a while do I actually remember the whole dream. I know I dreamed a lot about being with you – or Jeffrey – when you were in a coma, but I never remembered what happened in the dream when I woke up. I never spent much time trying to remember my dreams."

"You should start working on it. Try to remember your dreams as soon as you wake up, and write them down. Don told me that practicing lucid dreaming helped him to recognize when he was in a dream jump and not just a regular dream. When you are lucid in a normal dream, you can make things happen that wouldn't ordinarily happen and make yourself do things that aren't physically possible. But when you are lucid, yet find that you have no control over anything but yourself, then it is possible that you are in a dream jump." He shared with her everything he had learned about practicing lucid dreaming.

"So if I discovered that I was able to dream jump, what then? What would I do with it?"

"Whatever you want, I guess. I was using it to try to better understand what it was, and also to try to find you, or versions of you. Don was using it to try to access the Akashic record, or the knowledge of the universe. What you do with it is ultimately up to you. But always keep in mind that your actions in a dream jump will reflect upon the person you jump into, and they will have to deal with the consequences long after you leave them." Jenson remembered what had happened to Jamie, or rather, what he had caused to happen to Jamie. He remembered baby Jeffrey calling him Dada, and wondering if the Jenson of that world had heard him say those words before. He added, "It's someone's life you are playing with."

"Is it possible that my dreams about you were really dream jumps? Could I have actually been visiting with a version of you?"

"I think it's definitely possible. Maybe it's even possible that if they were dream jumps, one of them may have been you and I who were interacting. The probability of you and I ending up in the same world at the same time may be ridiculously low, but it isn't impossible. After all, I met up with someone from my other world in a dream jump."

"Why didn't you ever contact Kristine once you learned about dream jumping? You knew where to find her, and you knew she could dream jump. It seems like something you should've explored."

"I knew she could dream jump, but I don't think she knew that's what she was doing. You know me – well, in a sense – and even you had a hard time believing me when I told you about dream jumping. How do you think a complete stranger would react if I tried to tell them about it? She would've thought I was crazy and probably would've called the cops on me," Jenson rationalized.

"Yeah, I guess. If I were her, I probably wouldn't have believed you either."

"Even my ex-girlfriend didn't really believe any of it. She humored me, somewhat, but I knew she didn't think it was a real phenomenon. She referred to my interest in it as 'chasing butterflies.'"

Maggie looked slightly agitated. "It bothers me when you talk about your ex-girlfriend. I don't like thinking about it. I was ok with it when I thought it was all your imagination, but now that I know it was real…I just don't want to talk about it if we don't have to," Maggie said.

The thought had not occurred to Jenson that talking about ex-Maggie could hurt Maggie. If he was Jeffrey, then it would mean that he was in a relationship with another woman in another world while he was still married to Maggie in this world. He still thought of himself as Jenson, and his mind still viewed his life in his other world as being unrelated to this one. He hadn't meant to make Maggie uncomfortable.

"I'm sorry, I didn't even think about the, um, conflict of interest. I didn't mean to upset you."

"It's a weird, confusing situation. I don't hold you at fault for it. It isn't entirely logical for me to feel this way, given the circumstances, but like I said before, feelings don't have to be rational. It wouldn't bother me if we knew that you weren't Jeffrey, but if you are Jeffrey…no, I just don't want to think about it." Maggie shook her head as though it would clear her mind of ex-Maggie. "Change of subject!"

"Do you want to stop talking about dream jumping?"

"No, just something not related to your other world. Oh, here's something. Do you think it might be possible for two people to dream jump together? Not just to randomly end up in the same world together, but to actually plan a jump and travel there together at the same time?"

"You mean into the same person?"

"No, I mean to the same world, into the parallel versions of ourselves in that world."

Jenson considered it. "I don't know. I suppose if it were two people who had exceptional control over their abilities it might be possible. I never thought about actively trying to dream jump with someone. The only other person I know well enough to even attempt that with would be Don, and I know neither of us has enough control in our jumps to make it work. Besides, that would be awkward with Don. If you ever met Don, you would understand. He's an odd duck. He makes everything awkward," Jenson said with a chuckle.

"I want to try it," Maggie announced.

"What?" Jenson looked at her in surprise.

"I know I've never dream jumped, or at least knowingly dream jumped, but I want to try it. If you dream jump tonight, you might not come back. I want to know where you go, so that if you don't come back to me in this world, maybe I can go and find you in your world or whatever world you end up in. If you leave, I want to go with you."

"Maggie, that's crazy."

"This whole thing is crazy," Maggie pointed out. "There's no reason we can't try it. I vowed on my wedding day to follow my husband to the ends of the Earth and beyond. If you are Jeffrey, then I want to go with you so I don't lose you again. If you aren't, then maybe you will help me come one step closer to finding him. Either way, I'm going with you if I can."

"It isn't that easy. You have determination, I'll give you that, but if you are able to jump, it takes time and experience to be able to recognize that you are in a dream jump. You might not even be able to jump. I still can't control where I'm going, and I don't expect that you would be able to control it either if you did jump. It isn't like you just fall asleep and go wherever you want.

It's more like you fall asleep and *end up* somewhere. It's not as simple as you are making it out to be."

"I don't care. Even if I fail, at least I will have tried, and I will continue to try. 'In great attempts, it is glorious even to fail.'"

Jenson nodded. "I can't disagree with you on that. Ok. We will try it. I have no idea how to even approach this, but let's give it a whirl."

"You've told me all about your world, so maybe if I think about it, really focus on what I know about it, I will be able to go to it. That's where we're going, isn't it?"

"I think it's our best bet. I'd like to see what's happening there and how long I've been gone. If I'm able to get back there, I might be able to really focus on probing my mind to see if I can find any hint that I'm being shadowed or that I've taken over a body that didn't belong to me in the first place. Don't ask me *how* I'm going to do that, but I'm going to try. Also, I'd really like to hear Don's thoughts on this whole conundrum."

That night, Maggie insisted that they sleep in the same bed in order to better facilitate a connection. They lay in bed, side by side, in the darkness.

"I feel like I'm focusing so hard that I'll never fall asleep," Maggie whispered.

Jenson reached over and found her hand under the covers. He held it gently. He was surprised at how that simple touch could make his heart race. She turned her head to him.

"Try to find your way back to me, ok? I will be heartbroken if I wake up in the morning and find out you're gone."

"I'll do my best, Maggie. And for the record, regardless of who I am or where I came from, I want you to know that I care deeply for you. I will always try to find my way to you in whatever world I end up in."

She leaned over and kissed him on the cheek. Soon after that, as he was thinking about how badly he needed answers for both himself and for Maggie, he felt himself drifting off to sleep.

He suddenly felt jostled. It wasn't his body that was jarred, but rather his mind. The sensation was strange, and it reminded him of the sudden disorientation he felt when he was on an amusement park ride and the ride abruptly changed direction. There was a flash of brilliant white light, then…nothing. Not darkness, not light, just nothingness.

Chapter 13

He was present somewhere, yet it was like he wasn't anywhere at all. He had his thoughts, but no body with which to feel or eyes with which to see. He could draw up images in his mind, but he wasn't actually *seeing* anything. He wondered if he should feel panicked, or awe-stricken, but he felt no emotions at all. He tried to think about happy memories, and painful memories, but the emotions he had previously associated with those memories did not follow. The closest thing he could equate his present state to was contentedness, though it wasn't exactly that, either. He was in a blank, emotionless state of pure thought.

When he thought about his current predicament, his identity crisis, he found that he was able to ponder it clearly without all of the emotional attachments. He was no longer hoping to be Jeffrey so he could stay with Maggie, nor was he hoping to be Jenson just because he felt that he *was* Jenson. He was simply accepting to whatever truth may be discovered. As he worked through the problem, he noticed that he was able to access knowledge to which he hadn't previously been privy. He suddenly knew that the consciousness that had originated from the body in the coma world was currently inhabiting his body in his other world. Therefore, he was *not* Jeffrey. He was Jenson. It would seem that he and Jeffrey had switched places. He was neither shocked nor relieved, but accepted that this was the truth he sought. When he tried to contemplate his next course of action and what he wanted to do now, however, he found he was unable to do so. He could understand that there were many options before him, but he also understood that this decision required emotional content. Emotions weren't present in the Akashic record because they were a manifestation of the body, not the consciousness. Emotions are an evolutionary adaptation, a survival mechanism, and nothing more. They are unnecessary to the information of the universes. Right and wrong, morality – they are relative and situational, differing from culture to culture and world to world. Information is unconditional, and while information is the only thing necessary for the Akashic record, emotions are necessary for life. His decision regarding his future actions weren't a matter of truth, but rather a matter of what would be most beneficial to him emotionally, and thus could not be deliberated here.

He became aware of the sensation that he was moving shortly before he saw another bright flash of light. He felt instantly overwhelmed by sensory overload. His pulse was crashing loudly in his ears, and the fabric of the sheets was tearing at his skin. The light in the room was blinding him even through his closed eyelids. The taste of his morning breath made him gag, and the scent of the fabric softener on his pillowcase was overpowering. His emotions flooded through him at full force, and he felt the extremes of happiness alongside those of despair.

This strange condition lasted but mere seconds, and then it faded quickly. He was in a cold sweat when everything returned to normal. He opened his eyes slowly, hesitant to discover what he might behold. He was greeted by the beautiful face of a peaceful, sleeping Maggie. He had returned to her after all. He looked around the room to make sure he was in the world he had been in the night before. Everything appeared to be the same, right down to the shorts and t-shirt he was wearing.

"Maggie," he whispered. He gently stroked her lovely dark hair.

She began to rouse from her slumber. She opened her eyes sleepily, and when she saw that he was awake, she smiled at him.

"You came back to me." She curled her fingers around his hand and sighed. "I don't think I went anywhere last night. I don't remember anything."

"I did. At least, I think I did. It was the strangest experience I've had yet. I didn't return to my other world, but instead I felt a weird jolt, and then ended up in a place where I didn't have a body."

She furrowed her brow. "You were just floating around, like a ghost?"

"No. It wasn't even a place, exactly. I saw a flash of light, then there was nothing. It was like I was in a trance or something…no, that doesn't explain it well either. I don't know how to describe it to you. There was nothing in this place but my own thoughts. I didn't even feel any emotions. I felt like a computer, just processing data. I also had access to knowledge that I didn't know before, and I was able to figure out who I really am."

Maggie sat upright, suddenly alert. "Who are you?"

"I'm Jenson. I'm not Jeffrey. What's really strange is that I learned where Jeffrey was when I was in this 'place.' He's in my body in the other world."

Maggie's face contorted into an expression of extreme shock and confusion, and she pulled her hand from his. "What?! That's ludicrous!"

"I know. It made perfect sense to me when I came upon that knowledge, but now that I'm out of that place, it seems like utter ridiculousness. I feel like it couldn't possibly be true, but I know that it is. It's been burned into my brain as a fact. I don't know why he is there or how long he's been there, but that's where he is. It doesn't seem like pure chance that he would end up in my body and I would end up in his, though. There has to be some connection that sent me here and him there, don't you think?" Jenson rationalized.

"He's been gone for three years. Maybe he was dream jumping from world to world in that time, and when he jumped into your body, it sent you to his when you tried to jump back home. Weren't you in a series of jumps right before you came here?"

"Yeah, I was kind of all over the place for a bit there. When I fell asleep in the world before this one, I was focusing on trying to go home. I woke up here, instead. You might be right. I might've been sent here when I tried to return home to a body that was being controlled by someone else. What I don't understand is why I wouldn't have just returned to my body and kicked Jeffrey out. I've taken over bodies that were right in the middle of their daily activities, so I know it's not impossible to do so. What's so different about this situation that I wouldn't be *allowed* to return to my body?" Jenson felt troubled. "I wish I had tried to learn more about it when I was in my 'thinking space,' but my sense of curiosity was rather dampened." He had a sudden thought. "I wonder if that place I visited last night was something like Don's Akashic record. It kind of fit the bill. Damn, I wish I could talk to him about this."

"What exactly is the Akashic record?" Maggie wanted to know.

Jenson exhaled loudly. "Well...I don't know exactly. Don explained it to me as a dimension of knowledge, where information is stored. I guess you could think of it as the internet of the universes, except with real information instead of a bunch of cat videos. He thought that we all had limited access to it through our consciousness on a daily basis. He thought that if he could somehow 'visit' it in his dream jumping, he could access all the information of the universe and gain unlimited knowledge."

"And you think that's where you went?"

"I think it's possible. But I don't know if referring to it as a 'place' is really the right way to describe it, now that I think about it. It's more like an absence of 'place,' if that makes any sense."

"It doesn't. I'm going to call it a place," Maggie replied bluntly. "Do you think you can return to it? Now that you've been there, maybe you can find your way back to it and get some more answers."

Jenson remembered how traumatic it had been when he woke up from his dream jump this morning. It had been excruciating. He was certain it was a result of experiencing the complete nothingness of where he had been. Even if he could return to that 'place,' he wasn't sure that he was ready to endure the painful return from it again, at least not yet.

"I don't think I'm ready to go back to it right now. The return was incredibly unpleasant. Rather than try to understand why Jeffrey is there and I am here, though, I'd like to try to figure out what we want to do from here, especially now that you know I am not your husband. What is it that *you* want?"

Maggie was quiet. She looked away from him uncomfortably.

"You want Jeffrey back," he surmised.

She nodded, still avoiding eye contact with him. He felt a sting in his heart, but he knew he had no right to be upset with her decision.

"It's ok, I understand. He is your husband, after all, and I'm just a stranger in his body." He tried to hide the disappointment in his voice. He smiled, only because he knew that if he didn't, his face would reveal his pain.

Maggie finally looked at him. "You aren't a stranger, not exactly. But you're right - you aren't my husband. I guess I was holding on to hope that you were actually him. Now that I know for certain that you aren't..." she let her voice trail off without finishing her sentence. She didn't need to. He understood her meaning. *I don't want you here.*

He remembered how she had pleaded with him the night before to return to her, and how she had assured him that even if he wasn't Jeffrey, she still wanted him around so she wouldn't have to be alone in this world again. Now he understood that the only reason she had felt that way was because, in her heart, he *was* Jeffrey. She thought she had meant the things she said until she'd learned the hard truth about his identity. How quickly a heart can change.

"So what do you want me to do?" he asked her directly.

"I want you to return home. Maybe if you can get back into your own body, it will send Jeffrey back here to me."

"I will try, but what if it doesn't work? What if I can't get back home?"

"Then you keep trying." Maggie was suddenly distant. She seemed to have a hard time looking him in the eye. She climbed out of bed and left the room without another word.

Jenson swung his feet over the edge of the bed, but he didn't rise from it. He sat alone, wallowing in his own sorrows. He had hoped he would be able to stay here and be loved by the woman he had fallen in love with. A part of him had hoped that he was Jeffrey, because if he was, he had a happy life to look forward to. What was waiting for him in his own world? All he had to look forward to upon his return were hospital bills, no home of his own, no love of his life, and no reliable source of income. At least, that was how he had left it.

What was Jeffrey doing with Jenson's life right now? How long had Jenson been gone? He wondered if time in this world moved more slowly than time in his own, considering the fact that this world was over two years behind his own. If that was the case, then that might mean that Jeffrey had been in control of Jenson's life for more than the week or so that Jenson had been here. He wondered if any of his family could tell that the person in Jenson's body wasn't really Jenson. Did Jeffrey even know that he wasn't Jenson? Would Jeffrey have access to his memories? The only way for him to know what was happening was for him to return, but could he?

Jenson thought about the last two jumps he had made – the jump that had brought him here, and the one to the "thought realm." Both times, he had been completely focused on returning home, and both times, he had felt a strange jarring sensation before he woke up in a world that was not his own. Those were the only two times he had ever felt anything of the sort while making a jump. He didn't understand what it was. He recalled it as the sensation of a carnival ride quickly switching direction. Was it because his consciousness, in its travel to his own world, had somehow been pulled in a different direction, to a different world? Why would that happen? He couldn't answer that, but he had a feeling it was related to his inability to return to his body.

Something was keeping him away from it, for what purpose he had yet to discover.

The day passed slowly. Maggie had very little to say to him, and she seemed sullen. She had begun to address him as "Jenson" now, but she always made a slight grimace when she said it. It pained him to see her so unhappy, and even more so to know that he was the reason for it. However unintentional it had been, he had hurt her. He'd helped her to find her happiness again, then ripped it away from her. Poor Maggie had already been through too much in this life, and this was just another blow. He wished he could find a way to make things better for her, but the only way he could do that was to give her what she wanted. He loved her, and he wanted to show her that he could make her happy if she would give him a chance, but it wasn't what she wanted. If he truly loved her, he needed to do everything in his power to send Jeffrey back to his own body. He had to put his own feelings aside and focus on what was best for her.

That night, Maggie made the bed in the guest bedroom for him. When it seemed that she had been in there an inordinate amount of time, he went in to investigate. He found her sitting on the edge of the bed, tears running down her cheeks. She wasn't sobbing, but silently weeping.

"Maggie, what's wrong? Is it me?"

She quickly swiped her tears away. She looked embarrassed that he had seen her crying. She stood up and looked directly at him for the first time since that morning.

"Do you have any idea how hard it is to look at someone who is supposed to be my husband, yet I know that it isn't? To know that my real husband is far away in some other universe, living someone else's life, and might not even remember me? To know that he might not be thinking about me when all I have thought about for the past three years is him? To know that there is no way for me to reach him, to make him come back to me? It was bad enough to have to go through something like this once, with the coma, but now I'm forced to go through this again. And it's worse this time, because here you are, walking, talking, acting like my husband…and you aren't really my Jeffrey. I feel angry with you, but I feel guilty about my anger because I know this isn't your fault. I feel sad, too, because you seem to care a great deal about me, but I can't care about you the same way. I love my husband too much, and you aren't him. However like him you may be, you still *aren't* him."

Jenson stood silently. He wanted to go to her and hug her, but he knew that would be the wrong move. She didn't want to be comforted by him. She wanted Jeffrey. She walked past him, out of the room, saying a quick "goodnight" on her way out.

Jenson closed the door and changed into a pair of shorts. As he lay in bed, he realized that he had never felt so unwanted in all his life. Maggie didn't want him. Ex-Maggie didn't want him. Hell, even his own body didn't seem to want him. He had no place in this world, and it seemed that he didn't really have a place in his own world either. He had become a lonely drifter, and it was an unfulfilling existence. He'd hoped that his dream jumping would somehow bring him the things his life had lacked, and that it would be wonderful and full of adventure and help him discover what his life was supposed to be. Instead, it had brought his life great strife and caused him to constantly question what was real, where he belonged, and who he was. Socrates had said, "The unexamined life is not worth living," but Jenson was beginning to think that an over-examined life was really no better.

When Jenson woke up, he was in an unfamiliar bed in an unfamiliar room. He quickly understood that he had jumped again. He'd felt no jolt or jarring this time, but then again, he hadn't been focusing on going home before he fell asleep. He'd just been absorbed in his own sadness when he'd drifted off. He took it to mean that the jolt he'd started feeling was connected only to his attempts to return home.

As he climbed out of bed, he stepped on a big, hairy mass and lost his balance, collapsing onto the floor. He heard a yelp, and when he looked up, there was a startled and severely overweight black Labrador retriever standing next to him. It looked down at him and started licking his face. He "remembered" that the dog was his, and his name was Ardie. He sat up and patted the big brute's head.

"Sorry, buddy," he apologized as he stood up. Ardie wagged his tail and followed Jenson out of the room. He knew he was supposed to feed Ardie now. He went directly to the kitchen, already knowing his way around this house, and poured the dog the amount of dog food he knew he was supposed to feed him. He also knew that it was entirely too much food for the big fatty. He seemed to be able to access this body's knowledge much more freely than any body before. He wondered if it was because his skill was improving. He made himself some coffee and rummaged through the cupboards while it brewed. He was impressed at the variety of healthy food he had available to him, especially considering he was a bachelor. His cupboards and fridge were filled with fresh produce, granola, yogurt, protein bars, rice cakes, and whole grain breads. There wasn't one pack of ramen noodles or one box of macaroni and cheese in his kitchen. He ate a protein bar, then poured his coffee and went to the living room to watch some morning news.

He glanced out the window before he sat on the couch, and was surprised to see greenery outside. It was summer here. He absentmindedly scratched an itch on his stomach as he stared at the quiet street outside his home, and was startled by the hardness of his own body. He lifted up his shirt and gazed at his own well-defined abdominals. He made a mental note to start eating healthier when he returned to his own world.

He turned on the television, and as soon as he sat down, Ardie bounded into the living room and dove into his lap, spilling coffee everywhere.

"Dammit, dog!" he shouted as he pushed the great beast off of him. Ardie tucked his tail between his legs and slinked off to the bedroom. "This is why I don't have a dog," he said as he went about cleaning up the mess. His body's memories told him that this was a common occurrence in this house, and the multiple cans of carpet and upholstery cleaner in the closet attested to this fact.

Jenson got a fresh cup of coffee after he'd changed his clothes and sat down in front of the television, keeping a wary eye out for the kamikaze dog. He learned from the news that time in this world was slightly ahead of his own world, but only by a few months (assuming he had been gone for only a week or so). He also learned that this world was in a better economic state than this own, but that religious rivalries and atrocities were still rampant. The most abundant stories, however, were those of crime and politics, much like the news in his own world. It appeared to him that human nature as a whole did not vary in the worlds he visited. He wondered if there were other worlds where humans had evolved in a way that didn't make them so prone to violence and manipulation. Then again, would they really be considered humans if that were the case?

Jenson turned off the television. He wanted to try something he hadn't tried before. He closed his eyes and began rummaging through his new body's brain, trying to see how deep he could dig. He quickly realized that he had access to everything. His name was Neil. He lived in Brighton, Michigan. He found memories of this body's childhood, his first love, his first car, his job. He was a forester, and he could find all the information in his brain he needed to do such a job. It was all there. He'd never had such open access to memories in a first-person jump, and it made him wonder if the person he'd taken over was still present. He wanted to try to detect some hint of Neil's consciousness, but he wasn't sure how to do it. He didn't know what to look for, or to feel for.

He cleared his mind and sat completely still, trying to achieve a meditative state. He thought if his mind was quiet enough, he might be able to detect the stirring of another consciousness, like a hunter in the woods listening for the movement of wildlife. When he cleared his mind and focused all of his energy inwardly, he realized that he *did* feel it. It was such an infinitesimal sensation that he almost missed it completely. It was the feeling of being watched. He likened it to the way it feels when you sense someone standing right behind you. It made the hair stand up on the back of his neck and his eyes shot open. He looked around, just to make sure there wasn't someone else in the room.

Now that Jenson had sensed it, he couldn't make the feeling go away. He needed a distraction from it. He knew there was an outdoor, pet-friendly coffee shop up the road that Neil liked to go to, so he grabbed his phone and wallet, put a leash on Ardie, and left the house.

The warm sun and fresh air felt wonderful. After the bitter cold of the U.P. winter in his previous world, this felt like the Bahamas. Ardie made sure Jenson didn't enjoy himself for long, though, as Ardie had places to go and things to pee on. He zigzagged down the sidewalk, pulling Jenson with the power of a team of oxen. Neil might allow such behavior, but Jenson wasn't having it. He gave a short, loud shout, which caused the dog to stop and look at him. Jenson wound the leash around his hand, leaving only enough slack for Ardie to walk directly beside him. Ardie fought him a little when Jenson resumed at his own pace, but he was a smart dog, and after a little while, he was following along obediently.

"See, Ardie? You're not such an asshole after all," Jenson said. Ardie wagged his tail.

When they arrived at the coffee shop, Jenson sat at an open outside table. He knew better than to try to tie Ardie to the table or his chair, as his memory told him that it had ended badly last time he'd done that. He would have to hold the leash. A tall, slender young man in a uniform and apron approached the table and handed him a menu while reciting the specials of the day. Jenson handed the menu back to him and ordered a black coffee.

The server hesitated. "But you always order a latte. You don't want a latte today?"

"Nah, it's nice to change things up sometimes."

"Very true. I'll bring that out in a jiffy, Mr. Hawking."

Jenson pulled out his phone and started an internet search for dream jumping. He had already gathered from his mental reconnaissance of Neil's brain that this version of himself did not dream jump, but he was curious to see if there were theories about it in this world. Before he had a chance to look into it, however, he was interrupted.

"Aw! Can I pet your dog?" a female voice asked. He recognized that voice. He looked up and saw Maggie – or

Andrea? – standing near his table. Ardie stood up and wagged his tail excitedly.

"Yes, of course. He's friendly." Jenson quickly put his phone back in his pocket. "His name is Ardie. I'm Je-" Jenson almost slipped up and gave her the wrong name. "I'm Neil, by the way," he quickly corrected.

"I'm Stephanie," she replied, flashing him her beautiful smile briefly before turning her attention to Ardie. "You're just a big sweetie, aren't you?" she said to the dog as she kneeled down in front of him and ruffled his ears.

"So I take it you're a dog person?" Jenson asked her.

"Actually, no. I was attacked by a dog when I was a kid, and I've recently begun trying to get over my fear of dogs. I've found that interacting with them is the only way I'm ever going to get over it. If all dogs were this nice, I'd have no problem!" she said, giggling as Ardie licked her face.

"I'm sorry to hear that. But now you have a friend for life, I think," Jenson said, gesturing toward Ardie. "Please, sit down. Join us for coffee."

"Thank you," Stephanie said, smiling at him again. When she turned her head to place her handbag on the back of the chair, Jenson noticed a long scar on the side of her face, from her ear down to her jaw. He wondered if it was from the aforementioned dog attack. He quickly drew his eyes away from it so she wouldn't see him looking at it. He'd had a friend in college who had a facial scar, and he remembered how she had always felt like people were staring at it. He imagined Stephanie probably felt the same way, and it would be inconsiderate of him to make her uncomfortable.

The server returned with Jenson's coffee and asked Stephanie if she needed anything. She smiled pleasantly at the server and ordered a cappuccino. Everything she did, from her simplest movements to her smile, even the air around her, was full of life and energy. She was different than the parallel version of herself in the coma world, yet very much the same. She had similar mannerisms, but this version didn't seem to carry the weight of a difficult life. He wondered if Maggie had been this way before the loss of her child and Jeffrey's coma.

"So what are you doing on this fine Saturday?" Stephanie asked him.

"I don't know yet. This was as far as my planning took me. How about you?"

"I'm going to the lake with my friends. There's nothing better after a long work week than washing away your troubles at the lake."

"What do you do for a living?" Jenson asked.

"I'm a long-term care nurse."

"Wow, that sounds like a demanding job. Do you like it?"

"I really do. It's not easy, especially when you lose patients that you've become close to, or when the ones with Alzheimer's and dementia forget who you are every day. And then there's Miss Doris, who throws her mashed potatoes at me at least once a week because she thinks I took her cat." Stephanie laughed good-naturedly. She leaned toward him conspiratorially and whispered, "I told them to stop serving her mashed potatoes, and you know what happened? They gave her a baked potato. I took a baked potato right to the face that day. Needless to say, she gets mashed potatoes again, and I spend every Wednesday evening picking mashed potatoes out of my hair."

Jenson laughed. He enjoyed her sense of humor. The server brought her the cappuccino she'd ordered, and she thanked him politely.

Jenson continued the conversation. "You should start wearing one of those attractive plastic caps they wear in the operating room."

"I honestly asked my boss about it, but he told me it was a bad idea because it might upset some of the patients! One of our main goals is consistency because it's in the best interest of our patients if we try to keep things as familiar to them as we can from one day to the next. They don't handle change well, even minor changes. There was an old man I was taking care of who used to get scared of me every time I got a haircut. He's no longer with us, but I still remember the look of horror on his face when I'd walk into the room the day after I got my hair cut. Every time. It'd take him a good week before he'd warm up to me again. I had to befriend him all over again every three months or so."

"I could never do a job like that. I commend you for being able to do it."

"I love it. Like I said, it's hard sometimes, but it is worth it. I make a difference in those people's lives, whether they remember it or not. What I do means a lot to their families, and it is rewarding in its own right. Plus, I enjoy hearing their stories. They are living pieces of history, and I'm fascinated at the things they've lived through, the things they've seen during their time on this earth. I wouldn't trade my job for anything," she said sincerely. She took a sip of her cappuccino. "So what do you do?"

"I'm a forester. I manage timber stands for a paper company."

Stephanie's smile wavered slightly. "Does that mean you are the one who decides if an area is clear cut or not?"

"It depends on which species we are working with," Jenson answered, drawing from the knowledge of Neil's brain. "Some tree species are extremely shade-intolerant, so you need to cycle them with clear-cuts, or they won't grow. A lot of people have an aversion to clear-cutting, mostly because it isn't visually appealing, but there are ecological benefits to it just as there are to select-cutting. I manage a variety of stands, and I am always mindful of more than just growing and harvesting as many trees as we can as quickly as we can. There's a balance involved. I alternate clear-cut swatches of land with buffer zones and select-cut stands. I swear, I'm not just an asshole running around chopping down the entire forest," he said with his hands raised defensively. He was pleased with how much information he could access in Neil's brain.

Stephanie looked skeptical. "I just thought clear-cuts were a careless, thoughtless scar on the landscape. They always make me cringe when I drive past them."

"They don't look pretty at first, I'll give you that. But it isn't the death of the forest – it's regeneration. It isn't the destruction of habitat – it's creation of new habitat. Any deer hunter will tell you that whitetail love to frequent clear-cut areas.

So do a lot of other animals, like grouse and turkey. There are benefits and drawbacks to each of the different methods of harvesting. But our goal in every case is to regenerate the forest once the timber is harvested. It isn't like we are cutting down the trees to build a shopping mall."

Stephanie smiled again. "Alright then. I guess I can get on board with that. After all, I'm reasonable."

"I'm glad to hear it. A lot of people aren't so reasonable. They want the paper for their printers and the wood for their hardwood floors, yet they don't want to see a tree get cut down. The hypocrisy can be maddening."

Jenson was enjoying his conversation with Stephanie and he hoped he could persuade her to stay and visit with him a while longer. The server returned to the table to check on them. Stephanie asked for a glass of water, which Jenson took to mean that she wasn't planning to leave yet. He requested a second cup of coffee.

After the server brought their drinks, Stephanie asked, "So, can I assume that you are single?"

"Yes, I am. You?"

"Recently single, yes." She stared at him expectantly, a smile on her face. When he remained silent, she said, "I like you. I wouldn't be opposed to going on a date with you if you wanted to ask me out on one."

He chuckled. "Would you like to go on a date with me?"

"I might. Where are we going?"

He sifted through Neil's knowledge of the area. There was an Italian restaurant downtown that Neil seemed to like, so he suggested they go there. "When are you free?" he asked.

"I'm free tomorrow evening. I can meet you there at 6:30."

"Perfect! It's a date, then." Jenson sat awkwardly, not knowing what to say now. It felt like it was supposed to be the end of the conversation.

After a long silence, Stephanie asked, "Is there anything about you I should know before our date? Like, should I expect a crazy ex-girlfriend to barge in and start a fight with me? Anything like that?"

"No, nothing I can think of." *Except I won't be the same person you met today,* he thought. He wondered if he was making a mistake by asking Stephanie out on a date on Neil's behalf. Was Neil *actively* shadowing him right now? Did he even know what was going on? Would he remember any of this once Jenson left him? It wasn't like he could just *ask* Neil if he wanted to date Stephanie.

He decided he should go. If Neil didn't remember any of this, he would be at a great disadvantage on his date if Stephanie tried to bring up something from the conversation they had here today. He needed to cut it short.

"I'm sorry to split so soon, but I should go. I have a report to finish this weekend, and I want to make sure I get it done today so I don't have to rush it tomorrow. It was wonderful meeting you, Stephanie. I'm looking forward to seeing you tomorrow." He took down Stephanie's phone number and gave her his in case something came up before Sunday. He paid the server for both of their bills and hurried off with Ardie.

As he walked back to Neil's house, he felt like he had made a grave mistake. He was meddling in Neil's life, and it wasn't his place to do so. He was a visitor here, yet he was making himself too much at home. Again, he began to wonder how at home Jeffrey had made himself in Jenson's body. He wondered how much Jeffrey was meddling. He needed to get home and live his own life, even if it didn't have an Andrea/Maggie/Stephanie in it. Enough was enough.

When he got back to Neil's house, he let Ardie out into the fenced-in backyard while he went inside to write a letter to Neil. He tried his best to explain what had happened today, who he was, and how he had ended up in Neil's body. He apologized for making the date for him, but explained that Stephanie seemed to be a wonderful person and that he should give her a chance. When he was finished, he had filled up several sheets of paper. He hung them on the fridge with a magnetized clip, hoping Neil would see it as soon as he went into the kitchen. Jenson let Ardie back into the house, then went to lie down on the couch. As he closed his eyes, he convinced himself that he was going home this time.

Jenson felt a quick jolt and his eyes shot open. His jump had happened so abruptly that he hadn't been prepared for it. He felt like he had been in Neil's body only moments before, yet here he was...where? He looked over and saw Maggie sitting on the side of the bed with her back to him. Her shoulders were trembling, and he could hear her crying. He was back in the coma world yet again.

"...no, not again..." she sobbed.

He reached out to her and touched her shoulder. She jumped in surprise and whipped around. "Jeffrey?! Is it you?"

Her hopeful expression broke his heart. He shook his head slowly. "Still Jenson."

Her face crumpled and she broke into tears again. "But...but...you were gone. I thought you were gone. You weren't responding." She gasped for breath between sobs. "When are you going to send Jeffrey back?"

"I'm so sorry, Maggie. I didn't make it home. I was somewhere else. I will try again in a little while."

Maggie nodded and wiped the tears from her cheeks. Jenson looked at the clock on the wall. It was 8 AM. He hadn't been in the other world for very long, a few hours at most, yet the entire night had passed. He wondered if time had passed that much differently between the two places, or if his jump hadn't happened until very early in the morning. He also wondered why he wasn't called back to this body when Maggie had tried to rouse him. He remembered back to his Kristine dream, when he had been pulled out of his dream jump by his alarm waking his body. He supposed that it wouldn't work the same in this world, because he wasn't naturally tethered to this brain and body the way he should be to his own. Hell, he didn't seem to be tethered to his own body right now, either. What he wouldn't give to hear his own alarm going off right now...

"I'll make you some breakfast," Maggie said, drawing him back from his thoughts.

"Thank you. I'll come down and help."

"No, it's ok." She turned and started to walk out the door, then hesitated. "Jenson?"

"Hm?"

203

"I'm sorry if my actions are hurting your feelings. I don't mean to make you sad. I know we are both having a hard time with this."

Jenson smiled at her. "Don't worry about me. I just want to make this better. I want you to be happy."

"I know," she said. She gave him a warm smile which he hadn't seen in a while, then left the room.

After he showered and dressed, he sat at a barstool at the counter in the kitchen. He was surprised to see that Maggie had made him bacon pancakes. Maggie saw the surprise on his face.

"You didn't really get a chance to try them, so I thought I'd make them for you again as a thank you for being so understanding and selfless in this situation. I know you care about me, and I know a part of you was hoping that you were Jeffrey. I just want you to know that I appreciate what you are trying to do for me."

"It's the right thing to do. I will do my best to send Jeffrey back here to you."

Jenson ate his fill, knowing that he may very well never have Maggie's bacon pancakes again. When he was finished, he put his plate in the dishwasher.

"Good luck, Jenson," Maggie said to him as he headed back to bed.

Jenson lay in bed and closed his eyes. He thought about home. He found it strange that he wasn't really homesick. He just knew he needed to return. He needed to *will* himself back. He needed to get through whatever barrier was keeping him out and force his way back into his own life. *I am going home no matter what,* he thought as he started to fall asleep.

He woke up in a dark room. He sat up in bed, waiting for his eyes to adjust to the darkness. In the quiet stillness of the night, he heard a faint voice.

Dammit, he came back.

It hadn't come from inside the room. It seemed to have come from inside his head.

Chapter 14

Jenson looked around the dark room for the source of the voice, even though he was certain he was alone. He got out of bed and ran his hands along the wall, looking for a light switch. He wasn't in James's guest bedroom, and he had no idea where the lights were.

Almost there, cupcake.

Jenson halted. There was that faint voice again. "What the hell is that?" he wondered aloud.

Holy shit, he can hear me?

"Yes I can hear you! Where are you? Who are you?"

Well this is awkward. I know you very well, but you don't seem to know me in the slightest. I'm in here with you. My name is Jeffrey.

"What exactly do you mean by 'in here with you'?" Jenson asked the empty room, still standing in the dark with his hands on the wall.

I'm pretty sure you know what I mean. I'm in your body with you. You like to call it "shadowing." Now go find the light switch already. It's about five feet in front of you.

Jenson did as he was instructed and found the switch. He turned on the lights. "Where am I?" he asked as he looked around a room upon which he had never before laid eyes.

Home.

"My home or your home?"

I guess now it is "our" home.

"Is this the Jeffrey who was in a coma in the world I've been trapped in? Am I back in my own body now?"

Wait, you know who I am? You went to my world?

"Do I have to keep answering out loud, or can you read my thoughts?"

I don't think I can read your thoughts, but try it. We'll see.

Jenson thought, *Why would I be able to hear your thoughts but you couldn't hear mine?* He waited for an answer.

Are you trying it?

"You didn't hear that? You can't access my thoughts?"

I guess not. I never could before, but then again, you could never hear me before. I wonder why you can hear me all of a sudden.

"What do you mean I couldn't hear you before? How long have you been in here?"

I've been trapped in your body for a long time, Jenson. I was here long before you even knew what dream jumping was. I ended up here after I was stuck in a coma for a while. But before I answer any more of your questions, you need to answer mine. Did you go to my world?

"Yeah, I was stuck there for over a week, almost two weeks I think. I woke your body out of a three-year coma. When I told Maggie that I wasn't you, she didn't really believe me. She had even convinced me that I might actually be you, and all my memories of being Jenson were creations of my mind when I was in a coma."

Oh, my Maggie! How is she? Is she well? Is she happy?

"She was happy only when she thought I was you. Then I dream jumped to a weird place and learned that I wasn't you, and that you were here. After that, she wasn't happy anymore. She wants you to come home, Jeffrey. She needs you. She's been by your side through the entire coma, and it's taken its toll on her both mentally and physically. I left her with a promise that I would do everything I could to return you home to her."

I can't get back. Trust me, I've tried everything. I'm stuck here. I don't know how I got here, but I know that so far I haven't been able to get out. Even when I had control of your body, I tried dream jumping home, but I can't do it. I just keep waking up here, in this place.

Jenson sat down on the bed, feeling dizzy. This was all too much.

You ok there, buddy? I feel dizzy. It's a lot to take in, I know. But hey, you should be used to such craziness by now, shouldn't you?

"You don't hear my thoughts, but you feel what I feel?"

Yep. I can feel what the body feels, even some of the stronger emotions. When you got mad at your Maggie, I could feel the anger. When you felt really depressed, I was depressed too. When you were really happy, it was awesome. But you weren't really happy very often. Most of the time, I just felt my own despair at my situation. You never seemed to be able to detect me at all, my thoughts or my feelings. I have basically just been along for the ride this whole time. There were times when I was screaming at you to notice me, but you never did. Not until now. I wonder if it has something to do with the fact that I've had control of your body for the past three weeks. Maybe it has created some kind of bond in the brain that allows me to communicate with you.

"You've been controlling my body for *three weeks*?!" Jenson exclaimed. "What have you been doing?!"

First and foremost, I've been trying to keep you out until I could master dream jumping. I don't think I can do it from this shadowing state, but I thought that if I had enough time, I would be able to do it when I had control of your body. I felt you trying to come back a few times, but when I focused my energy on maintaining full awareness of my connection to this body and brain, it kept you away. It was selfish, I know. But you have no idea how much I miss my wife and how badly I want to go home. I thought this was the only way.

"So that weird jarring I was feeling in my jumps…that was you blocking me? I didn't even know such a thing was possible."

I didn't either. But when it worked the first time, I just kept doing it. The only reason you got in this time was because I was sleeping and I didn't detect your return. Every other time you tried to come back I was awake.

"What else have you been doing? What happened in the three weeks I was away?"

Let's see...I was here for your art show –

Jenson interrupted him. "My art show...did you see a woman that looked like your Maggie at the art show? In one of my jumps, I saw the woman I've been looking for at the art show, and I wanted to make it back in time to see if she showed up at the art show in my own world. Was she there?"

I didn't see her. Trust me, I would've noticed someone who looked like Maggie. She wasn't there. Otherwise, the show went very well. You made enough money for us to get this apartment. I didn't do any painting or anything because I'm not very artistic. By the way, James has been asking about his custom painting. I knew you'd be back eventually, so I told him I needed to get more supplies before I could work on it. I don't think anyone suspected that I wasn't you. I've been shadowing you long enough to know how to be you. Hell, I've been shadowing you long enough to BE you. You have rubbed off on me a lot more than I'd like to admit.

Also, I took the liberty of securing you some future income. Your Maggie had contacted you and said that you have a lot of hospital bills coming in at her apartment, so I figured you'd need to earn some more cash. Like I said, I knew you'd be back, so I took on several orders for paintings at the art show that you could do when you returned. I have a folder on the counter with all of the details enclosed for you. I wasn't expecting to be able to just tell you all about it, so I have been keeping a journal for you of my day-to-day activities so you wouldn't be lost when you came back. I really am a nice guy, though I'm sure you aren't very happy with me for blocking you from your own life.

"It was frustrating to not be able to come home, but I understand your reasons. Your Maggie is a wonderful woman, and I would be doing everything I could to return to her too. You know, your Maggie is one of the parallel versions of that Andrea woman I was talking about in my dream jumps."

She is? You didn't fall in love with my wife, did you?

"I'm not in love with your wife, exactly. I'm in love with whatever it is that makes her *her* in every world I see her in. I met a version of her in another world recently, and she was just as great there, too. I think I could be in love with whichever version of her I encountered."

Then why didn't you stay with Maggie? Not that I'm complaining, as the idea of you taking my wife is infuriating, but I don't understand why you wouldn't stay there if you were in love with her.

"She didn't love me. She loves you. When she found out for certain that I wasn't you, she was angry with me for having taken over your body. Just looking at me and knowing that it wasn't you was causing her pain. The thought had crossed my mind that perhaps I could persuade her to grow to love me, but I knew that wasn't the right thing to do. I would never be you, and it wouldn't be fair to either of you or to myself to try to force her to love me."

I think you and I must share some kind of deep connection, because not only do you and I love the same woman, in a sense, and not only have we switched bodies, but while you were gone, I had a dream that is very symbolic of the situation you just described to me even though I had absolutely no knowledge of it. I didn't understand the dream until right now.

"It wasn't a dream jump? Just a regular dream?"

Definitely not a dream jump. It was just a dream where I was watching things happen and wasn't actually present. It started out with a young girl of about twelve, and she broke into an internment camp of some sort to try to save a man imprisoned inside. The man was someone she knew and trusted. When she found him, she let him out of the prison cell he was being kept in, but he tricked her into going inside the cell and he locked her in. It had all been a ruse to lure her there so he could keep her locked up because he wanted to marry her when she was an adult, and he thought this was the only way. From there, the dream took on a montage-like quality, and I saw and understood that at first, the girl was hurt and confused. Then, in her teenage years, she hated the man who was keeping her prisoner and was full of anger toward him. Finally, as she grew into adulthood, she had begun to show symptoms of Stockholm syndrome and had come to love her captor. By that point, however, the man had realized that he couldn't love the woman she had grown into. For some reason, when she reached adulthood, her forearms had transformed into these strange, long, crab-like pincers that dripped with venom. Anyone who touched the venom would die instantly. All she wanted to do was hold the man she loved, but if she did, it would kill him. And now he no longer wanted her because she wasn't the woman he had hoped she would be.

I thought the dream was just a weird creation of my mind, but I see parallels in it to your – our – situation: the idea of being trapped and then keeping this woman with him in hopes that she would someday love him; of her being confused at first, then angry, then finally falling in love with him; of him wanting to love her, but realizing that he couldn't love her. Maybe the venom and pincers were representative of Maggie's residual love for me, keeping you from being able to love her and get close to her even if she did grow to love you.

Am I reading too much into this? Now that I put it all out there, I feel like it might sound ridiculous.

Jenson was thoughtful. It didn't sound ridiculous to him. He saw the parallels, and he understood the underlying meaning of the dream. If he had tried to stay with Maggie, to take Jeffrey's place, that was how it would feel.

"It isn't ridiculous, Jeffrey. It's actually quite spot-on. I don't know how you could possibly have created such an accurate, albeit strange, interpretation of my situation from a different world, but that seems to be what has happened. I wonder if you being in my head with me for so long has caused us to form this connection."

I wonder that too. I think it was random chance that sent me here in the beginning, like your first random dream jumps, but I've been with you so long that I find it more unlikely that we wouldn't form a connection eventually.

"You said you were trapped in a coma for a while before you came here. What was that like? I was in the coma for a few brief moments, and it was horrible. It was terrifying."

It was horrible. Nothing but darkness, stuck with only your thoughts, unable to feel your body except for a kind of...heaviness, I suppose. I used to think of it as being on an anchored raft that the current was trying to pull away, but you can feel the heavy tug of the anchor holding you in place. I could hear things sometimes, but it sounded like I was hearing it from under water. I didn't really sleep, but I did go through periods of haziness. It was during one of these hazy periods when I left. I was just suddenly here, following you around. At first I thought I was having a weird dream, but when I found out I was able to "sleep," and then I woke up in this same situation over and over again every morning with you, I came to understand that this was someone else's life. I thought maybe I was a ghost, but since I couldn't leave you, that didn't seem right either. Then I started to feel the things you were feeling. The first time it happened was when you were in the shower. I suddenly became aware of the feeling of the hot water on our skin, and it was glorious. I hadn't felt anything *in so long. It escalated pretty quickly from there, and before long I was connected to all of your physical senses. I didn't start feeling your emotions until much later, though. That happened within the past eight or nine months.*

"What was it like to finally be in control after all that time?"

I woke up in the morning and just lay there. Normally I wake up when you do, so I was waiting for you to get out of bed. Then I realized that I was the one controlling your eyes. I tried to move your body, and when it did everything I wanted it to do, I was elated. It took a few minutes to get accustomed to having to do everything myself, though. I had gotten so used to you controlling everything that it took a conscious effort to keep from retreating into my mind and staring off into space. I know I must have been slightly awkward that first day, but luckily I had gotten the hang of everything by the time I went to the art show. I have to admit, though, that now that I've become used to controlling your body, it is a little frustrating to be back in the backseat again. It feels weird. But at least this time I'm not alone. At least I can talk to you.

"I know it's a frustrating feeling. I've been in a few shadowing situations, and it was annoying to be screaming something at the person in control to no avail."

I remember you talking about it. It was the one when you went to a past universe. You were able to take over control for a minute, though, right? I wonder if I could ever do that.

Jenson was quiet. He wasn't sure he liked the idea of Jeffrey randomly taking over while Jenson was present.

I'm assuming from your silence that I made you uncomfortable. Be assured, I'm not going to try to take over your body. I was just wondering if it would be possible.

"So what are we going to do now?" Jenson pondered. "We can't stay like this forever. We need to find a way to send you home."

With you here, and me here, does that mean my body is back in a coma in my own world?

"Well, as far as anyone would know right now, it would probably seem to be sleeping. But if someone doesn't return to it soon…" Jenson felt no need to finish the sentence. They both knew it wouldn't be a good thing.

I don't know how to get back. I couldn't even dream jump when I had complete control. How am I supposed to return?

"I don't know. We need to figure it out, though. I wonder if I can go back and let Maggie know what's going on. If I try to do that, you aren't going to block me when I try to come back, are you?"

I promise I will not block you. Can you control your jumps well enough to be able to get back to my world?

"I'm pretty sure I can. I feel a connection to that world now. I'm going back." Jenson knew it was something he had to do. He still didn't know if he could trust Jeffrey completely, but he had no choice.

Tell Maggie that I love her and I miss her. Tell her these wild horses are a lot stronger than I had anticipated, but I will find my way back to her.

"Doesn't that seem a little bit corny?" Jenson teased.

The fact that you would ask that tells me that you still don't know Maggie very well. Maggie loves all things corny and cliché.

"Well, then she's bound to love that one," Jenson chuckled.

Jenson got up and shut the light off again. He lay in bed and closed his eyes, focusing his thoughts on Maggie.

Good luck, Jenson.

Soon, Jenson felt the shift. He opened his eyes, and he was back in Jeffrey's world. He was pleased with himself at how well he was beginning to control his jumps. He went out into the living room, yelling for Maggie.

"What? What is it?" Maggie sounded alarmed as she came running to him.

"I found him! Jeffrey is stuck in my body in my world. I came back to tell you."

Maggie's eyes welled up with tears. "When is he coming home?" she wanted to know, hopefulness returning to her.

Jenson scratched his head. "Well, we haven't figured that out yet. He can't jump. He's been trying, but he hasn't been able to do it. It turns out that he's been stuck in my world for a long time, just shadowing me, watching my world through my eyes. He was the reason I couldn't go back. He was blocking me because he thought that if he was in control of my body, he might be able to dream jump back here. Obviously, it didn't work. But when I made it home, I discovered that I was able to talk to him. I could hear him in my head. He sent a message for you." Jenson told her what Jeffrey had wanted him to tell her, and she smiled. "I told him it was corny, but he said you'd like it."

"They played that song at our wedding. It was something he always said to me, that wild horses couldn't drag him away from me. It really is him." She wiped the tears away from her eyes.

"Now, this next part is going to be hard, Maggie. I need to get back home so he and I can work out how we're going to accomplish getting him here where he belongs. In the meantime, this body is going to be empty again. You are going to have to call an ambulance and get this body back to the hospital after I leave."

"Can't we just go now? We can tell them you've been feeling strange lately, and you can jump once we're there."

"I can't just make a jump willy nilly. I need to be able to fall asleep, or something close to sleeping. I don't think they're going to let me fall asleep while they're examining me."

Maggie looked worried. "But what if something happens to his body before the ambulance can get here? What if his body dies without anyone in it?"

"I was gone a few times, and nothing happened to it then. I have no reason to believe that anything will happen to it now. But if it's going to be uninhabited for any length of time, it's going to need special care. It's basically going to be back in a coma. You're going to need to be strong through this, Maggie. I know it's asking a lot of a woman who has already been through so much, but at least now we have a goal in sight. I will try to return periodically to let you know how things are going and to make sure this body is still functioning properly. It might confuse the doctors, but it's the only way I can keep in touch with you. We are going to figure this out, Maggie. I promise." Jenson was determined, but he didn't honestly know if it was a promise he could keep.

"Ok. I can do this. If this is what it takes to get Jeffrey back, I'll do anything."

He smiled at her. "In case this is the last time I see you, I just want you to know that you are a truly wonderful person, and it was a pleasure knowing you. I wish you all the happiness in the world."

She leaned in and kissed him on the cheek. "Tell Jeffrey I can't wait to see him. Thank you, Jenson."

Jenson lay down on the couch and returned to his own world.

When he knew he was home, he didn't even bother opening his eyes. "I gave her your message," he said out loud. "She said she can't wait to see you."

We are going to figure this out, right?

214

"We're going to do our damndest."

He was tired, so he let himself sleep. Jeffrey was quiet.

The next morning, he was greeted with a cheerful voice inside his head.

Good morning, Jenson!

"Good morning, Jeffrey." Jenson got out of bed and walked around his new apartment, finding the bathroom first, and then went on to the kitchen. Jeffrey told him where the coffee was and chastised him for having a cookie for breakfast.

I made breakfast bars yesterday. They are just as tasty as a cookie but so much healthier. You should've had one of those.

"You bake?"

Hey, there's nothing wrong with a guy who can bake. I'll teach you if you want.

"No, that's quite alright. They have bakeries for guys like me."

Suit yourself. So what's on the agenda for today?

"I'm going to call Don. Don is definitely going to want to hear about all of this, and he might have some insights for us."

I like Don. He's kind of a kooky old fellow, but he's a good guy. I love listening to your conversations with him.

"It'll be nice if I can meet with him today. But remember, I can't talk to you in public or people will think I'm crazy. You can still talk to me, but don't be offended if I don't respond to you directly."

I won't be offended. But I can't promise you that I won't try to make you laugh in public, purely for my own entertainment. Or make random jabberings while you are trying to speak.

"Are you sure you *aren't* me?" Jenson mused. "Because that sounds like something I would do."

I told you, you've rubbed off on me. I didn't say they were all admirable qualities that I've picked up.

"Ok, you need to be quiet now. I'm going to call Don." Jenson sat down at the kitchen table with a hot cup of coffee and called Don.

Don answered the phone on the first ring. "Jennie, my boy! Where on earth have you been? Or should I say, where in the universes have you been?"

"Not in this one. It has been an exceedingly strange stretch of time since I spoke with you last. And now that I think about it, this version of you isn't even the last one I spoke with."

"You talked to a parallel version of me?"

"Yeah, but it was pretty much the same as talking to you. He was excited to be able to talk to a Jenson from another world."

"Well that sounds fantastic! Tell me all about your travels."

"This could take some time. I was wondering if I could meet with you. I live closer to U of M now, and I could make the trip easily."

"You seem more serious than usual. Why so serioussss?" Don asked, mimicking a popular comic book villain.

"I have a bit of a problem. You see, there is someone…stuck in me."

"Oh dear. Jennie, you do realize I'm not that kind of doctor, don't you?"

"Not like that! I mean that there is a consciousness within my head that belongs to someone else!"

Don was silent.

"Don?"

"Does it talk to you?" Don asked hesitantly.

"He didn't before, but he does now."

"And you are completely certain that it is a *real* voice?"

"Yes! I'm not crazy!"

Oh man, I could've messed with you so badly if I had thought of that earlier. Jenson, this is God. I want you to do my bidding.

Jenson smirked and shook his head but didn't respond audibly.

"Ok, just wanted to make sure. For a while there it was iffy, especially when you were freaking out about being lost in your dream jumps."

216

"So can we meet today? Wait, what day is it?"

"Are you sure you're ok?"

"I just got back last night. I was gone for three weeks. Excuse me for being a little out of sorts."

"It's Sunday. We'll meet at the Rookie Pub for lunch."

"A pub that's open for lunch on a Sunday?"

"Yep. My kind of church."

"I'll see you around noon, then. Thanks, Don."

"I assume this will be wildly entertaining. Bring some good stories."

Jenson ended the call and sipped his coffee. He browsed through the folder of orders that Jeffrey had taken for him at his art show while Jeffrey told him about each one. He then went through the diary that Jeffrey had been keeping, and Jeffrey commented on it. Jenson was beginning to see that Jeffrey talked *a lot*. Then again, he couldn't really blame him. If he'd been trapped in silence for years, he'd probably have a lot to say, too. He hoped that Jeffrey wouldn't be offended if Jenson had to ask him to quiet down once in a while. He'd cross that bridge when he came to it.

Jenson and Jeffrey conversed throughout the drive to the Rookie Pub. It was beginning to feel like they were old friends. After all, Jeffrey had known Jenson for quite some time and knew some of the most intimate details of his life. Jenson didn't know Jeffrey nearly as well, but he was an affable fellow and Jenson had quickly grown to like him a great deal.

"I know you've been in my head for a while, but do you know exactly how long?" Jenson asked.

I'm not entirely sure. It's been at least a year and a half, but probably more like two years.

"Damn. That's a long time to be locked away in somebody's head. How have you not gone insane?"

I don't know. There were times when I thought I might, but I managed to pull through it. It's not exactly solitary confinement, but pretty close. If I had been forced to stay in my own body in a coma, I probably would have been a little insane by now. At least here I was able to see and experience things, even if I wasn't actively part of it. I think things will be much

217

better now that I can express myself, though. The hardest part about shadowing was not having anyone to talk to. Plus, now I have some hope that I might be able to return home. A little hope can do wonders for one's spirit.

"Yes, it can. I am glad you are hopeful. I have to think that if you were able to make the jump to this world, there must be a way to send you back."

I agree. I am hopeful, but at the same time, I do wonder what is going to happen with us if I can't return. If I end up stuck here in your head forever, how will we cope with that? I can't imagine that having a voice in your head is something that someone can live happily with for an extended period of time.

"I know. The thought has crossed my mind. It would be difficult, but we would have to find a way to make it work. What other choice would we have?"

If I don't return, eventually Maggie is going to have to pull the plug on me.

"No, she wouldn't. I can go back there to check up on things, to let her know that you are still with me. She wouldn't pull the plug if she knew you were still out there somewhere, trying to get home."

I know she wouldn't want to. That's not what I was getting at. What I'm trying to say is that I think if we can't find a way to return me home, maybe she should *pull the plug. You can't live like this forever, and neither can I. It would be the only logical solution.*

"Whoa, whoa, slow down there, captain. Nobody's pulling the plug on your body. We will figure this out. We will send you home. I don't want you to start thinking like that already before we've even tried anything." Jenson wanted to keep Jeffrey in a positive state of mind.

I wouldn't ask that unless we've exhausted all options, of course. But we need to think about this realistically. We need to be ready for whatever the situation might bring us. I just want to make sure that you know this is what I will want if we fail.

"If we fail once, we try again. If we fail twice, we try again. We just keep trying until we get it right. Failure isn't an option here. If we don't succeed right away, it doesn't mean that we won't figure it out a little later. Besides, who's to say that you wouldn't be stuck here anyway, even if your body did die? You share a connection with me now, so don't you think it's possible that you might not move on?"

I remember the conversation you had with Don about dying while in a dream jump. I'm of the same mind as Don on this one. I think if my body dies, so do I, regardless of where my consciousness resides. We get one body, one life. Though it may be an immeasurable distance away, I still feel that my body is my life source. If it is extinguished, then I will be forced to move on.

"Move on to what, though? What do you think there is after this? Aren't you the least bit afraid of what happens when you die?"

Not anymore. I used to be, but after my experiences with being in a coma and shadowing, I find that there isn't much I'm afraid of now. The only thing I fear is what it will do to Maggie if she is forced to sit idly by and wait for me for the rest of her life. She has an entire life ahead of her that she needs to be able to enjoy. She's had a rough go of it lately, and she needs to find peace again. She will never be at peace if my empty body is there keeping her emotionally tied to a husk.

"I don't want to talk about this anymore. Talking about it makes me feel like we've already given up. I am not giving up, no matter what."

I haven't given up. Not by a long shot.

"Good, because if we are going to do this, I need you to be confident and to think positively. We need to be the Little Engine that Could."

I think I can, I think I can, I think I can.

"Exactly. I'm glad you have that book in your world, too, otherwise I would've sounded pretty stupid just now."

It's funny to me sometimes how alike our worlds are. It's easy to forget that this isn't my own world, but then I see or hear one little thing that is so completely different from mine that it occasionally surprises me. Of course, I can't even imagine what has changed in my own world in the three years my body has been in a coma. Perhaps it is even more like this world now.

"It is a lot like this world. I couldn't tell you what has changed, though, because I have no idea what your world was like three years ago."

So you couldn't access any of my brain's memories when you were in my body?

"Not one. I don't know if it is because of the coma, if the brain is truly in an amnesiac state, or if it is just because your consciousness is not present."

Does that mean I might forget everything once I'm reconnected to my own body?

"I don't think so. You remember everything now, so why would you forget it?"

Well, maybe I remember it now because I remembered it when I made the jump. But what if, due to the coma, my physical brain hasn't retained all these memories? Reconnecting to it might erase the memories from my consciousness. It could be as though my brain has been reformatted. It might be like trying to put a motherboard from one kind of computer into a computer that is of a completely different format. The information is still on the motherboard, but when it is in the new computer, it is basically useless. In order to make the motherboard compatible, you'd need to reformat it, which would erase all the information on it.

"Well shit, I never thought of it like that. But why wouldn't it erase my memories, if that were the case? I'm not formatted to fit your brain."

But it also isn't your body. You may not have connected with it the way I do. You were controlling that body, but you weren't actually part of it. You have a healthy brain here that you are connected to. You remembered everything about you while you were away, and then you returned and reconnected easily. I remember everything right now, while I'm away, but once I try to reconnect to my own brain, that might be a different story.

I could be way off, I know. I'm just trying to think of all the obstacles I might have ahead of me.

"I think you're just worrying yourself too much. You're getting ahead of yourself. Let's focus on the task at hand, and worry about the details later. First and foremost, we need to get you home." Jenson pulled into the Rookie Pub parking lot. "Now let's go get wasted at noon on a Sunday."

Chapter 15

Jenson spotted Don as soon as he walked into the pub. He was seated at the same booth as when he'd first met Don. He went to the booth and sat down.

"Ah, Jennie, you look well. Are you feeling better after your accident?" Don asked jovially.

"I am, thank you."

The server approached the table with a pitcher of beer and a glass for Jenson.

"I took the liberty of ordering us a pitcher," Don explained when Jenson gave him a questioning look. "You sounded like you needed a drink. Thanks, Smiley." He bowed his head to the server, who sneered and rolled her eyes. As she walked away, Don said, "She really likes me, I can tell."

"It goes without saying," Jenson replied sarcastically.

"Tell me about your travels. And about your new friend. I am very interested in your mental squatter."

I'm so far out of my mind that I'm in yours, Jenson heard Jeffrey joke.

Jenson smirked at Jeffrey's joke. He told Don, "He hears everything I hear, sees what I see, he feels everything this body feels, and he can even feel some of my emotions. But before I get into all that, let me start from the beginning." He told Don about his two jumps to the worlds similar to his own, and described how he was able to tell that each world was not his own. He talked about the conversation he had with parallel Don, and how Don had helped him to realize that he was exerting control over his jumps. He then told Don about waking up from a coma in his third jump. He explained how he had become confused about who he was, and told him about Maggie's conjecture regarding how he may have come to think he was Jenson in the first place.

Don was intrigued by the idea of stealing someone's identity. "It had never occurred to me that someone could actually be made to believe they were someone else. The idea of actually accessing someone's memories and assuming they were all your own is fascinating. If that were to happen, how would you know that it wasn't really you? You wouldn't," Don answered his own question. "You would essentially *become* that person. We are a collection of our genetics and our experiences. The body provides the genetics, and if you stole someone's memories of their entire life, you would be completely convinced that this was the person you had always been. You wouldn't even have an inkling that you had ever been anyone else."

"That was the problem. I had no way of knowing if I had been Jeffrey before I was Jenson." He discussed how he had planned to use dream jumping to figure out who he was and to possibly find Jeffrey to confirm that Jenson wasn't Jeffrey. He then brought up Maggie's request to dream jump together. "Is that something that would even be possible?" Jenson asked.

"I suppose it would be possible for two people who had excellent control over their jumps to be able to jump to the same universe. I don't see why not. But I don't know how likely it would be for someone who has no experience with jumping to be able to just latch on to someone else's dream jump and 'follow' them to another universe. I won't say it's impossible, but I'd think there would need to be an incredibly strong connection between the two people. It didn't work for you and Maggie, I am assuming."

"No, it didn't. But I did make an interesting jump that night." He told Don about visiting the place where he learned about Jeffrey inhabiting his body. Don's eyes lit up.

"Amazing! You may have tapped into the Akashic record! What else did you learn while you were there?" Don asked excitedly.

"Nothing, really. I didn't go there specifically seeking any knowledge other than who I was, and that seemed to be all that I was interested in learning. I had no desire to learn anything else or to see what kind of information I had access to. I had no real sense of curiosity. I was looking for a truth, I found it, and I left, basically. But when I returned to Jeffrey's body, the sensory overload was excruciating. It was kind of like when you have the television on at a high volume all day and you get used to it, and then you shut it off and sit in silence for a while. When you turn that TV back on to the same volume it had been, it suddenly seems like it's blaring loud after experiencing silence. Now imagine that, except with all of your senses at once, and multiply it by one thousand. That was how it felt to go from nothingness back to the real world. It didn't last long, but it was horrible."

"You didn't think about anything else while you were there?" Don asked.

"I tried to think about what I should do when I returned to Jeffrey's body, but I couldn't focus on it. I knew all of the options I had, everything that I *could* do, but I had no way of finding a *right* choice because it wasn't a matter of truth or fact. It was a matter of how I felt about each choice that would drive my future actions, and as I mentioned, there were no feelings in that place. It was kind of like asking your GPS which restaurant you should go to. It can tell you all the options, which is closest to you, which one serves which foods, but it can't tell you which one will be most satisfying to you. You need to use your own feelings and desires to decide that. The place I visited, if we want to call it the Akashic record, is only a place of facts and truths. I could go there and find out how to do something, but I would never be able to contemplate whether I *should* do it while in that place. There is no right or wrong. There are no morals or ethics. There is no purpose. It isn't a place to go to look for meaning or wisdom. There is only information. And from what I could tell, you could only access the information you specifically sought out. It wasn't a flood of knowledge like I imagined the Akashic record would be."

"This is beyond exciting," Don said. He was smiling like a kid at Christmas. "You just thought about your query, and the answer was there? Just like that?" Don snapped his fingers for emphasis.

"Just like that. I just suddenly knew the answer. But it wasn't completely direct. It wasn't like I just suddenly knew I was Jenson without any further explanation. The information I received was that Jeffrey was in my body in my world, and that was when I knew that I was Jenson."

"That's probably because you wanted to know where Jeffrey was. I wonder if you would've discovered that information if you hadn't been concerned with finding Jeffrey in the first place. If all you wanted to know was whether or not you were Jenson, maybe you would've just been given knowledge that you were Jenson without learning of Jeffrey's fate."

"I think you're probably right about that. I think you have to go into the Akashic record with a good understanding of the information you need. Not that you need to understand the information beforehand, but that you need to know exactly what you are looking for, if that makes any sense," Jenson said.

"You'd have to go into the Akashic record knowing what you'd want to get from it. You couldn't just go in blindly and hope that some kind of wonderful knowledge would fall into your lap. It isn't how I imagined it either, but now that I see it this way it makes sense to me. Could you imagine how overwhelming it would be to just have all the knowledge of the universes suddenly explode into your consciousness? It would be too much, like watching every single TV channel all at once and expecting to make sense of it. There's no way you could process it all. No, you'd have to take bits of it at a time. There are limitations to our abilities of comprehension." Don reasoned. "Now all I need to know is how the hell did you find the Akashic record?"

"I don't know. I went to sleep focusing on trying to get home to get answers, and I was sent there. Actually, to be more accurate, my consciousness tried to return home, but I was blocked by Jeffrey, and then I was sent to the Akashic record."

"Blocked? Explain this," Don requested, his brow furrowed.

"Jeffrey was able to sense my consciousness returning, and he blocked me from my body. He described it as focusing all of his energy on maintaining his connection to my body and my brain, and it kept me out. I don't know how it worked, but he was able to block me several times. I was only able to sneak back in when he was asleep and his vigilance was compromised."

"My oh my, you have had one hell of a go of things, haven't you!? You've experienced coma, visited the Akashic record, tried a paired dream jump, questioned your identity, been blocked from your own body, and now have someone else's consciousness trapped in your body with you! What are you going to do next, Jennie?"

"I'm going to Disney World," Jenson quipped.

"Let's not get carried away. You didn't win the Super Bowl."

"Who knows, in some universe I might have."

Can I ask something? Jeffrey interjected.

Jenson nodded without speaking, and held up his hand to silence Don when Don started to reply. Don looked at him quizzically.

Something has been bothering me. I was under the impression that nothing in the universe could move faster than the speed of light. How is it that our consciousness is able to jump from one universe to another so instantaneously? Doesn't that break the laws of physics?

"Sorry, Don. Jeffrey was asking me something. I wasn't trying to be rude."

"The answer is yes, Jeffrey. I am aware of how completely delightful I am. Thank you for noticing."

"You and I both know that no one in any universe would ever call you delightful."

"But I am delightful. I'm like that little ray of sunshine that bursts through the clouds on a rainy day and makes a rainbow."

Jenson laughed. "And you are like the joy in a child's laughter, right?"

"Obviously," Don said.

"Ok, now that we've established the extent of your delusions, Jeffrey had a question. A real question. He wanted to know how it's possible to instantaneously dream jump from one universe to another when the laws of physics state that nothing can move faster than the speed of light."

"Remember when we talked about quantum entanglement? The effects of entanglement move faster than the speed of light. When one particle is affected, the other particle responds instantly regardless of their distance apart. If your consciousness is connected, or entangled, with another, I think it's completely possible that it can jump from one body to the other without defying the laws of physics.

"In addition, there is the idea of the Einstein-Rosen bridge, or wormholes, which act as shortcuts through space-time. These wormholes would allow for the travel through space faster than it would take light to travel that distance without the shortcut. You wouldn't be breaking the light-speed barrier, you'd just be shortening the distance you had to go. Let's consider a spinning black hole, which describes every black hole that has been detected in space up to this point in time. Spinning black holes do not collapse into a single point, but rather a rotating ring. Centrifugal forces keep it from collapsing. Everything that approaches that ring is stretched out and 'spaghetti-fied,' but this holds no consequence for something without material, such as a consciousness. Gravitational forces would be great, but not infinite. Like a laser or x-ray, even if those wavelengths get stretched out and distorted by the extreme gravity, the information is still present. Now, think of that spinning ring as a rim to a mirror, and if you pass through that ring, you could enter into a parallel universe. If spinning black holes really could be gateways, or wormholes, then they would be fairly common in the universe. There are also theories of negative energy that would allow for such travel and the stabilization of black hole gateways.

"We like to think of the speed of light as the speed limit of the universe, but there are findings now that indicate that particles called neutrinos may travel faster than light. As is the case with much of quantum physics, there are ways around some of the traditional laws of relativity." Don finished his beer and poured himself another, then topped off Jenson's mug with what was left in the pitcher. "Now that we have that out of the way, tell me about Jeffrey."

Jenson took a drink from his mug, giving himself a moment to gather his thoughts. "When I was finally able to return to my own body, I could hear a faint voice in my head. It was Jeffrey. He was surprised that I could hear him all of a sudden. He told me that he's been shadowing me for possibly as long as two years. He was present during his coma for a while, just alone with his thoughts and unable to use his body. Then he was suddenly here, with me. At first he could only hear and see the things I did. He was later able to feel things I felt. But he couldn't access my thoughts or memories, and he couldn't communicate with me. I had no idea he was with me. I wonder now, though, if I would have been able to sense him if I had known to look for him. I'd made a dream jump the night after visiting the Akashic record, and in that jump, I was actually able to sense the consciousness of the body I had taken over. When I quieted my mind and focused inwardly, I could feel it. It was the sensation of someone watching me. If I had been able to do that earlier, I might've learned to open up communication with Jeffrey long before now."

"Were you able to communicate with the consciousness of the body you'd taken over?" Don asked.

"No, I wasn't. But I didn't try. I only wondered if I could sense it, and when I did, I didn't like the way it felt. It was an uncomfortable feeling, so I tried to ignore it. I didn't know at the time that communication with a shadowing consciousness was possible. All I knew was that I had full access to his memories and knowledge."

"Do you have full access to Jeffrey's memories and knowledge?"

Jenson paused. "No, I don't. But then again, that's probably because this isn't Jeffrey's brain."

"Then I wonder why he doesn't have access to your memories? Did he have access when he was controlling your body?"

No, I didn't.

"He didn't. He and I had a discussion today about why I couldn't access any of his memories when I was in his body. We were wondering if it was just because he wasn't present, or if it's because his brain doesn't actually hold any of those memories anymore. He is concerned that when he returns, his memories will be lost when he reconnects with his brain." He shared Jeffrey's computer analogy with Don.

"That's an interesting way of looking at it. Maybe he should email his memories to an internet account to be downloaded later," Don said. He sounded like he was joking, but his face was completely serious. When Jenson just stared at him, Don continued, "Obviously I don't mean that literally. What I'm saying is that perhaps his memories aren't attached to any physical part of his being in such a way that they could be erased without having access to them. I had mentioned a while back, when we first met here, that consciousnesses might be linked, like a network. Maybe Jeffrey's memories are such that regardless of the 'format' of his brain, his consciousness will still be able to access them because they are within this network."

"If they're in the network, then why wouldn't I be able to access them when I was in his body?"

"He must have them password-protected," Don said. He then added, "Again, I don't mean literally." He raised his hand to get the waitress's attention and pointed at the pitcher, indicating that they needed another.

"You do realize it is the middle of the day, don't you?" Jenson said, referring to the amount of alcohol that Don was consuming.

"I realize that it is the middle of the day on a *weekend*. There's a difference. Tell me, Jennie, how are you able to communicate with Jeffrey? Is it all in your head? Does he read your thoughts?"

"No, I have to actually speak to him out loud. He talks to me in my head, but I can't do the same."

"Are you reading his thoughts, or does he have to make an effort to project what he wants to say to you?"

I have to say things directly to you. It's the same as when you know you want to say something versus just thinking something. I still have my own private thoughts.

Jenson relayed Jeffrey's statement. "I'm a little confused about why information is so easily transferred in some cases, but not in others. I've been able to access memories from shadowing states and in first-person jumps, but for some reason Jeffrey and I are unable to access knowledge from each other."

"It is puzzling. It's also puzzling that you can communicate so freely. I have never encountered anything like this before, and it isn't even something that I thought to be within the realm of possibilites. It's just a strange situation all the way around, and I hate to say it, but I'm at a bit of a loss," Don admitted.

"It is strange, indeed. But the strangest part of this whole thing is that Jeffrey can't return to his own body. He's stuck in this world. The reason he had blocked me once he had control of this body was because he thought that he could finally perform a jump if he was out of the shadowing state. He couldn't do it, though. He's tried many times to escape, but he doesn't seem to be able to make the jump. I was hoping that you might have some suggestions for us to get him back to his own world."

"Get outta my dreams," Don started singing. "Get into my car..."

"That isn't helping," Jenson said as Don continued to sing a few more verses.

I'm beginning to question our choice to come to him for answers, Jeffrey said jokingly.

The waitress brought them another pitcher of beer. "This isn't a karaoke bar, Don," she said. "I shouldn't have to keep reminding you of that."

"It is my civic duty to share this angelic voice with the world. I'm pretty much the best singer I know."

"Who sings that song?" she asked. When he started to answer, she interrupted him with, "Then let him sing it."

Don chuckled as she walked off. "She's just jealous." He poured himself another beer, then looked at Jenson. "So, we need to figure out how to evict the squatter. Have you come up with any ideas yet?"

"Not really. We thought you might have some."

"Does Jeffrey sleep while in the shadowing state?"

"He mentioned that he does. He usually sleeps when I do."

"Does he dream when he sleeps?"

No. I was only able to dream when I was in control of your body.

Jenson told Don what Jeffrey had said. "Is that significant?"

"Well, I think it might mean that it will be easier for him to attempt a jump while in control. Maybe you should try jumping and leave him in control to attempt his own jump. You'd want to go somewhere other than his world, though, because it might be harder for him to return to his body if you are in it." Don was thoughtful for a moment. "But then again, maybe not. If his consciousness has become strongly connected with yours, as I suspect it must have by now, then it might be easier for him to find his way home if he can draw himself to your consciousness. You would provide a beacon for him. Do you think you'd be able to return to his world again? Has your control over your jumps become that skilled?"

"I can return if I wish. I've formed a connection to that world, and I have already been able to return to it once from this world. I had to go back to tell Maggie that I found Jeffrey."

"Excellent! Then I would say to try it both ways. Hell, you could even try that paired jumping thing you were talking about earlier. If you two have a strong enough connection, you just might be able to get it to work even if Jeffrey isn't a skilled jumper. You could try to drag him along with you."

"So you don't think that he'll be able to jump from his shadowing state?"

"I don't know, really. This is an unprecedented case. I'm just thinking that he'll have a better chance if he's in a situation where he can sleep and dream. Given the fact that he hasn't been able to jump in the two years he's been shadowing, I'd say it's time to try something else, that's all."

"That's true."

"Bear in mind, though, that it could take a long time to get it right. He's an inexperienced jumper, so who knows how long it will take before he can even make a jump. Even then, it might not be to the right place. And there's always the possibility that he just can't make it happen. Have you considered what you will do if he never returns home?"

"We've talked a little about it, but I'd rather not start worrying about that just yet. I'm confident that if he was able to make a jump to this world, he should be able to do it again."

"For your sake, Jennie, I hope you're right. I can't imagine what it would be like to live with someone else inside my head. Having a roommate is hard enough, but to have a bunkmate in your brain may prove to be maddening."

"Well, he and I are basically just two sides to the same coin, so I think we'll manage just fine."

"It's the people who are most like us that tend to drive us the craziest," Don pointed out.

"In your case, I could see that being true."

"I thought we established that I was delightful."

"No, we established that you are delusional," Jenson corrected.

"Can't both be true?"

"They can, but they aren't in your case."

"Oh come now. I can't be that bad. You seem to like me just fine."

"I know. It's just another great mystery of the universes that has yet to be explained."

"Speaking of mysteries of the universes, are you planning to visit the Akashic record again? If you did, you might be able to find the answer to how to return Jeffrey to his own world."

"I would like to, but I don't know if I can control a jump to it yet. It is something that I will try to find again, even if it was a horrible experience coming back from it."

"I have faith in you, Jennie. If you found it once, you'll find it again."

Jenson visited with Don for a while longer, then headed back home. He was eager to try the methods they'd discussed to return Jeffrey home, as was Jeffrey.

Jeffrey was surprisingly quiet on the ride home. Jenson asked him if something was wrong.

No, I'm just thinking about home. Thinking about Maggie. Hoping that I can return to her someday.

"You will. We can do this. I am sure we can do this."

Jeffrey was silent again, so Jenson let him be.

When they arrived at home, Jenson made himself a sandwich and discussed with Jeffrey what they should try first.

"How do you want to do this? What do you think will be our best shot?" Jenson asked.

Maybe we should try the paired dream jump first. That way, if it doesn't work, you'll already be in my world and I can then try to follow you from my own dream jump. I'll try to focus on your energy and try to connect with you. We've got to make the most of each attempt, because it's not like we can try this over and over again. You can't just sleep all day every day.

"That sounds like a good plan. But first, we should try an exercise. I'll focus all of my attention on trying to sense your consciousness, like I did in my other dream jump. You do the same. If we are able to sense each other's consciousness, it might help to strengthen our bond. It might help you to hone in on my location after my jump if you learn to sense my energy."

That looks good on paper, but I don't know how feasible it is. I don't know how to 'sense' a consciousness.

"Sure you do. You were able to sense me returning, weren't you? That was how you blocked me, wasn't it?"

It wasn't so much that I was sensing your consciousness exactly. It was more like a feeling that someone was rushing up behind me, and I instinctively knew what it was. But I couldn't say for certain that I would've been able to tell it was your consciousness specifically. It could've been anyone, really.

"Still, the fact that you were able to sense it at all is a big step in the right direction. Focus on how that felt. Focus on the 'otherness' within this body."

I'll try, but I'm still not sure how I'm supposed to do that. Everything in this body is 'otherness.'

Jenson finished his sandwich and retired to the couch. He lay down and closed his eyes. He tried to find a calm, meditative state by clearing his mind and focusing all of his attention on trying to feel the foreign energy in his body. He was surprised at how quickly he zeroed in on Jeffrey's consciousness. It was a different feeling than when he had sensed Neil's consciousness. Neil's consciousness had felt looming, ominous, and watchful, like an unknown entity lurking just behind the fence in his brain. Jeffrey's consciousness felt different. It didn't seem hidden or ominous. It felt more like a friend waiting in another room. He focused on that feeling, trying to create a signature of it in his mind, and trying to reach out for it. He could feel it, but it didn't feel like he was making any kind of connection with it. They were still two completely separate entities, which made him think that a paired jump might not work. It could only work if they were able to connect. He waited, focusing on Jeffrey, hoping to feel a sense of Jeffrey's consciousness reaching out toward him.

I don't feel anything, Jeffrey said after a while, breaking Jenson's concentration. *It just feels like I'm trying to fall asleep.*

"I could sense you. I was trying to connect with your consciousness, but it wasn't working. It felt like you were in a different room, and I couldn't quite get to you. I think we're only going to be able to connect if you can sense my consciousness."

To me, this is as impossible as if you asked me to use the Force. I don't think I'm capable of doing the things that you can do.

Jenson could tell that Jeffrey was already discouraged. "It's ok. I don't expect you to get it right away. In time, and with practice, I think you'll figure it out, though. We'll have to keep trying."

I want to try a jump. Let's just see what happens. If you were able to sense me, maybe you'll still be able to bring me with you when you jump.

Jenson was doubtful, but he tried to hide his uncertainties. "Ok, we'll try it. I'll try to take you with me to your own world. If it doesn't work, I'll stay there a while to give you an opportunity to find me." Jenson closed his eyes and tried to focus on Jeffrey's consciousness. When he felt it, he tried to hold onto his awareness of it while simultaneously seeking out Jeffrey's world. It was too difficult. To make the jump, he needed to focus too much of his attention on Jeffrey's world to maintain awareness of Jeffrey's consciousness. He made the jump without him.

He woke up feeling hazy. He didn't feel well. He was weak and incredibly tired. He turned his head, which took great effort, and saw Maggie asleep in the chair near the bed.

"Maggie," he whispered, but his voice was hoarse and barely audible. He tried again, but he couldn't make his voice any louder. He already felt out of breath. Something was wrong.

Chapter 16

Jenson mustered all the energy he had in his body and called out to Maggie one more time. She lifted her head and looked over at him with heavy eyelids. When she saw his eyes were open, however, she was instantly alert.

"Jeffrey?!" She rushed to his side and grasped his hand.

He slowly moved his head from side to side, too weak to say, "No."

"Jenson." Maggie's disappointment was palpable. "Jeffrey's body is failing. After you left, Jeffrey's body had a seizure. His blood pressure is dropping little by little every day, and the doctors fear the worst. At this rate, if things stay the way they are, Jeffrey's body isn't going to make it through the week. Please tell me that you have good news for me."

Jenson wanted to tell Maggie that it would all be ok. He wanted to hold her and stroke her hair. He wanted to reach up and wipe the tears from her cheeks. But he couldn't do any of those things because Jeffrey's failing body couldn't perform those functions. He felt tears in his eyes. Jeffrey was running out of time, and he wasn't at all certain that he could bring Jeffrey back before his body gave out.

Maggie saw the tears, and she shook her head as she began to sob. "You said you'd bring him back!" she shouted angrily. "I want him back!"

Jenson opened his mouth and tried to speak, but no words came out. He was overcome by extreme fatigue, and he was expelled from Jeffrey's body.

Jenson didn't know what to tell Jeffrey when he returned. When he sat up and didn't hear Jeffrey's voice right away, he had a moment of hope. Maybe he had been expelled because Jeffrey had found his way back to his body. Then again, maybe…

It didn't work. And you came back too soon for me to attempt a jump.

Jenson felt his heart sink. He put his head in his hands.

You are severely saddened. I can feel it. Tell me what's going on.

"I don't know how to tell you this, Jeffrey."

Is it Maggie?! Is she ok?!

"It isn't Maggie. It's you." Jenson took a deep, shaky breath. "When I jumped into your body, I could tell something wasn't right. It was weak and tired, and I could hardly speak. Jeffrey, you're body isn't going to make it much longer."

Jeffrey was silent for a long time.

How long do I have?

"A week, maybe." He told him what Maggie had said, leaving out the angry outburst. He knew that Maggie's pain would only further upset Jeffrey. "I'm sorry, Jeffrey. I thought we would have more time."

I need to get back. Even if it doesn't keep me from dying, I need to at least be able to see Maggie's face one more time. I need to be able to tell her goodbye.

"I don't think I'll be able to jump back into your world. I couldn't stay in your body for very long before I was kicked out. I think you're going to have to find it on your own, unfortunately."

It's ok. Thank you, Jenson. You are a good man. I have no words to express the depth of my gratitude for your kindness. In the time I've spent with you over the past two years, I've come to think of you as my closest friend, even though you were unaware of my existence for most of that time. I've seen the type of person you are and been with you through some of your most trying moments. You are a kind person, a thoughtful person, and if I am unable to return to my Maggie, I can think of no other person that I would rather spend my last few days with.

Jenson felt tears welling up in his eyes. He was touched by Jeffrey's kind words, and he was heartbroken that there was nothing he could do to save him. He was helpless. All he could do was step aside and hope that Jeffrey could find his way home in time to say goodbye to his one great love. He may not have known Jeffrey for very long, but he had lived Jeffrey's life, and Jeffrey had lived his. He felt close to him, deeply connected to him. He wasn't sure how he was going to cope with this loss.

"That means a lot to me, Jeffrey. I know I haven't known you long, but I feel like I've known you for ages. I will do everything I can to help you get home. If you want, I can even try to stay in dream jumps so that you can have every bit of control in the time you have left. You can use all of that time to do whatever you wish. You can spend it all trying to get home, if that's what you want. You can use whatever finances I have to visit somewhere you've always wanted to go. I don't care. I just want to make sure that your last days are the best days they can possibly be."

No, I don't wish for that. I would like to spend as much time as I can trying to get home, but I don't want to spend all of my time alone. I don't want to die alone. If I can't make it home, I don't want to live a borrowed life. I always thought I was living on borrowed time to begin with. There have been many times that I've wondered why I didn't just die in the accident, and thought that it was a fluke that I was still here. But now that I know it's coming to an end, I'm afraid. I had said that nothing really scared me anymore, but I was wrong. This scares me. I don't want to go through this all by myself. Give me some time to work on dream jumping, but then I want you to come back.

"Ok, Jeffrey. If that's what you want, then that's what I'll do. I'm going to go for now, and I hope when I return, I find that you have made it home."

But if I'm not here when you return, how will you know I made it home? How will you know that I haven't just...passed?

"I get the feeling that I will just *know*," Jenson said honestly. "I wish you all the best, Jeffrey."

Jenson went into his bedroom to lie down. He felt uneasy, and he hoped that his uneasiness wouldn't keep him awake. He needed to leave for Jeffrey's sake. He tossed and turned for a while, but eventually his mind began to wander, and he started to doze off. He knew he needed to jump, and he didn't care where he jumped to. He just let it happen.

When Jenson completed his jump, he found himself in an already awake and alert version of himself. He was sitting at a table in a house, looking at ex-Maggie. She was yammering on about furniture, browsing through a magazine, and when she glanced up at him, she did a double-take.

"Jenson, are you alright? You have a surprised look on your face."

"Hm? Oh, no, I'm fine. I just…don't quite feel myself all of a sudden."

"What the hell does that mean? Are you sick?"

"No, I don't think so. Well, maybe. I'm going to go lie down for a bit."

Jenson hadn't jumped into a fully alert body in a long time. It used to happen a lot in his earlier jumps, but it was different now that he understood what was happening and knew that he wasn't dreaming. As he walked down a hallway to where he knew the bedroom was, he tried to dig for information in this body's brain. In this world, he had married ex-Maggie. They'd bought a house. He'd given up his painting to become a graphic designer for a big company. He also discovered that this version of himself was a dream jumper as well, but that he'd given up his pursuit of knowledge on the subject at ex-Maggie's request. This version of himself didn't even allow himself to dream jump anymore. He'd given up everything that he was passionate about just to make her happy. And he was miserable. He could feel the regret so deeply ingrained in this body that it was making him upset. He didn't want to stay here, but he knew he needed to stay out of his own body long enough to allow Jeffrey time to work on jumping.

He sat down on their king-sized bed and looked at all the ridiculous throw pillows arranged so decoratively upon it. The walls in the room were covered with abstracts and still-life paintings, but none of them were his. Ex-Maggie hadn't hung one piece of his art on the walls in their entire home, he learned. All of his unsold artwork, and even art he had made for himself, sat in a neat stack in a closet in the basement. It was as though ex-Maggie had tried to erase everything about him that made him who he was, and replaced it with what she wanted him to be. And, unfortunately, in this world, Jenson had allowed her to do it. He knew that this was the life he would have had if he had stayed with her.

"Jenson," ex-Maggie said as she stormed into the room. "What is going on? Don't just walk out of the room without explaining yourself."

"I said I was going to lie down. What more explanation do you need?"

"How about *why* you feel you might be sick, or *how* you don't feel yourself all of a sudden?"

"Am I the same person now that I was when you met me? Doesn't it bother you to know that I've given up my art, my dream jumping, my *dignity* for you? I mean, what kind of man sleeps in a bed with this many throw pillows? What kind of artist lives in a home without any shred of his artwork on display? This is not me. This is you. Everything about this life is just you."

"Jenson! How dare you! We built this life together! What has gotten into you?!"

"What's gotten into me? Some sense, to begin with. You have beaten down this version of me so much that I think he's completely forgotten who he is. He's basically just become a sad shell of the man he used to be."

"Have you gone completely insane? Why are you talking like that? This *version* of you?"

"Oh, remember that dream jumping thing he used to do? Well I still do it. I am not the Jenson you know, thank God, but I've managed to jump into this world from a different one. And I

240

happen to be going through some things right now, and I just don't feel up to dealing with this today."

Ex-Maggie stared at him, wide-eyed. "You're going to make up stories and lie to me just so you can argue with me? Blame it on the parallel Jenson so you can say whatever asinine things you want? Do you think I'm really that gullible?"

"I honestly don't care what you do or don't believe. I'm not going to try to prove it to you. Just let me be by myself for a while."

"I will not." She walked up to the bed and sat down next to him. "Just calm down. Tell me what kind of things you are going through."

Jenson looked at her in surprise. His ex-Maggie had never cared what was bothering him unless it directly affected her, and she usually walked away from a fight instead of trying to resolve it. This Maggie seemed to be very much like ex-Maggie, but perhaps she wasn't as cold-hearted. He had no one else to open up to right now, so why not just tell her his problems?

"In my own world, I'm losing a friend right now. He has less than a week to live, and there's nothing I can do to save him. Then, I jump to this world, and I see what this version of myself has become. It's depressing. I see nothing of him in this house and this life, and I can feel how sad it makes him. Have you not noticed that your Jenson is unhappy?"

Maggie looked surprised. "You really aren't Jenson, are you? Jenson would never be this frank with me. Well, there was a time when he was, but not anymore. I haven't seen this kind of fire in those eyes since before the accident."

"In my world, you and I broke up after the accident. I can see from this Jenson's memories that he chose a different path. He gave up."

"Gave up? Gave up on what?"

"Himself."

"That's where you're wrong. He didn't give up on himself. He just chose not to give up on love."

"That was what he thought he was doing at the time, but he's since come to understand that it was just himself that he gave up on. He changed who he was just to make you happy. He figured that if he wasn't going to be happy, there was no point in you being unhappy as well."

He saw her eyes begin to redden. "Is he really this miserable?" Jenson nodded. "I had no idea. I thought I was improving him. I thought he was finally making changes because he could see that the path he was on was the wrong one."

"That's a very selfish way of thinking. It wasn't the wrong path. It was *his* path. Just because it didn't line up perfectly with what you expected of him didn't mean it was a path he shouldn't have taken. If there's one thing in life that I've learned, it's that you need to be true to yourself. Cliché, I know. But being true to yourself doesn't mean that you selfishly do whatever you please, either. You make compromises, yes, but you never lose sight of who you are. Love should be about give *and* take, but in this case, I see a whole lot of one-sided giving without much in return. You need to allow him to be him without making him feel guilty about it or ashamed of it. If you love him, then you need to find out who he really is. You can't just love what you think someone should be. You have to love the person that they are."

"But I do love him. I thought things were going well for us. We haven't had an argument in a long time. I thought he was happy with the way our life was. If he was so miserable, then why didn't he tell me?" Maggie's voice began to crack, and she was on the verge of tears.

"How would you have reacted if he did? How did you always react before when he mentioned that he didn't like how things were going? You'd put him on a guilt trip. You'd make it about you, and make him feel selfish for having feelings and for having a mind of his own. My Maggie did that too. After years of being made to feel that your opinions and thoughts don't matter, and that they're wrong, you start to believe it. You start to second-guess every unpleasant emotion that you have, thinking that you might be selfish for wanting something other than what your significant other wants. Your Jenson has gone so deep down that rabbit hole that he truly believes that his misery is a selfish emotion."

Maggie carefully wiped tears away from her eyes, making sure not to smudge her makeup. She looked down at her hands for a few moments before saying, "I didn't know I was doing this to him. What am I supposed to do now that I know how much he hates this life?"

"He doesn't hate it, Maggie. He just isn't very happy right now. He loves you, he just doesn't love the way you've made him feel about himself. He doesn't love how much you control his choices. What you do is up to you. I'm just telling you what he's been too afraid to tell you, because I know it is something you needed to hear. This is never going to get better for him unless you know what he's going through. And now you know."

"I guess I should've seen it. Maybe I did see it, but I didn't want to admit it. When the fighting stopped, I thought it meant that he had come to the conclusion that I was right. Now that I think about it, I remember him saying a long time ago that a couple that never fights is a couple that doesn't care. I thought it was ridiculous, but I guess it was true for him. He resents me, doesn't he?"

"There is resentment, yes. But it isn't something you two can't overcome. Like I said, he loves you. I can tell that he loves you deeply. You just need to let him be himself so that he can love himself again."

Maggie slipped her hand into his and squeezed it tightly. "Thank you."

They sat in silence for a while, and Jenson could tell that Maggie was thinking over all the things he'd told her. He had meddled in someone else's life once again, but he thought it necessary in this situation. He knew the Jenson of this world had wanted to say those things to Maggie, but he didn't have the courage to do so. Now that she knew his true feelings, they had a chance to improve their marriage and their life. Of course, Jenson couldn't fix their problems for them, but he felt he had at least opened up a line of communication for them to work from. He couldn't fix his own problems with ex-Maggie, but he felt that this Jenson and this Maggie could work it out. They seemed to love each other, which is something he didn't think he'd ever really had with ex-Maggie. He felt he'd done a good thing today.

"When will my Jenson come back?" Maggie asked him after a while.

"When I leave. But I can't leave right away."

"Why not?"

"It's complicated. Let's just say that I'm buying time for someone right now, and it's important that I stay in a dream jump. I will probably be here all day. I hope that doesn't interfere with your plans for today."

"Well, it's not a problem for me, but it might be for Jenson. I'm going to be leaving for work in half an hour, and he's supposed to work today too. You caught us having our morning coffee. That was you, wasn't it? That weird look on Jenson's face was you taking over, I assume."

"Yeah, that was me. Can I call in sick? Does he have sick days he can use? I could probably do his job by accessing his memories and knowledge, but I'd hate to do something at work to mess things up for him. I've already messed with his life as it is," Jenson said.

"Call in. I'm sure it'll be fine. His phone is on the table, and the number is in it. If you don't mind, I'm going to go ahead and get ready for work. I'll talk to Jenson about our conversation when I get home if he is back then. Is he going to know anything about our conversation, or am I going to have to explain it to him?"

"I'm not sure. I still don't know how shadowing works for the people I jump into. I'll leave him a note, if that helps."

"Thank you. And thank you for telling me everything. I'd always been skeptical of dream jumping, but I can't really deny its existence any longer. I know my Jenson...or at least I thought I did. Regardless, I know that you aren't him. But I'm glad I got to meet you. I think things will be better for him, for us, after this."

"I'm glad I could help. If only I could fix my own problems so easily."

Maggie smiled at him. "Take your own advice. Be true to yourself. You'll find a way, of that I have no doubt." She squeezed his hand once more and rose from the bed. "Oh, and if you do decide to lie down on the bed, could you be a dear and not rest on the throw pillows? It will make them lumpy. Just put them in a nice pile on the bench at the foot of the bed. You can put them back on the bed when you get up, and maybe you could smooth out the comforter at that time, too." With that, Maggie walked out of the room.

Jenson lay back on the bed after pushing all the throw pillows to the opposite side, watching a couple of them fall onto the floor. He made no move to pick them up. This Maggie was different from his ex-Maggie, but apparently not *that* different. As he lay there, he wasn't sure what he should be doing right now. He was just biding his time. He thought about ex-Maggie, and how she was just different enough from this Maggie to make his relationship with her unworkable. It made him wonder if there were versions of Jeffrey's Maggie, or his Andrea, that were also different enough to make a relationship impossible. Obviously a relationship with Jeffrey's Maggie wouldn't have worked, but it wasn't because she was incompatible with him. It was because she was in love with Jeffrey, and now that Jeffrey was dying, he would never see her again. He couldn't jump to a world without a corresponding body.

Jenson felt a lump in his throat. This was the first time he'd actually realized that he would never see Jeffrey's Maggie again. Her last words to him had been words of anger, and those were the last words he would ever hear her say. He wondered what her last words to Jeffrey had been before his accident. Were they words of love, of endearment? Were they something inconsequential, like "We need a gallon of milk"? Were they words of anger, like the exchange between him and ex-Maggie before his accident? Jeffrey might never get to hear his Maggie's voice again. He might never again hear her tell him she loved him. He might never again be able to say those words to her, either. And once Jeffrey passed, Jenson wouldn't be able to go to her and tell her everything would be alright. She would be alone.

Jenson blinked his tears away as he heard Maggie of this world leaving the house. She yelled goodbye to him before he heard the door close. He remembered that he had to call in sick, so he did so. Then he sat by himself in the empty house. This is what it would be like every day in his world once Jeffrey was gone. He would be completely alone in an empty apartment for the first time in his life. Before, he'd always had roommates, or Maggie, or his brother, or Jeffrey. Soon, though, it would just be him – alone in his head, alone in the world. It was an unbearable thought for him at the moment.

He decided to write a note to parallel Jenson as he told Maggie he would. As he went to the office room and started rummaging around for paper, it dawned on him that he should try communicating with the Jenson of this world as he did with Jeffrey. He hadn't tried it in Neil's world, but it didn't mean that he couldn't. He went back to the bedroom to lie down and attempt a connection with this Jenson. As soon as he cleared his mind, he was quick to find parallel Jenson's consciousness. It felt different from both Jeffrey and Neil, which made Jenson think that each consciousness must have its own signature "feel" to it. They may all be connected on a cosmic level, but they were all still unique in their own way. Jenson tried to connect with it the way he had tried to connect with Jeffrey, and he found that this parallel version of himself was reaching for him in return. He felt a sensation similar to a static shock, and he was flooded with all of parallel Jenson's thoughts and questions and emotions. It was overwhelming to have two different minds swirling together haphazardly in a disorganized mess. He had to gather himself and try to hold back his own thoughts and emotions, like a mental firewall. Parallel Jenson was also able to rein it in eventually, though it took a little longer. Finally, when Jenson felt the wave of thoughts subside, he made an effort to send a message directly to parallel Jenson's consciousness.

Can you hear me? Jenson asked.

What is going on? I've never had this happen before! Is this what it was like for all the people I took over in my dream jumps? Did they experience everything I was doing in their place? parallel Jenson questioned.

I don't know. I think some people retreat so deeply while shadowing that they don't really know what's going on. I've never had it happen to me, either, so I can't say for certain. I've always been the one doing the jump. What's it like for you? Jenson asked.

It's similar to most of my other shadowing experiences, except more…intense, I guess. Also, I couldn't access your mind until now. It's weird to have someone suddenly take over like this. I don't know how I feel about you opening up to Maggie like that, by the way. It wasn't your place to do that.

I know, but don't you think it's better this way? How could you live the rest of your life in such misery? I'm sure that eventually it would've all come out, but by that point, would it have been in a rational conversation, or would it have been an explosion of pent up anger and resentment? Jenson reasoned.

This isn't your life. It wasn't your choice to make. It might feel a lot like your life, but it's mine. How is what you did any better than what Maggie does? Everybody wants to make my decisions for me, thinking it's what's best for me. I am my own man. I may not be happy with my life right now, but it doesn't mean that I need someone to come in and fix it for me. How would you feel if I went and messed with your life?

Go ahead, it's already pretty damn messy. Have a look if you'd like. I know you can see into my mind now, Jenson invited.

I know, but…I just wish you hadn't done that. I'm sorry for what you are going through, but not everybody needs to be saved. I am capable of saving myself from my mess with Maggie in my own time. I'm not emotionally ready to deal with it yet, but now I have to.

The clock is always ticking, so there's never a good reason to wait to do something you know needs to be done. We've all got things we aren't ready to deal with, but sometimes you have to bite the bullet and just do it. The longer you let your wounds fester, the harder it is to heal them. And there's always the chance that you might wait too long. You don't want to waste your life being miserable, thinking you can change it later, only to find out that there is no 'later.'

I appreciate your concern, and I will take your words to heart, but when can I have my body back? I *understand that you are trying to help your friend Jeffrey right now, but I really don't like shadowing myself. Is there any way that you can be the one shadowing? Is there a way to switch this around?*

Jenson hadn't thought of that. There had to be a way. He'd taken over a parallel body from a shadowing state before, so he knew it was possible, at least temporarily. And then there was Jeffrey, who had maintained control of a body that wasn't his by focusing on his awareness and connection to the body. He shared what he knew with parallel Jenson and instructed him to try taking control. It might end up sending Jenson back to his own body, but he had no other choice at this point. He had to at least try it. He would do everything he could to keep from returning to his own body for Jeffrey's sake, but he couldn't just steal parallel Jenson's body for the day against his wishes. If they could make this switch work, it would be a win for everybody.

Jenson felt nothing at first. He tried to remain passive and kept his attention focused inwardly rather than on the body. He felt a tingling, like his limbs had fallen asleep, but as soon as he took notice of it, it captured his attention, and it went away. He was still in control. He needed to try to ignore it. He waited, and he felt it again. He focused not on the feeling of it, but instead he imagined that he had no limbs. He imagined the feeling of being weightless, of having no body, but tried to remain present *in* the body. He felt parallel Jenson's consciousness suddenly being severed from his own. For a moment, he thought he was being cast out, so he instantly focused his attention back to the body. The body sat up, but Jenson didn't have control anymore. Yet he was still here. They had succeeded. When he tried to reconnect with parallel Jenson's consciousness, he was unable.

Parallel Jenson sat on the bed for a while without moving. Then he said, "Well, he must be gone."

Jenson assumed that parallel Jenson couldn't sense that he was shadowing him now. He wondered how that could be, seeing as they had been mentally connected only moments before. Perhaps parallel Jenson just wasn't as skilled at sensing other consciousnesses as was he. Why was it so easy for Jenson to do these things when other versions of himself didn't seem to possess those skills? He supposed practice had a lot to do with it.

He followed parallel Jenson throughout his day. He found himself often retreating into his own thoughts, though, and when he did so, he discovered that he had completely missed what had been happening in parallel Jenson's world. It was like daydreaming while someone is talking to you. You know they're talking, but you don't hear one word of it. Jenson worried about Jeffrey, worried about Jeffrey's Maggie, and worried about what he was going to do with his life from this point on. He would still paint, of course, as it was his livelihood and he had orders to complete and hospital bills to pay. But what about dream jumping? Knowing what he knew now, could he continue to dream jump with a clear conscience? It was changing people's lives, and not often for the better. He couldn't get things right in his own life, so what gave him the right to jump into other people's lives and meddle? Nothing he had done had been done out of malice, but even when he tried to help people, things had a way of going wrong.

Jenson tried to focus on the good he had done, but for every good thing, he could think of several negative things. He'd probably caused confusion and chaos at the very least, even in the worlds where he hadn't directly meddled in the course of someone's life. He'd taken over several versions of himself that may have left them feeling helpless and upset when he did. This parallel Jenson didn't like it, so he had to assume that the rest didn't either. He'd tried to help this parallel Jenson fix his problems with Maggie, but he'd only managed to anger him. He'd tried to tell Natalie from the apocalypse world that he'd met her in another world, but he'd ended up getting that version of himself hurt or killed. He'd set Neil up on a date with Stephanie, but who knows if he really wanted to go on a date with her? He'd reconnected Maggie and Jeffrey, in a way, but had that really helped anybody? Now Jeffrey's body was dying, and he had no way of knowing if it was his fault. Maggie had gone through an emotional rollercoaster because of his jump, and now she was angry with him.

However, he had helped Jeffrey, hadn't he? If he hadn't done everything he'd done, Jeffrey would still be a lonely, shadowing ghost, stuck in a world in which he didn't belong with no solace from his own despair. Then again, if he hadn't meddled, maybe Jeffrey wouldn't be dying now, and maybe he would've eventually found his way back to his body on his own. Jenson might not have helped him after all. He might have killed him.

Dream jumping wasn't a blessing. It wasn't a beautiful, fantastic phenomenon. It was a curse.

Jenson realized that Maggie was home, and she and parallel Jenson were talking about him. Parallel Jenson apologized to her about what Jenson had said, and told her that it was all a lie. Jenson was disappointed. He hadn't anticipated that parallel Jenson would take that route. He hoped that even though parallel Jenson had denied feeling the way he did, maybe Maggie would still remember his words and try to take parallel Jenson's feelings into account in the future. It would be hard for her to do that, though, if he didn't share those feelings with her.

Jenson spent the entire night shadowing parallel Jenson. Jenson didn't sleep. Even when the body was sleeping, and he was just lying in darkness, he was lost in his thoughts, wide awake. It startled him when parallel Jenson woke up and opened his eyes, and he was no longer in darkness. But soon, he was daydreaming again, oblivious to parallel Jenson's life. He didn't care anymore about what happened to parallel Jenson. He was going to do what he was going to do, and Jenson no longer found a reason for it to affect him.

As parallel Jenson went about his day at work, Jenson watched him for a while, comparing his work to what he had learned in college about graphic design. Suddenly, he felt a strange tugging on his consciousness, like something trying to draw his attention. He fought it, trying to stay in this world. Then, he heard Jeffrey.

Jenson! Come home!

Chapter 17

Jeffrey was beckoning Jenson. He could hear the urgency in his voice. He didn't know how he could hear Jeffrey, but that wasn't important at the moment. He quickly made the jump back home.

When he returned, he was lying in his bed. He felt a lingering sense of distress, which he assumed must've been from Jeffrey.

It's happening, Jenson. I can feel it. I think I'm dying right now.

Jenson felt panicked. It had only been a little over a day. He wasn't ready for this yet.

"Stay calm. Did you ever make it home?"

No. I've been here the whole time. Jenson, I'm scared. I feel tired, but not the kind of tired after a long day. It's a kind of tired that snakes through all of your being. It feels like wanting to just give up on everything and going to sleep forever.

"It's going to be alright, Jeffrey. I'm here for you."

Do you think I will be able to see my baby boy? You know, on the other side? Did Maggie tell you about little Jeffie?

"Just a little, but it was too painful for her to talk about. You don't have to talk about it either. I don't want you to spend your last moments in grief."

No, it's ok. If you never talk about someone, it's like they never lived. The stories are what keep them alive in your heart. Little Jeffie was our son. He died in his crib one night. He'd managed to pull one of the eyes off of his stuffed teddy bear after he went to bed, and he choked on it. We didn't hear anything over the baby monitor. It was completely silent. When Maggie checked on him a couple of hours later, around the time we were heading to bed, he was already gone. He was only 10 months old. It was devastating, and I thought Maggie would never recover from her grief. It was only three months after that when I was hit by the truck. Poor Maggie. I hope she can move on after all of this is over. Maybe it will comfort her to know that Little Jeffie and I might be together once again. If you ever see her again, tell her that I love her, and I'm sorry for everything.

"Jeffrey, I don't think –" Jenson had started to tell Jeffrey he couldn't visit Maggie anymore, but decided against it. What purpose would it serve to tell him that? Instead, he said, "If I see her again, I will tell her. I'm so sorry for the things you both have had to endure. You are wonderful people. Things like this shouldn't happen to people like you and Maggie."

Jenson, I can't feel bodily sensations anymore. I can't see through your eyes. I can hear you, but it isn't like it was before. It's more like I'm simply understanding what you want to say to me. I don't know what to do. I feel like I could drift away at any moment, but I don't know where I'm going... Jeffrey was suddenly silent.

"Jeffrey? Are you still here?"

I feel so strange all of a sudden. It isn't peaceful, it isn't tumultuous...it isn't anything. It's strange because it's nothing. I don't feel anything, Jenson. I'm not scared anymore. I'm...

And he was gone. Jeffrey was just gone. Jenson felt the moment that it happened. It was nothing spectacular – no strong sensation to indicate that Jeffrey was being ripped away from him. He just disappeared, as though he had never been there in the first place.

Jenson allowed himself to cry. It wasn't a sobbing, slobbering, snotty mess, but rather a few silent tears shed in an act of mourning. He cried for Jeffrey, who never got to say goodbye to Maggie. He cried for Maggie, who had to cope with Jeffrey's death alone. He cried for himself, because he'd not only lost a friend, but he'd let down two people he'd come to care deeply about. He'd broken his promise to both of them, and he could never tell them how sorry he was.

Jenson went to the bathroom to get a tissue. His apartment felt so empty. He felt empty. He walked around aimlessly, looking at his artwork on the walls, the arrangement of his sparse furniture, the food in the cupboards. Everything in this apartment was the way it was because Jeffrey had placed it there. Jeffrey had put that food in the cupboards and arranged that furniture and hung his artwork on the walls. There were leftover meals in the fridge that Jeffrey had prepared. Jeffrey had made this apartment his home, and now he was gone. And the saddest thing was that no one in this world, aside from Jenson, ever knew him. Don knew about him, but he didn't really know him. People had met him, but they never knew he was Jeffrey. He'd left a mark on this world, however miniscule it may have been, for which he would never receive credit. And he'd died here, and no one but Jenson would mourn him. There would be no funeral for Jenson to attend, and no headstone for him to visit to pay his respects. It was as though he never existed but within Jenson's own mind, and Jenson would mourn his death alone. For this, he cried.

The next several days were painful. Jenson was an emotional mess. It wasn't just the death of Jeffrey that had taken its toll on him, but also the never-ending "what-if's" that buzzed in Jenson's head. What if he'd never gone to Jeffrey's world? What if he'd never started dream jumping? What if he'd stayed in Jeffrey's body instead of trying to return to his own? What if he hadn't broken up with Maggie? Every decision he'd ever made was suddenly up for scrutiny, and he couldn't stop it.

He didn't want to dream jump any longer. It had brought pain and suffering, of a magnitude he'd only recently begun to comprehend. The only place he could go where he could be certain not to interfere with anyone's life was the Akashic record, but what need did he have for that place? His pursuit of knowledge was what had brought him to his current state of desolation. The Akashic record held no knowledge that would bring him peace, did it? What could he possibly learn that would ever make this experience less painful? It couldn't tell him whether his decisions had been the right ones or the wrong ones. It couldn't tell him what to do next. He needed guidance and consolation, not facts.

He began to wonder where Jeffrey had gone when he died. Did Heaven and Hell exist? He'd never thought that they were real places, but it didn't mean that they weren't. With all he had learned about dream jumping and multiple universes, he supposed that Heaven and Hell couldn't be definitively disregarded. They might not be the places that people tended to think they were, but there could be some resemblance of them out there in the universes. Was Jeffrey in one of them now?

It was with that thought that Jenson realized he did still have use for the Akashic record. It could tell him where Jeffrey went after he died. That was information, wasn't it? He probably wouldn't be able to tell if Jeffrey was happy or not, but if he knew where he had gone, it was something he might be able to surmise once he regained his emotions when he returned to his body. The question now, though, was whether he truly wanted to know. If he learned that Jeffrey was in a terrible place, it would only cause him more pain. At this point, he felt like Jeffrey was in a "Schrödinger's cat" situation. He was both at peace and in agony until Jenson observed his fate. He decided that he needed to know, regardless of the outcome.

Jenson spent the next few days seeking out the Akashic record. When he accidentally jumped to other places, he left immediately. He didn't want to interfere with anyone else's life. He came to some strange places, and a few times, his curiosity almost got the best of him. But as soon as he thought about Jeffrey, and all the bad decisions he'd made, he found the resolve to leave without further investigation. After several days of this, however, he was becoming irritated with his inability to find the one place he sought.

Finally, though, as his frustration mounted and his determination to find an answer was at its peak, he found it. As soon as he saw the bright flash of white and realized he was there, he also realized that he had answers. It had been instantaneous. He knew that Jeffrey was *here*. He had become part of the information in the Akashic record, as do all conscious beings upon the death of their physical bodies. The Akashic record was a warehouse for not only the information of the universes, but also the energy of all consciousness. Jeffrey's life, his memories, and his knowledge were all here. His life force was here. Jenson wasn't exactly speaking to Jeffrey, but he knew that Jeffrey was able to "see" everything now. Jeffrey knew what was going on in Maggie's life at any given time. He knew what was going on in Jenson's life. Jeffrey had become one with the Akashic record, and thus, had complete access to all of the information therein. Jenson knew that the energy of Jeffrey's life force would at some point be recycled to make a new consciousness for a new being, but the Jeffrey that once was would always be – as part of the Akashic record. To where that life force would go, to what being it would create, there was no knowledge. The Akashic record did not foretell the future, as events were never set in stone, and fate and destiny did not exist. Free-will was not simply an illusion. The Akashic record could only provide knowledge of which possibilities were relevant, and this knowledge was constantly changing as events took place in all the universes that affected the likelihood of those possibilities coming to fruition. Jenson's questions had been answered, and when he sought no more, he was returned home.

When he reentered his body, he wanted to scream from the pain, but he knew the sound would exacerbate his condition. The sensory overload was unbearable. He writhed in agony, but with every movement he felt like his body was being ripped apart by his bed sheets. His eyes felt like they were going to explode, as did his eardrums. When the excruciating pain finally subsided, he vowed to never return to the Akashic record. The sensory overload had seemed to last much longer this time than it had last time, and the intensity was far greater. He was fearful of what kind of return he would face if he made that jump again. If it was any worse than this time…he didn't even want to think about it. He thought there must be some way of accessing knowledge from the Akashic record without actually visiting it, but he had no intentions of ever attempting it for fear that he might accidentally slip back into that place. No amount of curiosity was worth this kind of torment.

Once he had calmed down, he thought about the information he had received in the Akashic record. Jeffrey wasn't at peace or in agony. He simply *was*. Jenson remembered how Jeffrey had described his last moments, and it now made sense. He'd started to feel nothing because he was going to a place of no feelings, no senses. It was true that those who have passed do continue to "watch" over the living, but they do so without any feeling of sadness, regret, or even happiness. They become part of an all-"seeing," unfeeling eye. Jenson had experienced the nothingness of that existence, so in a sense, he had already experienced death. Twice. Granted, he hadn't actually merged with the Akashic record, but some day he would. And he was not afraid.

Jenson was not disheartened by the idea of living out eternity without ever feeling joy or happiness again. When you feel no emotions, you don't miss feeling emotions. You don't miss anything because the act of yearning for something you no longer have *is* an emotion. He also realized now that he had no sense of time when he was in the Akashic record. Eternity wouldn't stretch on and on like a boring car ride, rather it would be forever and an instant, all at once. With this knowledge, Jenson would enjoy the life he had, but he would go forth knowing that there was no reason to fear what comes with death.

He wondered if he should share his knowledge. For someone who has never experienced the Akashic record, who has never experienced an emotionless state, the knowledge of what comes after death may not be comforting. People want to pretend that the afterlife will be blissful, peaceful, and happy. They want to think that they will have a joy-filled reunion with those who died before them, and that they will be able to look in on their loved ones to provide them comfort. They want to think that those who are bad or evil will be punished for their misdeeds, that they will go to a place of eternal suffering when they die. How would people react if they knew that everyone goes to the same place, regardless of how their life was lived? Would morality continue to exist with such knowledge?

Jenson's morality hadn't changed. He still had a distinct sense of right and wrong, but it didn't mean that this would be the case for everyone. Was human nature such that we would thrive with such knowledge, or destroy ourselves in greed and violence? Are humans inherently kind, social beings, or are we prone to being driven by selfishness and greed? Are we in a Lockean or Hobbesian state of nature?

Jenson knew that he could argue himself in circles if he continued with this line of inquiry. None of it mattered, either, because it wasn't as though anyone other than his family and Don would believe him. Even then, he wasn't sure that this knowledge was meant for them. His life was largely unaffected by his knowledge of the "afterlife," but this might not be so for those who haven't experienced the Akashic record. It is only with experiencing it that understanding of it can be complete. He decided that this was information that was best kept to himself, at least for now.

He needed to talk to someone, though, as his loneliness was becoming unbearable. He didn't want to burden his brothers with his depression, and he was afraid that his mother would worry excessively if she knew what he was going through. The only person he could talk to about this was Don. He decided to call him.

"How are things, Jennie?" Don greeted him.

"Not so good."

"That seems to be the story of your life. What's going on now?"

"Jeffrey died."

"I'm sorry to hear that. How did it happen?"

Jenson told him everything except the final visit to the Akashic record.

"He was able to call out to you?" Don asked. "How did he manage that? I thought you two couldn't make a connection."

"I don't know how it happened. I wasn't able to make a direct connection with him while he was shadowing me, but I still felt connected to him in a way. Maybe it wasn't that he was able to call out to me in a different universe, but that I was able to hear him calling me from my own world. Remember when I was able to hear the alarm in the Kristine dream jump, even though the alarm was in my own world and I wasn't? I think it was like that. I could hear him calling for me because he was doing so from my own body, and I still shared a connection with it, and with him."

"That makes sense. So he just disappeared? That was it?"

"Right before he disappeared, he said he couldn't see or hear or feel anything anymore. He described it as 'nothingness,' and said that he wasn't scared anymore. Then he was gone. Poof, gone."

"It's odd that he would describe feeling nothing. Most people describe a feeling of peace."

"Maybe some people interpret it as a feeling of peace, when really it is just the lack of feeling or emotion. Jeffrey had described it as not being peaceful or tumultuous."

"It sounds a lot like how you described the Akashic record. Is it possible that he wasn't actually dying at that moment, but instead visiting the Akashic record? Maybe that's what happens before you die. Perhaps you visit the Akashic record as a final step before true death. Or maybe you just become part of the Akashic record when you die. I think we talked about this a little bit a while back, when we first met."

Now that Jenson thought about it, he remembered Don saying something about that. He wondered if he should tell Don that he had been right. "Don, if there was a way that you could find out definitively what happened to you when you died, would you want to know?"

"As a scientist, I welcome all knowledge. Of course I would want to know. That's one of the big questions of humankind. Who wouldn't want to know?"

"Think about it, though. Would knowing what would happen after death change the way you lived? Would it affect your quality of life? Would it affect the choices you made?"

"Depending on what comes after death, I suppose it could. If I knew for certain that I was going to Hell if I didn't go to church every Sunday, I would definitely start going to church. Real church, not the pub."

"What if you learned that there was nothing after death?"

"I don't think my choices would be affected. It is something I have considered. Of course, there's a part of me that wants to think that there is some great afterlife waiting for all of us, but I find it much more logical to assume that our energy just goes back out into the universe to become part of the Akashic record or that we simply cease to be. 'This parrot is no more. It has ceased to be.'"

Jenson understood the reference. "This isn't a time for jokes."

"It is the perfect time for jokes. You are depressed. You need to laugh a little. I know it isn't easy to deal with a death, but you need to continue to live your life. Mourning is a thing we do only for ourselves. The person we mourn has already passed, and it does them no good to be sad about their passing. I understand that mourning is an important part of coping and eventually moving on, but it doesn't mean that you can't allow yourself to be happy sometimes, too. It's time to start being happy again, Jennie. You have been in turmoil for far too long. What is keeping you from contentment? You have your life back now. You don't have to fear losing yourself in dream jumps any longer. You've got a fresh start again, so don't weigh yourself down with the sadness of your past. It's time to put it behind you."

"I don't know if I can. I keep wondering if I am the reason that Jeffrey died. I keep thinking about how devastated his wife must be. I'm upset that I wasn't able to reunite them. Worst of all, I keep thinking about how much I have screwed up other people's lives with my dream jumping. I don't think I can do it anymore."

"Then don't. But fretting about things you can't change isn't helpful. It only causes you unnecessary stress. Perhaps it went the way it had to, the way it was always going to. You worry so much about how you have affected the lives of your parallel selves, but have you stopped to consider that many of your parallel selves are doing the same thing to each other? Isn't it possible that if it hadn't been you who messed with their lives, it would have been another version of you who did? You may have been the lesser of two evils. Not saying you are evil or anything, but I think you get my point. Regret is a part of being human, but you can't let it consume you. Instead of living with regret, try living with purpose. Learn from your mistakes. Turn them into something positive, and focus on the things you can change," Don encouraged. "Maybe a break from dream jumping will be a good thing for you. It will give you time to work on your own life, to reevaluate who you are and where you want *this* life to take you."

Jenson was surprised at how uplifting Don's words were to him. Don was right. It was time to move on. He needed to accept that he had made mistakes, and use what he'd learned from those mistakes to make better choices in the future. His journey had been a difficult one as of late, but he had learned a lot about himself from these experiences. Rather than letting it destroy him, his memory of past misfortunes would fuel his future fortitude.

"Thanks, Don. That was exactly what I needed to hear right now."

"I know it was. I might be a weird old jackass, but I'll be damned if I let a friend put himself through such self-inflicted torment. I know you don't want to dream jump anymore, but that doesn't mean you can't call me just to chat. I do expect you to keep in touch. Don't make me come find you."

When Jenson ended the call, he was surprised at how much better he felt. It wasn't just Don's advice that had helped him, but the reassurance that, even if he *lived* alone, he wasn't truly alone. It was time to get back to living his own life.

***

Seven months went by, and Jenson didn't dream jump once in that time. He had gained such control over it that now he never "accidentally" jumped. It would only happen when he wanted it to happen, and at this point, he still didn't want it to happen. He had spent his time painting and expanding his exposure by doing art shows in other cities, attending craft shows all around Michigan, and collaborating with businesses. He found that living alone was actually a blessing. He had no one to answer to, no other schedules to work around, and no distractions. He was doing well for himself, and he had begun paying off his sizeable hospital bills from his accident. He was in a good place. No, he was in a great place. For the first time in a long time, he felt like he had a place in this world.

One day, as he sat in front of a fresh, new canvas, he thought about how much a blank canvas reminded him of that day Don had steered him out of his depression. He had started his life anew that day, and much like this canvas, the possibilities were endless. He alone held the brush, and he controlled what went onto that canvas, and what didn't. He would draw from his talents and his experiences to make a new piece of art, and it would be his own creation. No one would tell him what to paint, or how to paint – he could make of it whatever he chose. And it would be beautiful.

As he started to apply background color, he heard a knock at the door. He put his brush aside and went to the door. When he opened it and saw who was standing on the other side, his heart leapt into his throat.

Chapter 18

There she was. It was the woman for whom he had been searching the universes. It was the woman for whom he had given up looking, because he had come to see her as an unobtainable treasure. She had been his unicorn. Yet here she was, in his world, at his door – it was his Andrea.

She said, "I'm looking for the Jenson Thorne who briefly went by the name of Jeffrey Tyson, and who lived with Jeffrey Tyson after his coma. I've spent the last six months looking for him, in places you might not even be able to imagine. Are you him?"

Jenson stared at the woman standing before him. "…Maggie?"

An expression of relief and joy spread across her face. Her eyes began to well up with tears.

He asked, "Is it really you? Are you Jeffrey's Maggie?"

"I can't believe I found you, Jenson. Yes, it's me."

"But…how?"

"I'm a dream jumper now. I may have been all along, but I was finally able to harness it and understand it. God, Jenson, I've searched everywhere for you."

Jenson was flabbergasted. "Please, come in," he said, still in disbelief.

Maggie walked into the apartment and hugged him tightly. He hugged her back, and when the scent of her hair drifted up into his nostrils, he felt the calmness of familiarity wash over him. She stepped back and looked him over.

"You look just like him. Well, just like he looked before his coma. Most of the others did too. It's still so strange to see people that look like him, but aren't him."

"How many places did you visit before you found me?"

"At least a hundred. I never thought in a million years I'd actually find the real you in the vastness of the universes. I didn't even know if a version of me existed in your world. But I had to try to find you."

"Why?" he wondered. "Not that I'm complaining. You wouldn't believe how happy I am to see you. But I don't understand. Why would you be looking for me?"

"I have many reasons for wanting to find you. The last time I saw you, I was upset and I lashed out in anger. I have been deeply bothered by that. I wanted you to know that I don't blame you for what happened, and that I'm not angry with you. I wanted to thank you for trying to help Jeffrey and me. Secondly, I wanted to know if Jeffrey passed on in peace. I wanted to make sure he didn't go out of this world full of regrets. And thirdly, I wanted to repay you for your kindness, understanding, and selflessness. You tried to bring my Jeffrey to me, so I wanted to bring your Andrea to you. And her name is Andrea, believe it or not."

Jenson invited Maggie into the living room to sit and talk with him. He was having a hard time finding words, though many questions swirled in his brain. He decided to tell her about Jeffrey's attempts to make it home to her, and about his last moments with him.

"He died peacefully," Jenson added when he was finished. "I never thought I'd be able to pass on his message to you, but I didn't have the heart to remind him that I couldn't jump to a world where I had no compatible body. But here I am, talking to you. I'm glad I was at least able to do that for him."

"Do you think he really is with Jeffie now?"

263

"I have no doubt," Jenson answered truthfully. "He is with all of those who have passed before us, and we will join them when we pass as well."

"How do you know?"

"I just do. I can't explain it, but I know." He could explain it, but he wouldn't. He still believed that it was knowledge better left unshared.

Maggie was quiet for a moment. "I'm glad his suffering is over. I miss him dreadfully, but I think this was the best thing for him if he couldn't come home."

"That was how he felt about it as well. He'd told me that if he couldn't make it home, he wanted to pass on so everyone could move on with their lives. He didn't want you to spend your life waiting for him."

"I would have, too. I would have waited forever for him. But I wouldn't have regretted one minute of it. He was a man worth waiting for." Maggie dabbed the corners of her eyes with her shirt sleeve. Jenson brought her a tissue and allowed her time to regain her composure. "I had a hard time after he died. I put all of my time and energy into trying to dream jump just so I could see him again in other worlds. When I finally discovered I was able to do it, I realized that my objective was flawed. I could visit other versions of him, and you, but they weren't really him. It was causing me more pain to try to find him in those other versions of him. That was when I understood what I should be doing. Instead of trying to find false comfort in these parallel worlds, I should be using my new-found skills to repay my debt to you. You were there for us in a way no one else ever could have been, and you asked nothing in return. You fought selflessly to bring us back together. For that I thank you, and I have brought Andrea to you. It wasn't easy, and in some worlds, I couldn't find a version of you at all. I think it's a good sign for us that in this world, your Andrea only lives thirty minutes away from you. Perhaps you can find with her what Jeffrey and I had together, and what so many of the other versions of you and Jeffrey have with the other versions of me."

"How did you find me, anyway?"

"I searched for 'Jenson Thorne' on social media. There weren't many people named Jenson Thorne. When I found the profile with pictures that matched what I know all your parallel selves look like, I used the information in your profile to look up your address. You'd be surprised at the things you can find on the internet. It's funny, though, that you can find someone's home address, but not a number to their cell phone. It didn't always work in other worlds, and in some places you lived too far away for me to make the trip in one dream jump. In those worlds, I sent you a message over social media, and often didn't hear back in time before I had to leave. When I did hear back, they seemed confused, and I figured it wasn't you. But lucky for us, I was able to contact you in this world."

"How did you know that the other versions of me weren't actually me?" Jenson asked.

"Some of the Jensons quite obviously weren't you, given what I knew about you and what you'd told me about your life. In some worlds, our parallel selves were already together, so I didn't interfere. Sometimes I ended up in worlds that I knew right away weren't even your world. But occasionally, everything seemed to fit the bill...until I started talking to those parallel versions of you. Some of them seemed happy to see me, as I think they were looking for versions of myself just as you were, but when they were perplexed by my mention of Jeffrey, I knew it wasn't you. But I've finally found you. Of all the infinite universes in existence, I managed to find the one with you in it."

"I still can't believe it myself. I thought I'd never see you again. I had given up. I gave up dream jumping, and with it, my pursuit of you and Andrea. I had to give it up because I couldn't live with the knowledge that I was messing with other people's lives. I felt guilty for everything I put you and Jeffrey through, and wondered if things would have been better for both of you if I hadn't jumped to your world at all. But I found a way to put it behind me, to move on. I had come to believe that dream jumping would never bring me joy or happiness again, but now it has."

"I am grateful for you coming into my life. If you hadn't jumped to my world, I wouldn't have known about what had become of Jeffrey or about dream jumping. I would've still been wondering why he wasn't waking up, if he was suffering, if his soul had passed, and what I should do with my life while I waited for him. You helped me find answers to those questions. You gave me purpose again. And you were there to comfort Jeffrey in his death when I couldn't be. You have nothing for which to be remorseful."

"It means a lot to me to hear you say that. Thank you, Maggie."

"Now, I have a question for you. Do you know if Andrea can see what I see, like Jeffrey did with you? Will she know about the visit you and I had today?"

"I don't know. I think some people do, and some people don't. When you leave, she may not remember any of this. She might have no idea who I am."

"Damn, I was afraid that might be the case." Maggie was thoughtful for a minute. "I can't just leave her here, in case she wakes up and has no recollection of how she got here and who you are. That might be a bit traumatizing for her. How do I get her to understand what has happened?"

Jenson assumed it would be too much to ask to have Maggie try to connect her consciousness with Andrea's. Then he remembered what he did when he had set up a date for Neil with Stephanie. "You could leave her a letter. Tell her who you are, what has happened, and that I would like to meet her. Leave it somewhere she will see it right away. You could even hold it in your hands when you leave – that way she'll wake up with it right in front of her." Jenson gave her a time and a place to tell Andrea to meet him. He gave her his phone number, too, in case Andrea wanted to call him. Maggie put the number into Andrea's contacts on her phone, and even snapped a photo of Jenson to accompany the contact information and further verify her story. Maggie asked if Jenson wanted Andrea's phone number.

"No. I want to leave this up to her. If she is completely freaked out by this, and doesn't want anything to do with me, I don't want to call her and rattle her even more. This should be her decision. If she doesn't call me, I'll be waiting for her at the restaurant. If she doesn't show up, I'll know that it just isn't going to happen for us and I'll give up on it. I won't try to pursue her if I know she doesn't want this."

"Maybe it would be easier if I just gave you her address, and used her memories to tell you all the places she frequents. Then you could just casually run into her and meet her that way."

"I want her to have all of this information up front. She needs to know what happened today. If she can see what's going on right now, she will already know everything. If that's the case, she might not appreciate me indirectly stalking her, especially if she's already decided that this is not what she wants. No, it's better to tell her everything, and leave this in her hands."

"I see where you're coming from. I think you're right. It's best to be transparent with this." Maggie looked up at the clock on the wall. "Well, I should go. I've got a lot of writing and explaining to do before I leave this world."

"What are you going to do from here? Now that you've found me and you did what you set out to do, what's next for you?" Jenson wondered.

"I'm going to move on with my life. I feel like I finally have closure, and I'm ready to start fresh. My life has basically been on 'hold' for almost four years, and it's time for me to start living it again. Like you, I'll probably give up dream jumping. I've accomplished what I needed to do, and I have no further use for it. I don't need to escape my own life anymore. Thank you, Jenson, for everything you've done for me and for Jeffrey. Even now, when I came here to help you, I've found that you've helped me. You helped me finish my quest, to find peace once again. This is a bittersweet ending for both of us, but it's also a new beginning. I hope that Andrea becomes part of your new beginning, but if she doesn't, don't hold back on life. There is much joy to be found in the worlds in which we live, and we don't necessarily need one particular person in order to find it. Find your joy, Jenson. Good luck."

Jenson walked Maggie to the door, and he embraced her, holding her close for the last time. She kissed him on the cheek, smiled warmly at him, and then walked out of his life forever.

Jenson had four days before he was to meet Andrea. In that time, he didn't receive a phone call. He was slightly discouraged, but not disheartened. If she didn't show up at the restaurant, he would be sad, but he wouldn't be broken. He had everything he needed within himself to push on without regrets. If she didn't show up, he would know that it was not meant to be. Fate and destiny might not exist, but there was something to be said for accepting the way things were. There was no point in trying to change the unchangeable. No force in the world could make someone love you if they didn't want to love you. Whether or not she showed up, it would be an end to his own journey he had started what seemed like ages ago. If she was there, then he had finally found her and completed what he had sought to do. If she wasn't, then he knew that he no longer needed to look for her. Maggie had been right that it was a bittersweet ending. They would both have completed their quests.

When the day arrived, Jenson searched through his closet carefully, choosing an outfit that would have met with ex-Maggie's approval. She may not have had many good qualities, but her fashion sense was impeccable. He brushed his teeth and styled his hair. He looked at himself in the mirror and said, "I might not get the girl tonight, but hey, at least I'll still have my good looks." He gave his reflection the pistol fingers and left for his date.

When he walked into the restaurant, he told the hostess he was supposed to be meeting someone and he wasn't sure if she had shown up already. He gave her Andrea's description. She informed him that no one had arrived alone recently. She showed him to a table, and he sat down. He scanned the room, but Andrea was not there. He looked at his watch. He was right on time, so there was still plenty of time for her to show up. When the waiter approached him, he ordered only a water and told him he was waiting for someone. He sipped his water and waited.

And waited.

And waited.

He waited for thirty minutes, but Andrea didn't show.

The waiter approached him again, for the third time that evening, and said, "Sir, if you don't order something, we're going to have to ask you to give up your table for a waiting party."

"I am a waiting party," Jenson mumbled under his breath, feeling overwhelming disappointment. "Fine, bring me the tallest mug of whatever you've got on tap and…do you have pie?" The waiter nodded, giving him a strange look. "Bring me some pie. I don't care what kind."

Jenson downed half his beer in one long drink, and started in on the apple pie the waiter had brought him. This was it. His quest was over. He felt unfulfilled.

As he finished up his beer, he looked around for his waiter to order another. That was when he saw her. The hostess was pointing Andrea toward his table.

She approached the table hesitantly, looking unsure of herself. Jenson stood up so quickly he accidentally knocked his chair over. He leaned down and righted it, and when he looked up again, she was standing before him. She held her hand out to him and smiled awkwardly.

He shook her hand, and she said, "It's nice to meet you…again." He pulled her chair out for her and she sat down. She stared silently across the table at him for a moment after he was seated.

She broke the silence with an uncomfortable laugh, and said, "This story is going to sound completely crazy…"

Jenson grinned and replied, "Sounds like my kind of story."

THE END

Epilogue

Dear Andrea,

I'm not exactly sure how to explain this to you, especially if you aren't aware of anything that happened today, but here it goes. My name is Maggie, and I am a dream jumper from a different world. I borrowed your body for a while today, and I'm sorry if it has caused you confusion or discomfort. Ok, that sounded creepy…I guess it kind of is. Let me explain.

There is a phenomenon that exists called "dream jumping." I won't get into all the technical details of it, but it's when the consciousness of one person from one universe leaves their body and jumps into the body of a parallel version of himself or herself in a parallel universe. I am a parallel version of you, and I jumped into your body today. I had a purpose for it, though. There is a man in your world named Jenson Thorne, and he is a dream jumper like me. He's actually the one who introduced me to it. Anyway, he used his dream jumping to help me through a very strange, very hard time in my life, and I am trying to repay him for his kindness.

He has been looking for you for a long time. He met parallel versions of you and me in different universes, and, well, he's fairly certain it means something. In many of these worlds, our parallel selves are in a happy, loving relationship with Jenson's parallel selves. I was one of them, actually. Anyway, I have been on a mission to locate him in his world so I could bring you two together. I've finally done it. Well, mostly. When I borrowed your body today, I went and found him to show him that you do exist in his world. We decided that if you two were to meet, it would have to be your decision if you wanted to meet him. And he made it clear that he wanted you to know everything that had happened today, hence this letter. I know I am leaving out huge chunks of information, but none of it is important right now. If you want to know more about it, Jenson can tell you everything. He will be waiting for you at the Kaku Two restaurant at 6:30 PM on Saturday. That's four days from today. If you want to call him to verify what I've told you, his number is in your phone along with the picture I took of him today. (You'll see that he's a very handsome man.)

Now, I can't presume to tell you what to do. But I would strongly urge you to meet with him. He is an amazing person. He is selfless, kind-hearted, funny, intelligent, handsome, and...well, he's just a damn good guy. That is why I am doing this for him. He deserves it, and I believe you deserve it too. I have had access to your memories while I was here, and I know the kind of relationships you've been through. Jenson is not like Ben or Mike. I was married to a parallel version of Jenson, and they are very much alike. So much so that I thought he was my husband at first. Again, he can explain this to you. Anyway, I can tell you from experience that men like Jenson make the best partner and friend a girl could ask for. If you are skeptical, just meet him for yourself and you will see.

I'm sorry for having sprung all of this on you. It's a lot to take in, I know. You have a lot to consider now, and I hope you do think it over. Give him a chance. If I had the choice, I would stay here with him. I would. But now you have the chance to seize an opportunity that I wish I had. Please don't let it slip through your fingers. Life is too short. Don't spend so much time looking for matches that you miss the fact that the candle has already been lit.

-Maggie Tyson

About the Author

I was born and raised in Michigan. I have spent most of my life in the Upper Peninsula, where I currently reside with my husband and our two children. I earned my Bachelors of Science degree from Grand Valley State University in 2008 and started my first book in early 2010. When I'm not writing, I teach painting classes, read, and enjoy being active.

I have been inspired by the works of a variety of both fiction and nonfiction authors, including Brian Greene, Michio Kaku, Carl Sagan, Stephen King, and Dean Koontz.

If you enjoyed *Dream Jumper*, check out some of my other books: *The Burning Side*, *Beyond Reason*, *The Time Thief*, and *The Time Thief: A Change of Face*.

Special thanks to my family and friends who have been so supportive and given me constructive criticism and ideas along the way. I couldn't have done it without you.